# BULLET THROUGH YOUR FACE

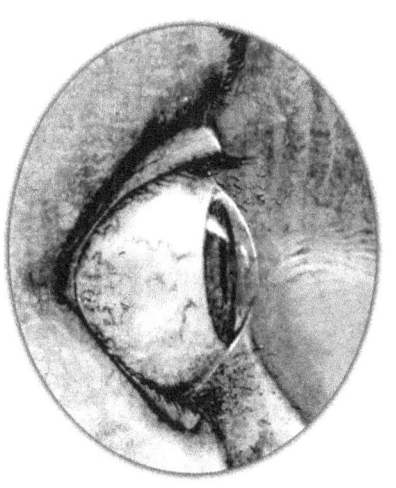

## EDWARD LEE

deadite press

DEADITE PRESS
205 NE BRYANT
PORTLAND, OR 97211

AN ERASERHEAD PRESS COMPANY
WWW.ERASERHEADPRESS.COM

ISBN: 1-936383-02-0

"Ever Nat" first appeared as a limited edition chapbook by Bloodletting Press, April, 2003.
"The Salt-Diviner" first appeared in THE USHERS AND OTHER STORIES, Obsidian Press, September, 1999.
"The Refrigerator Full of Sperm" first appeared in SPLATTERSPUNK, Sideshow Books, March, 1998.

Copyright © 2010 by Edward Lee

Cover art copyright © 2010 Alan M. Clark
www.alanmclark.com

Interior illustrations © 2010 Chrissy Horchheimer

All rights reserved. No part of this book may be reproduced or transmitted in any form or by any means, electronic or mechanical, including photocopying, recording, or by any information storage and retrieval system, without the written consent of the publisher, except where permitted by law.

Printed in the USA.

## CONTENTS

Ever Nat..................................................................5

The Salt-Diviner.......................................................55

The Refrigerator Full of Sperm....................87

# EVER NAT

Gray had seen the girl hitching down the Route several nights in a row. Pure-bred redneck, he could tell, but . . . *Christ, she's cute.* Faded cut-offs, halter top, sleek bare legs flashing in his headlights as she trod the road's gravel edge. He'd read in the county section that prostitutes were known to hitch on the Route . . .

Gray worked in the city: 125k a year now, assistant programming director for UniCorp. Not bad for 40. And switching him to 4-to-12s dropped another ten percent in his pocket as a night differential. The adjustment came easy: fewer people in the office, fewer distractions and ringing phones—more time to work. Gray had no wife anymore and had never really cared about a social life; the way he saw it, work was the only way to make anything of himself. *And I have,* he thought now. His car, in part, was proof. An onyx-black Callaway Twin Turbo Corvette: sixty grand. A $15,000 VTL/Apogee stereo at home. And home wasn't shabby either, a three-bedroom luxury condo, waterfront. The good things in life--that's what he worked for . . .

But at times like this, during these incalculable drives, he got to wondering. *What else is there?* Good question after two marriages and two divorces, plus the handful of nickel-dime relationships in between. Women always wanted something, at least it seemed to him. *Like I owe them a life in exchange for sex once a week.* He'd had it up with the whole ball of wax. *I don't need a woman in my life,* he considered, comfortable behind the padded wheel. *All I need is me . . .*

But was that really true?

There were other needs.

Four-to-12s had one more perk: no rush hour. Gray left the city at midnight, then took the Route to the interstate. With no traffic, he'd be back to his condo in less than a half hour. State Route 154 was a long winding flood emergency route through the dense woodland of south county. It was a pretty drive, scenic—especially at night, especially during the summer. The low moon followed him through the trees.

Crickets and peepers issued their steady, pulsating cacophony, and the stars glimmered like luminous spillage in the sky.

And here she was again. The girl he'd seen hitchhiking several nights in a row. The girl, and that rising need.

Yes, he'd read in the paper that prostitutes often walked the Route, but not like the hookers in the city—they were all drug-addicts, scary in their empty-eyed stares and sleazy getups. These Route girls, he'd heard, were just poor rubes—white trash, for the most part—looking to make a few bucks to take back to their broken farms. And this one here?

Just last night he'd passed her, hadn't he? She'd been walking just past the bend, and when Gray spotted her, something in his soul seized up. That trampy, hick beauty glared back in the swoosh of halogen high beams; a freeze-frame locked in his head.

*Oh, man...*

All slim curves and fine lines. Frayed cutoffs satcheled sleek, spread hips. Pert breasts, large for a girl of her delicate frame, swayed braless in the faded orange halter, and between that and her beltline, Gray lost his breath at the image of her tight, sloping abdomen and the tiny slit of bellybutton. Her face seemed to beam bright as the halogens: big brown eyes; a small, robust mouth; a peaches-and-cream complexion.

Hair the color of mature straw danced at her shoulders.

And all these details, yes, he'd managed to assess in the split-second glimpse as his Corvette rounded the bend. But one more detail nicked at him, more persistent than the others, and the detail was this: Her tanned arm extended, her thumb out.

*Pick her up,* he thought. *Maybe she'll...*

*Maybe she'll what? Proposition you?*

Was that what he was looking for?

The answer must've been yes, because a few tenths of a mile later, Gray was pulling a U. His heart seemed to pick up in its beat as he drove, scanning the lit shoulder. But—

*Ever Nat*

*Goddamn it!*

When he got back to the bend, another car idled at the line—a nicely refurbed '68 Camaro, ice-white. It was a small-block, with headers and chambered exhaust. Gray could tell by the healthy *chunk-chunk-chunk* of the idle. But something in his spirit seemed to collapse when he saw...

The girl was getting in. A final passing glimpse showed him the driver's face in the left window, some stubbled, long-haired redneck. *Goddamn rube probably changes tires for a living,* Gray thought in disgust.

So that was the end of that. Or—

Maybe not.

Here she was again, tonight, hitching along the same shoulder, barefoot, long tan legs stepping backward as she jerked her thumb out.

*Pick her up...*

It was something like a haze in his eyes when he pulled the Corvette right over. A shadow danced in his rearview, and then the passenger door was opening. The shadow slipped in, bringing a faintly musky scent in its wake. The door slunked shut.

"Hi," Gray said.

"Ha," she replied. That's what her redneck dialect turned the word "hi" into. "Wow, this, I say, this is some really nass car."

*Nass?* he thought, but then he considered the dialect again. She was saying nice.

"Thanks. So where you headed?"

"Tylersville, I means, if ya kin go all's that way. You's kin drops me off 'fore the highway ramp if ya's cain't go that far."

*Fuck.* Tylersville was all the way at the end of the Route, close to ten miles probably.

"Sure," he agreed. *What else have I got to do?* Gray thought. *Go home? Catch the end of Leno?* "It's not that far out of my way."

"Thank-ya, and I'se sorry if I smell like crabs."

The comment took him aback. "Smell like what?"

"Likes crabs. See, I'se work for Stevenson's Crabbers. They'se got a shack juss up the Route. That's where I'se walkin' home from juss now. I'se a crab-picker. See, they'se buy crabs by the bushel down the City Dock, and we'se pick all the meat out of 'em and put it in containers ta sells ta the city restaurants so they'se can make crabcakes'n newburg'n stuff. Pay's not bad, eithers—fifty cent over minimum wage."

What was that? About seven bucks an hour to pick crabs in some sweatshop all day. *I make that much in about five minutes,* he thought.

"Sounds like, uh, an interesting job."

"Ak-shure-lee it kinda sucks," she admitted, "but I gots a baby an' I don't wanna go on the welfare."

"Well, that's, uh, that's very commendable of you," Gray struggled for a reply.

"An', ya know, you'll'se see me hitchin' home from there this time most ever nat."

*Ever nat?* Gray tried to decipher and remembered yet again the dialect. *Ever nat. Every night.*

"Yeah, I, you know, I think I saw you last night, but—"

"I saws you too. Ain't no way I'd ferget a nice car like this. Wish ya'd picked me up, thoughs, 'cos the guy who did, it was this real cracker inna white Camaro. He weren't very nice."

Gray searched for a comment. What did she mean? But before he could think of something . . .

"'Corse I do more'n pick crabs fer money, ya know."

Silence. Gray drove with it. It was like a companion riding in the backseat, a preceptor sitting there and waiting to see how he would gauge and then react to the remark.

This was the moment, wasn't it? Put up or shut up.

His groin, suddenly, felt like some burgeoning *thing,* a husky, drooling animal dragging him around. He couldn't control it. He hadn't really even looked at her since she'd gotten into the car, yet something about her seemed to emanate: the musky, perspiry scent, the gentle drawl of her voice, the way her lithe shadow played on the dashboard.

"An' I guess you knows what I'se talkin' 'bout," she went on unabashed, "'n'less that's, like, a summer squash ya gots there in yer pants."

Gray, in spite of his nervousness, almost belted out a loud laugh. It reminded him of old high school jokes. *Is that the Loch Ness Monster in your pants, or are you just happy to see me? Shit. Some summer squash.* Six and a quarter inches, and that was on a *good* day. But it was time, wasn't it? *Time to get down to business.*

"I'm not a cop or anything," he felt the impulse to offer. Didn't they usually ask that first? He'd seen it on the cop shows and in the movies. If they asked and a decoy cop said no, there was some entrapment law they'd be violating? Gray wasn't sure.

"Oh, I know you ain't no cop," she said and laughed lightly. "Cops don't drive cars like this! 'Sides, I kin tell you's're a nass guy."

Hmm. *So. I'm a nass guy.*

"Well, thank you for saying so," he said. "You're a nice girl."

"And I'se kin tell ya, cops 'round these parts? They ain't nass. 'Specially them county sheriffs. They ain't nass at all."

Gray didn't know what to say. He was too excited to pursue small-talk. The pause that followed sounded hollow, mixed with the big engine's soft hum. He gulped and continued, "So, like how much money are we talking here, and, you know . . . for what?"

Her voice didn't hitch. "I'll'se give ya a good blowjob fer, like, ten bucks, if you'll drive me all's the way home."

*Ten bucks? Christ.* Gray was about to offer a hundred. He fished in his pocket—there was a twenty in there somewhere. He grabbed some haphazard bills and gave them to her.

"I don't know what that is," he said. "Twenty, thirty, something like that. You can have it."

"Dag, mister!" Her nimble hands counted the bills in the

moonlight on the dash. "This here's twennie, not ten. Plus a five."

"You can have it, you know, for—"

The feel of her hand on his groin silenced him. At first it felt as though a little bird had landed there, but then the bird gave a soft rub and then a harder squeeze. Gray nearly came.

Her lilting voice hushed as she leaned over. The hand rubbed him more intricately. "I mean, I don't wants ya ta think I'm juss some whore're anything. But I'se never seed nothing wrong with a gal taking some money long's she's willing ta give something'n return. Ya know? Mue-cher-all agreement."

Gray's breath lodged in his chest. "I . . . agree . . ."

"Tells ya what," she whispered. Now her face was so close to his crotch, he could almost feel her breath on it. "You's juss keep yer hands on the wheel an' con-ser-trates on yer drivin', an' I'll'se do the rest."

Gray gulped, nodded mutely.

He felt his buckle come undone, then heard the rasp of his zipper. A sweet shock seemed to tremor, then, when he felt her fingers push his slacks down and then prise out his scrotum and already hard penis. She gently squeezed his balls, and, next, harder, she squeezed the shaft. Gray felt a small reservoir of pre-ejaculate form at the glans.

"You's juss drives me all the way down the Route. Turn left on 3 ta Tylersville, an' I'se'll suck ya the whole way."

Gray was about to come right now, not ten miles from now, and she hadn't even taken it into her mouth. *I don't think. . . . I'll quite . . . last that . . . long,* he thought, his teeth grinding.

Her right hand cupped his balls as her mouth sucked, first the glans, then took the whole thing—all six and a quarter inches—down to the back of her throat. Gray's cock suddenly felt cocooned in a hot, wet gulf. At the base, her lips constricted to a tight O, then drew up. This was expert, this was phenomenal. That delectable wet O drew up and down again, up and down—

Thinking about baseball worked to a point, a destructive

distraction. Each time he forced an image into his head—Clemens' twenty-second win, or A-Rod post-season record breaker—Gray's orgasm was staved off for a moment. But he gnashed his teeth in objection—inviting such imagery seemed a horrible vandalism to the sensation. He wanted the sensation to be extended, though; hence, a brutal cycle of sabotage. He'd turn the image off and was about to come, so he turned it right back on: Swisher, Jeter, Texiera, etc. *Aw, Jesus!* When he summoned the image of C.C. Sabathia's face, his erection nearly died.

"Mmm, yeah," the girl paused to say. "You're lastin' a good long while. I wouldn't mind ya fuckin' me, neithers. Bet'cha'd make me come."

She slowly jacked it with her hand a few times, fingers playing over slick spit. Gray had to keep his eyes ludicrously wide on the road.

"I don't mind suckin' fellas off," she drawled on. "It's kind'a fun." She squeezed more crystal ooze out of the tip, then played her thumb over it. Gray fidgeted sharply in the seat.

"And you ain't like a lotta guys." More talk, more hand-play. "You know? Lotta guys talk real nasty while I'm doin' it, sayin' mean stuff. Like that fella last night? Kept callin' me pig'n bitch'n whore, sayin' 'suck that cock, ya little whore' and stuff like that."

Gray's legs were tremoring; he had trouble keeping his right foot controlled over the gas. "That's, uh," he gasped. "That wasn't very nice."

"Naw, but you are."

Her voice was erotic—that drawl, half innocence, half experience. Sabathia's psychological wreckage disappeared, and Gray was hard again, hard as metal pipe. She'd squeeze against the nerve-charged rigidity, slide her hand up, slide her hand down, with pain-staking slowness. A few more times like that and he'd come all over himself, probably squirt himself in the face. But just when that would happen, she let go and massaged his balls. Gray was definitely getting his money's worth.

She seemed to be considering something when she said, "Awright, I know what I'll do. But I don't usually do it, just so ya's know."

Gray was dismayed, face bloated and popping sweat behind the wheel. *What the fuck are you talking about? Keep sucking!*

She held something up she'd slipped out of her pocket. Gray heard the faintest tearing sound. He pulled his eyes off the road several times, sneaking glances, and saw that she'd just slipped a condom out of its packet. The rubbery lubricant scent wafted over.

"What, uh, what are you—"

"Shh," she replied. "You'll like this."

*What, she's gonna fuck me while I'm driving?*

"See, fellas all like it, they just never say so on account they don't want the girl ta think they're queer."

Gray remained speechless in his dismay as she rolled the condom over her right index finger. Then she was leaning over.

"What, uh, what are you—"

"In we go." She slipped her finger right into his anus, slipped it in deep.

Gray could not reckon such turmoil; he wanted to shout. But then it occurred to him only a second later that this "turmoil" was very interesting. Gray's entire being felt bloated in the strange, excruciating pleasure, and before he knew it she was fellating him again, with mind-boggling precision. He knew he'd last only a second longer like this, the mouth sucking his cock like she was drinking a milkshake through a straw and the finger roving. It didn't matter that he'd last only another second, because he knew it would be the best second of pleasure in his life.

Yes, in just another—

Gray seized up in the driver's seat and came anxiously into the hot wet wonderful spit-filled mouth. It was an explosive release. He thought of a tube of window chalk lying on its side and suddenly being smacked with a sledgehammer, its contents evacuated at once. He expected her lips to pop off at the first mammoth spurt, but they didn't. They stayed there, more quickly now drawing up and down. Gray's hips quivered, his asshole clenching around her finger, and then his buttocks rose off the leather seat as he struggled to remember he was driving a car down a winding road. So much semen spurted out of him he wondered how her mouth could hold it all. The orgasm supplanted him into another world; his eyes rolled in his head, and his knees shook to the point that he could barely control the foot pedals.

When she was done, she slipped her mouth off, leaned backed, and swallowed.

"Fellas like it more when a gal swallers," she said. "Don't know why, but'cha git used ta the way it tastes."

Gray barely heard her, nerves firing down. He felt like a big sack of dough in the seat. Then he flinched, nearly yelped aloud, when she slipped the condomed finger out of his anus. The aftersensation radiated, and as she'd been removing her finger, he felt some mysterious leftover of sperm ooze slowly out of his urethra.

*Holy motherfucking shit,* he thought.

She held her hand out the window, slipped the fouled condom off her finger. It flew away into the dark like an expectoration.

"Ya feel better now?" she asked him.

Gray tried to say yes but his tongue clogged his mouth. Sucking breaths, he nodded.

"I knew ya'd like it. My brothers tolt me 'bout it, 'bout how they'll come better during a blowjob with a finger up'n their ass. Some gland up in there, little gland that makes yer jizz er somethin'."

Gray could fathom absolutely no response. Had she said her *brothers?* Her *brothers* had given her a lesson in rectal anatomy? Gray didn't even want to guess, didn't want to imagine what kind of family she might have come from. But of course she'd been right, too. Her technical intricacies had provided him the best orgasm of his life. She rubbed his testicles some more and he was still spasming down. *A finger up the ass, huh?* Until then the only things to ever be up Gray's ass were turds, but he could hardly argue.

He slowed the car down, unaware until now how he'd been accelerating through the event. Finally he blurted out, "That was great."

"I wanna do things ya like, 'cos I like ya. If I do things ya like, then you'll pick me up agin, next time ya see me hitchin' home from the crab-pickers."

"Kuh—count on it."

"Cain't have ya thinkin' I'm a slob," came her next inexplicable chatter. Now she was rubbing his bare stomach, looking down at his groin. "Cain't be leavin' a mess on ya, ya know? I always clean up my messes."

Gray flinched, nearly yelped again when she abruptly popped his penis back into her mouth and sucked hard, sucking off those oozing remnants. His hips and thighs tingled fiercely as the last lingering semen was drawn out. His cock felt fat, half deflated but still buzzing in luxuriant post-climax. She sucked her mouth off again and simultaneously slid her hand back up the spitty shaft, squeezed tightly with her index finger and thumb collaring his corona. A final pearl of sperm appeared and she licked it right off.

*Good God...*

Gray eventually managed to get his mind back on driving. Her hand lingered on his balls, a finger teasing between them. *Jesus Christ, can she give a blow job...* Every aspect of his reproductive capacity—from nerve reaction to sperm supply—felt utterly drained, a bucket tipped over and emptied.

"You's shore came a lot," she observed next, smacking her lips, "and you gotta nice cock, a nice-looking knob, and it ain't all bumpy like a lotta of 'em."

All Gray could say to the most inane compliment of his life was "Thank you."

"And you're nice'n clean too," she kept chattering. "No

foreskin—not that I got anythin' against 'em but—Chrast—so many fellas don't wash it out and it's got all that smelly stuff in it. Yuck."

"I can't say that I know what you mean," he tried to joke, "since I don't have the benefit of your experience. So I'll take your word for it."

The attempt at levity went over her head. Another smack of her lips, then she poised in the seat, animated. "And, ya know, yer come tastes good, not like a lotta fellas, all bitter'n all."

*My come tastes good,* Gray repeated the remark in his mind. *Oh dear me, is this a night of revelation or what?* Maybe if he ever got a girlfriend again, he could tell her that on the first date. *By the way, I have it on some very qualified authority that my sperm tastes good.*

The girl stared out the windshield and stroked her chin as if pondering a puzzle. "I wonder if what'cha eat effects the taste of your come? Ya think?"

Gray's smile of incredulity bloomed on his face. "I . . . don't know. But I suppose it's an interesting question."

"Like, if all a guy eats bacon, does it make his come taste like bacon? Er-er-er, what if he eats lots'a candy?" Her stare beyond the glass deepened. "I wonder if it makes his come sweet."

"Perhaps it does." Gray could barely stifle a chuckle. *This is some conversation.* "You're really great," he finally said when he got his breath back. Now she was daintily rebuckling his slacks, tucking the shirt in, making sure the zipper's tab was right when she pulled it up.

"There ya go . . ."

"Look, you know, I mean," he began to babble, "didn't you say said you walk this way a lot?"

"Yeah. Ever nat. Ever week-nat that is."

"Well, see, why don't we make a deal? I drive home this way every night too, the same time, and I was thinking that maybe I could pick you up like this and drive you home, for, you know—"

She seemed elated. "You's'll drive me home ever nat fer a blow job an' gives me twennie five ta boot?"

"Yes," Gray said. "Why not?" The quiet calculation registered: twenty-five dollars a night, five nights a week. *A little over six grand a year. Piece of cake.* His two ex-wives were remarried now—no more alimony. "I mean, you need the money for your baby, and I, you know, I need—"

Her hand, perhaps unconsciously, squeezed his crotch. "That'd be dandy 'cos, like, most'a the guys who give me rides ever nat, they'se only pay like five'r ten bucks an' a lotta times they'se try to do things I never agreet to. They'se all mostly crackers, see, dirty fellas and mostly drunk. But I like you. An' you's say you give me twennie-five fer a blow? Ever nat?"

"Sure," Gray said. "Every night."

She lived way back in the boondocks, all right. An old county utility road took them deep into the woods. The moon had risen higher; it was a half-moon, a yellow lump hovering. Gray kept taking sideglances at it, for whatever reason, but it just made him more aware of the girl. For the whole time he drove, she never took her hand off his crotch. He could feel her hand's warmth through the material. Then she was rubbing more intently as her big dark-caramel eyes wandered over the scape of the forest. It didn't take long before Gray was hard again.

The Corvette's tires crunched over gravel. At the end of the road, a clearing opened, and a little two-story farmhouse sat wedged into sprawls of high weeds. Blistered once-white paint peeled back to reveal old, dull-gray wood, and there were dark shutters with slats falling out. An attic with one blank window peaked out of the structure toward its rear, some shingles missing from the small belfry-like roof. A large garage branched off one side, obviously a makeshift addition, and behind it, an expansive area surrounded by an eight-foot-high plank fence, more old unvarnished gray. Amid the weeds crawling around the house, Gray noticed orange bloated objects sitting lopsided, and then he realized what they were. *Pumpkins,* he thought. *Well that's damn appropriate, because this dump could pass for a Halloween house of horrors any day.* Gray didn't want to hang around. She had a kid, so she probably had a husband. And the husband must have a shotgun, to fit right in with the rest of this backwoods cliché.

He pulled up at the end of the gravel drive, stopped.

"Look," she said, "I means, you been real nice'n generous to me, 'specially offerin' ta pick me up ever nat, but, see, I lives here with my two brothers Jory'n Hull, but, see, they'se're mechanics, they'se work on cars."

"What about . . . I mean, aren't you married?"

"Aw, no, I'se ain't married!" she exclaimed as if it was an absurdity. "I gotta baby, shore, but that was juss by some fella who raped me once."

"Oh, wow," Gray said. "I'm sorry."

"Ain't nothin' ta be sorry 'bout 'cos she's a beauter-full baby." Her fingers, very daintily, tacked around Gray's crotch. Things were moving down there again, the tent struggled to rise against the tension. "I'se don't want ya ta think I'm greedy're nothing, but, ya know, seein's that yer hard again, I thoughts ya might wanna come in an' give me a fuck."

Just hearing the word—*fuck*—come from her mouth made Gray feel like he might come right there in his pants. His chest tightened. "But-but you said you had two brothers."

"Yeah, I'se do, but, see, they'se ain't here right now, won't be home till tuh-marruh nat on account they had ta go ta Pennsylvania ta buy car parts at some big car convention. So's you kin come in, an' we'se won't be disturbed. But, ya know, I'd have ta charge, like, maybe . . . forty?"

All reason was lost now. Gray turned off the motor and the lights, opened his wallet, and gave her a hundred dollars.

"Tarnations! Ya don't have ta give me that much!"

"Take it," he said. His words came out parched. "You're really just so . . . beautiful . . ."

Her face leaned forward in the dark. He couldn't see it as much as feel it—its softness, its warmth. She kissed him very lightly on the lips while her hand lingered at his crotch, his lust rekindled now full-force. Yes, so much lust for her, lust that felt like an inchoate, molten mass.

"Come on," she whispered. "I'll'se make ya feel real good. You ain't even gotta use a rubber if ya don't want."

Rubbers were the last thing on his mind just then. In fact, everything was—everything but her. Gray got out, almost fell over in some distractive euphoria. Did she giggle? She led him into the house, holding his hand. The front door creaked open; she switched on a light.

*What a dive,* Gray thought. This looked like the place Jed and Granny lived in *before* they moved to Beverly Hills. More dilapidated inside than out, a shit-heap. But then he scolded himself. Certainly she was underprivileged. No education? Picking crabmeat? And she'd do that to support her child rather than go on welfare. In a lot of ways, she was a better person than he.

"Sorry'se 'bout the mess," she apologized.

The words barely registered. Gray stood in a prickling fog, staring. His eyes seemed to be entities with minds of their own; he couldn't take them off her. She nonchalantly turned, tossed her head, gave a despondent smile. Then she took off the halter and, just as nonchalantly, stepped out of her cutoffs.

*God Almighty,* Gray thought.

Even in this tacky place, in this tacky lamplight . . . she was beautiful. It was a sporadic kind of beauty, an honest kind, utterly divorced from centerfold appeal and women's-mag chicness. Here was a real woman, however unsophisticated, full of real life. Even her flaws were beautiful: one upper front tooth slightly crooked, one distended nipple minutely larger than the other, an old scar on one knee. *Beautiful,* Gray thought in his daze. His mouth felt dry. She didn't seem the least bit inhibited about standing before a perfect stranger totally naked. Fine hair showed traceably from her underarms. A plot of dark-blond fur puffed from her pubis, and within it, just barely, he could see the lovely folds of her femininity.

The large, high breasts swayed as she stepped forward. "You ready?" she asked.

"Yes," he nearly croaked.

The vision entranced him, pulled him to his knees. Now he was face to face with the nebulous triangle of hair. Gray brushed the hair with his lips; it was so soft he barely felt it. Just as soft were the backs of her thighs, over which his hands glided until they found their way to her buttocks. His mouth urged closer, the hair tickling, and when his tongue slipped against the nugget of her clitoris, her ass clenched in his hands.

"I-I lack that," her whisper flittered down from above.

Lack. Like. Yes, he wanted her to like it, that most irrational part of himself. The other part was buried somewhere, interred in a sepulcher of modern common sense. Licking a prostitute's vagina wasn't something the upwardly mobile did in this day and age, but Gray did it anyway, reveling in her sharp taste and moist heat. He could hear her breathing faster. She tweezed her clitoris between two fingertips and gently pulled up. The action extruded the little acorn of flesh more directly, so Gray could lick it better. The fingertips of her other hand pushed the back of his head. She was gasping gently now, the knowing human noise turned Gray on more, and her own excitement couldn't be contested. He could taste it, that salty glaze beginning to flow from the folds beneath the downy hair. Gray couldn't have been more pleased with himself. He was a tekkie, a computer geek, yet here he was arousing this worldly woman of obvious sexual experience. If anything, her responses were very flattering.

But his own needs were raging—the needs he was paying for.

"Now, baby—"

Gray looked up, saw her face looking back down at him between the beautiful breasts. The face was flushed, the eyes narrowed with desire. Her hands were on his shoulders next, urging him to stand, and when he was back on his feet, the front of his pants bulging, she kissed him and ran her tongue between his lips.

"Git'cher cock out, baby," came the next parched whisper. Gray did, and was tempted to jerk it off right there when she turned around and bent over to clear off some space on the kitchen table behind her. His eyes ran up the back of her legs, over the tight, white rump, up the sleek lines of her back. When he squeezed his penis—just once—it didn't even feel like his. It was insanely hard, throbbing like some convulsant animal, a fat veined lizard.

Then she turned back around, almost dizzy now. She sat up on the edge of the table, lay back, and held her legs wide open for him, her feet poised high in the air. "Put it in me, baby. Juss stick it right in . . ."

Gray stepped up, slack and shorts down at his ankles. He eased in and out of her, biting his lip. *Not again . . .* The simple feel of her inside turned him into a hair trigger about to fall. Struggling, he summoned more baseball images.

"Hard. Do it hard."

Gray tried but—*Forget it.* Not even imagining being in the showers with Randy Johnson could hold off the inevitable. Gray's balls drew all the way up to the root; he gasped. The first spurt of his orgasm vaulted out of him and into her, a flood-gate knocked down, but before he could even be aware of the second spurt—

—some blunt object cracked him on the back of the skull. And Gray's world, as well as all of his desires and all of his dreams and all of his love, turned black.

He awoke, lying askew, on a gritty bare-wood floor. A bright light burned from above, but before it, two blurred shapes began to sharpen. "How's it goin' there, City Boy?" someone asked like a voice echoing from the bottom of a well.

Gray's head barked with pain. He squinted upward and focused. Two men in overalls grinned down, stubbled faces, mouths full of black teeth.

"'Cos that's where you's're from, ain't it? The city?"

Gray groaned at the pain in his head. Another pain, somewhere else, nagged at him, but he couldn't place it.

"*Must* be from the city, Hull," another voice, losing its well-bottom echo, speculated. "Them fancified city clothes, an' that Callaway 'Vette? An' he's got credit cards too. Only city fellas have them."

Gray strained his vision at the younger of the two overalled men. Mussed hair stuck up in spikes; he grinned as he ruffled through Gray's kidskin wallet.

"This here's my l'il brother Jory, and me? I'se Hull," said the other one. This was too proverbial: these guys were hicks, hayseeds, right down to their dusty workboots and denim overalls. *The girl set me up,* Gray realized, bringing a hand to his head. *And, Christ—what did they hit me with? A fucking refrigerator?*

"Bet'cher noggin hurts," said Hull, the older one, thumbing the straps of his overalls. Chest hair and muscles showed beneath the bib. "Jory jacked ya out a might hard." The man tittered. "Bet'cher backside smarts too, huh?"

Only then did Gray calculate that other pain. He leaned up and saw that his X'andrini black silk shirt had been removed, and his Italian slacks—$150 at Grenadi's For Men—had been pulled down. His anus seemed to throb in time with the pain in his head.

"What . . . what did you do?"

"Jory here, see, he already had hisself a nut up yer cornhole. While's you was havin' yer beauty sleep."

"Tightest boy-pussy I ever had, I still say," Jory added. He was still riffing through Gray's wallet. "Hey, Hull! City's got a couple hunnerts here!"

Gray groggily leaned up. The answer to his question had already been answered by the throbbing rectal pain. But Gray asked anyway. "Wait a minute, wait a minute. Are you saying that you sodomized me?"

The two rednecks belted laughter. "Sodder-mized? Shee-it, you really is from the city!" Jory exclaimed.

Then Hull: "We don't call it sodder-mee here, City. We'se real folks, and what we'se call it is cornholin'."

*Jesus Christ...*

"An' I 'spect," Hull went on, "Jory here's gonna have hisself another nut up yer cornhole, like, real soon. Me, I'se usually just good fer one nut a day s'bout. But a young fella like him? Got a hard dog three, four times a day, he does."

Gray couldn't believe this. *I've been abducted by homosexual rednecks.* Hull, he could see, was rubbing the front of his overalls like someone in a grocery testing avocados for ripeness. Jory, on the other hand, still had his penis hanging out the front of his overalls. He flicked off a little raisinette of shit.

When Gray adjusted his position on the floor, he heard a metallic clatter, and then he made the next—decidedly grim—discovery. A steel shackle girded his left ankle, and from the shackle a chain extended. A *heavy* chain. The chain looked about six or eight feet long. Its other end was padlocked to an iron ring bolted to the floor.

*I'm fuckin' chained to the floor!*

"Had to chain ya," Hull explained. "Caint have ya gittin' out. Sheriff's station ain't but five miles yonder, off the Route."

*I'm chained,* Gray thought again as if to finalize the reality. This fact probably meant that his hosts wouldn't be letting him out of here any time soon...

"Gits my dog hard juss lookin' at you, City," Hull went on. "Come on, now. Hands and knees."

Gray was incredulous. Hull was dropping his overalls, and so was Jory. "You got to be shitting me, man," Gray remarked. "You don't expect me to—"

Hull slapped him hard on the head; Gray reeled. Then he got into position, chain clattering.

"Hands'n knees now, like a pooch." Hull produced a buck knife for a little extra incentive. It glinted.

"Yeah," the other one chuckled. "Ever heard'a screwin' the pooch? *You're* the pooch."

"Look," Gray pleaded in a last effort, "do you guys really have to do this? I mean, you got the girl. I'm sure she'd be a hell of a lot better than me."

Gray shrieked when Hull slapped his head again. "What-choo talkin' 'bout!" Hull took exception. "Kari Ann? She's our sister! That'd be insesteriss! What kinda pree-verts ya think we is?"

Gray's brain felt like a single, throbbing blob of pain. *Pardon me for making the inference,* he thought, as pissed off as he was terrified, *but it's not like I'm seeing a whole lot of morality here. You just RAPED ME in the ass.*

"Shee-it. I oughts ta cut me off one'a yer balls juss fer sayin' such a dirty thing."

"Sorry," Gray sputtered.

But Jory railed, "Dag damn, Hull! I'se gonna have myself a good come up his this fella's backside. Second nut'a the day's always the best, I say." Jory knelt and turned Gray around, jerking up at his hips. "Feels good!"

"Best not ta fight it, City," Hull obliged. "We'se gonna have ya one ways're another. Don't make me git ta cuttin' on ya."

Gray's eyes widened in more truth. What could he do? Moreover, what would they do when they were finished? It wasn't like he was going anywhere, not chained to the fucking floor. The rationale of survival set its teeth: *I've got no choice . . .*

Hull flexed his hairy pecs. "You's gonna give me a peter-suck while's Jory here checks yer oil."

Gray, fully on hands and knees now, nodded grimly. He winced at the sound of Jory clearing his throat and expectorating into the cleft of his buttocks. "Gots ta slick ya up some, huh, City? Give that tight l'il boy-poon a good lubin'."

"Jory, see, he don't much care fer a peter-suck, says it tickles," Hull enlightened. "Pur-fers a cornholin' any day. But me? I'se just the opper-sit. Don't care to have a fella's shit on my stick much, ya know? But a good peter-suck—*that's* what I'se pur-fer."

"Time to park the car in the garage," Jory quipped, kneeling right up now behind Gray. Gray's cheek's billowed at the sensation: a wet nudge . . . forward pressure, then . . .

*slunk*

Jory's "car" pulled deftly into Gray's "garage." Gray blew out more air. The pain was not nearly as paramount as the sheer pressure. Jory's callused hands held Gray's hips as he began to draw in and out. *Christ, this motherfucker's huge!* Gray had no choice but to observe. *It feels like I'm taking a shit in reverse . . .*

"Luckys fer you that Hull don't fancy a lot'a cornholin', 'cos his dog's even bigger'n mine."

Hull chuckled. "Now come on, Jory. Ain't ya got no manners? When yer cornholin' a fella it's only proper'n courteous ta at least give him a reach-around!"

Jory pumped now in a steady rhythm, each stroke seeming to reach up into Gray's guts. "Aw, City, I'se truly do apoler-gize. That ain't very hospital of me at all, now, is it?" Jory reached under Gray's right hip and grabbed his penis and scrotum. He squeezed it probingly several times, as though it were an udder on a cow. "Shee-it, Hull, I say this boy ain't got much at all!"

Gray's genitals felt like a bag of dead flesh.

Hull grinned through rotten teeth. "He gittin' hard?"

"Shee-it, Hull! Hard? This here city fella here? Peter on him feels about as hard as a chicken liver! And I say, his nuts don't feel hardly no bigger'n a coupla olives!"

"Bet he don't come much neithers." Hull knelt before Gray's face, inched up closer on his knees, and fully pulled down his overalls. "Well, here's something for ya, City." He used his full hand to extract his genitals. "Like a big hot lollipop."

Gray's eyes opened to the size of Kennedy dollars. *You've got to be shitting me!* If Gray, on a good day, sported six and a quarter inches, well . . . you could add about three more inches to that and it still wouldn't be as big as Hull's, and who cares if it was a good day? What hung immediately before Gray's face was something that looked like an erect summer sausage—with a snout on the end. Folds of abundant foreskin looked like bunched lunchmeat. "You suck on this good, City," Hull said, then flashed the point of the buck knife toward his face. "Ands if you even think 'bout bitin' it, so helps me, I'll'se dig yer eyeball out'n make ya eat it. Hear me?"

Gray, puff-eyed, nodded.

Hull pulled back the foreskin—a veritable sheet of loose skin—to reveal a damp pink glans with a ring of smegma girding the rim. "Git yer yap open, City, like at the doctor's office, open wide'n say ahhh. And don't mind the dick cheese. Hail, a l'il cheese won't hurt ya. Give ya something ta taste, huh?"

Gray, mortified now, squeezed his eyes shut and opened his mouth, and what was then inserted into said mouth reminded him of a raw turkey neck. Only bigger. "Reach up'n give my balls a squeeze too," Hull eloquently requested. Gray had to lean all his forward weight on one palm when he did so. And what his hand enclosed felt like two kiwi fruits.

Only bigger.

"Come on, City! Shee-it! You kins suck a dog better'n that. Suck it like yer daddy taught ya."

*This may come as a surprise to you, sir, but my father DIDN'T teach me how to suck dick . . .* Gray reasoned that his survival just now might very well depend on the dexterity by which he performed fellatio on this unwashed hayseed. And unwashed was an understatement. With his mouth so full, he had no recourse but to breathe through his nose, and with each inhalation came the most nefarious fetors. *Jesus,* he thought. *I've never sucked dick before. How am I supposed to know how to do it?* But he thought about that, and came to a conclusion. *Suck it the way the girl sucked you...*

He tried to abstract, and formulate his own method of expertise. A few agonizing slaps to the head indicated that his initial efforts weren't satisfactory, but then . . . Then he abstracted further: He pretended he was fellating himself. He kept the inside of his mouth wet, his lips tight, and his tongue firm against the basal shaft.

He thought he must be getting the hang of it but then Hull sputtered, "Fuckin' useless piece'a shit. Might as well just kill ya now. Any guy gives head bad as you don't deserve ta live."

The comment was not encouraging, but at least it served as an incentive. *Just . . . suck his dick better, for God's sake!* Gray thought. He stepped up the tempo, his mouth vised open as if by a shoe-tree. He tried to suck harder, feeling a slimy leakage begin to form on his tongue.

"Hmm. Not bad, I say. Gittin' better. Keep goin' jess like that an' I might not cut'cher throat tonight. Naw, might even keep ya alive fer one more."

The rewards of perseverance. But Gray knew he couldn't let him get bored. Then an idea blinked on.

*Like the girl,* he thought.

He remembered. How could he forget? *Lubricant,* came the frantic thought. The cock plungering in and out of his ass gave him the answer quite quickly. Jory had used saliva. *So will I,* Gray realized. He momentarily uncorked his mouth from Hull's hot penis, then he laved his own index finger with his spit, then—

"City's got some brains after all," Hull chuckled when Gray reached his hand around and slipped his finger into the man's anus. It plowed through chunky feces. Gray re-jammed the cock into his mouth, wriggling his finger.

"Yeah, City! That's it! Now ya got it!"

"Bet Kari Ann taught him that," Jory deduced, picking up his own tempo. Gray grimly felt Jory's testicle's slapping his own with each thrust forward. "Bet she done the same thing'n sucked his little peter in the car."

"Bet so."

"Little jizz-head's always been dumber'n cow flop but at least we taught her how ta do *somethin'* right."

Mouth crammed with dick, Gray rolled his eyes. *Didn't these guys just crack me in the head for implying that they might be incestuous? Go figure.* All that mattered at this instant was that he wasn't getting cracked in the head *again,* for performing mediocre fellatio. His index finger tilled through more hillbilly shit, teasing the prostate, while his mouth was fastidiously fucked. Gray's ass was being fucked with equal fastidiousness.More smegma dissolved on his tongue—an acrid yet pale flavor—and he willed himself to think about smells other than those which wafted from Hull's groin. Roses. Cranberry Lambic. Vanilla extract and his mother's hot apple pie. Reflex, however, caused his rectum to flinch, via such an intrusive invasion, but then Jory approved, "Hull? I say this here fella's one hail of a butt-fuck. Squeezes up his butthole real tight on my bone! Why, I'se still say this boy's the blammed best cornholing I'se ever had!"

"And ya's know what, Jor?" Hull replied, stroking steadily into Gray's mouth, "he kin suck a peter like there's no tuh-marruh!"

"Shee-it, I'se-I'se-I'se think I'se gonna come alls-ready. Pinch that butthole, boy! Squeeze it!"

Gray squeezed it, flexing intricate muscles he scarcely knew he had. Then—

Jory's fingers dug into his hips, his strokes faltering. "Aw, yeah, I say yeah! I'se comin' in this fella like a firehose!"

Gray wasn't sure he agreed with the simile. More like a turkey baster full of hot egg-drop soup being aspirated deep into his bowel. Gray could feel it, he could feel the wet, gluelike heat spurt and then settle. And, next, Hull's own strokes accelerated. "Shee-it, git it, City, git it! I'se gonna—"

The entirety of Gray's face seemed to swell shut when Hull ejaculated into his mouth. It was a voluminous ejaculation. Long hot spurts, like velotic pieces of spaghetti, launched to the back of his throat.

"Fuckin'-A."

There was nearly an audible pop when Hull withdrew the deflating—and elephantine—member, then his hand snatched up Gray's chin. "Swaller it now, City. Be a good l'il cock-suck ands swaller it all. Swaller alls that good come right down inta yer breadbasket 'nless ya want yer eye digged out."

Gray didn't want his eye "digged" out, so he "swallered." And what it was exactly that he swallered was something that reminded him of a mouthful of hot, thin snot. He winced, nearly gagged, then gulped.

And down it went.

It left a warm, strangely minty aftertrail down his esophagus.

"Hail of a come, Jory. Fella sucks a peter better'n a fifty-year-old whore."

"Take a cock up the tail just as good, I say," Jory elucidated. "Ain't never, I say never, had me a cornhole so's good. Came enough ta fill a milk bucket, I did!"

Gray pulled his finger out of Hull's ass and was then allowed to collapse to his belly. Chain links clinked. He could smell the fresh excrement on his finger.

"Kinda neat, ain't it?" Hull speculated. "I means he gotta belly fulla my come, an' a butt fulla yers."

"Yeahs," Jory agreed. "Too bad it ain't winter. All that come'd keep him warm."

Gray's cheek lay against the floor. *Thank God it's over. But . . .*

Exhausted, he turned over on his back, his Italian slacks bunched at his knees. What he saw, absurdly, appalled him. Jory was using his X'andrini black silk shirt as a rag to wipe off his genitals with.

"Man, that shirt cost two hundred bucks."

"Worth it," Jory grinned. "You's the best cornhole I'se ever had, an' this city-faggot shirt's the best dick-wipe. Soft."

Upside-down, Gray watched Hull stick his fat, deflated penis back into his overalls. Then he stood up. "T'was a dandy nut, City. You done good. An' 'cos you done such a fine job'a takin' care'a us, we'll'se send Kari Ann up with some viddles fer ya."

"An' we'll'se visit ya agin tuh-marruh," Jory promised.

"Hopes ya like yer dinner, City." Hull chuckled, turned, then slapped his brother on the shoulder. "Come on, Jor. Let's git downstairs now'n git ta work on them cars."

Their booted feet clunked down the stairs. A doorlock clicked.

Then Gray passed out.

"Wake up. Hey."

Something in a dream patted him on the cheek, jostled him. But when Gray opened his eyes, he saw it was no dream at all. It was still the same nightmare.

Haltered breasts swayed. The girl's face hovered over his. "Wakes up there. I'se got some food'n water fer ya."

Gray leaned up. At least the pain in his head didn't feel as pronounced, and as for the pain in his anus--it felt more numb than anything. When he rubbed his face, he winced; he could smell his finger. When he sat up, the chain dragged a little. He could imagine how ludicrous he looked—in spite of the horror his predicament presented: he was naked, save for his t-shirt and black dress socks.

"Here ya go. Sorry I ain't's got no spoon. Yer's gonna have ta eat it with yer fingers."

Gray's vision focused on the object in her hand.

*A bucket.*

Actually, two buckets, one in the other hand. Just garden-variety buckets. Gray's chain dragged when he sat up. For some reason, he tried to pull his t-shirt down over his exposed groin, as if he should be modest. Or could it be the fact that terror and violation had shrunk his genitals to what must look like a five-year-old's? But the attempt was futile. He'd put on some weight lately; the t-shirt could only be pulled down to the top of his pubic hair.

"What's in the buckets?"

"This bucket here?" She held one up, then set it down in the corner. "It's fer—Well, you know."

"No, I don't know," Gray replied testily.

"It's fer ya to pee in, and . . ."

*A shit-bucket, great. Well what do you know? There's a men's room here. I wonder if there's an attendant to go along with it, to pump the soap for me when I wash my hands.*

His sarcasm served no purpose. The wood floor felt warm on his bare, ghoul-white buttocks. But what was that smell? No, not the awful smell of dried shit on his finger—there was a pale aroma in the room.

She set the other bucket down. It steamed.

"This here's yer dinner," she told him, and something close to delight tickled Gray.

"Thank God, I'm starving." After being abducted, beaten, and raped? After spending the night nearly naked and chained to a wood floor? You bet. Some sustenance was just what he needed to focus on his predicament, and think of a way to get out of here.

"What is it?" he asked. "It smells sort of familiar, but I can't quite place it," and then she slid the bucket to him.

"I cooked it up for ya. Don't really know how to, so's I figured I'd steam it."

Gray looked in the bucket. "You've got to be kidding me!" he outraged.

Slabs of pumpkin lay in the steaming bucket.

"Well, I'se sorry it ain't nothin' better, but that's all they'se said I could give ya. Hull says we gots ta save money, an' these pumpkins grow all over the yard."

Gray shot her a critical glare. "You don't *eat* pumpkin, not as is.

It's just used for flavoring in pies!"

"Hull says the Indians et pumpkin all the tam—"

*All the tam,* Gray thought, disgusted.

"—durin' famines 'n such when the pilgrims wanted 'em ta starve." Her eyes lit up, as if with enthusiasm. "But they *didn't* starve, see, 'cos they et pumpkin."

Gray just looked at her.

"It ain't that bad," she encouraged. "Er, at least, probably it ain't."

"Wonderful." He pushed the steaming bucket away, no longer even mindful of his shrunken penis and scrotum. "I can't possibly eat this."

"Well-well," she stammered. "Ya best eat it all, 'cos Jory says if ya don't, they'll come up here 'n ruck ya about somethin' fierce."

"Great." That's what this was all about, wasn't it? Maximum humiliation. Rape him, make him give blowjobs. Force him to eat *pumpkin.* And why? *For the hell of it,* Gray realized. *If I don't eat it, they'll just kick my ass some more . . . and that's not the only thing they'll do with my ass . . .*

"'Least it'll be somethin' in yer belly," the girl suggested.

*She's right about that.* Gray decided to think with some practicality. The pumpkin would provide some necessary nutrition, some energy, and he'd need that to get out of here. *I'm about to eat hot pumpkin, with my hands.* Or, *hand,* that is. The finger of one hand, of course, had been up Hull's ass, and he didn't want to be eating with that one. He reached in, pulled up a wedge. At least she'd seeded it. He took a bite, his face squeezing up, eating it like a watermelon.

It did *not* taste like watermelon.

"Is it good?" the girl asked.

Gray just looked at her. It was not good. It was slimy, no sweetness whatever, just a mushy texture. He tried to tell himself it would taste like eggplant.

But it did not taste like eggplant.

"Bet it tastes like pumpkin pie, huh?"

"No," he groaned. She'd pronounced "pie" as "pah." There was a pumpkin flavor, though, and at least he learned something. *Hot pumpkin tastes like shit.* In a constant wince, he ate the pumpkin's whitish flesh off the orange skin, choking it down. It was awful.

The girl was on her knees, leaning over as she watched. He could see her bare breasts inside the halter but just now even the most erotic image caused no reaction. As he started in on the second wedge, she kneed around behind him, rubbed his shoulders. "Anythin' ya want me ta do fer ya?" she offered. "You kin fuck me if ya wants."

Gray smirked, cheeks stuffed with hot mush. "No, thanks."

"Wanna blowjob?"

"No!" A chunk of pumpkin blew out of his mouth. "I'm not exactly in the mood, you know? Those animal brothers of yours raped me. And it's *your* fault."

"It's not!" Suddenly she was sobbing. "Just 'cos they'se bad don't mean I am!"

"You're worse," Gray blurted. "You set me up. You lured me here—for them."

"I ain't had no choice!" she nearly shrieked. "If I don't do whats they say, they'se'll kill me, and my baby!"

Now she was blubbering hysterically. Swallowing more mush, Gray considered her words. She was just a stupid hill-girl, born into poverty, abused and tormented and subjugated from day one. What could Gray expect?

*And don't be an asshole,* he told himself. *You need this dumb cracker bitch to get out of here.* "Look, I'm sorry," he said, turning to her. He hugged her, a phony gesture, yes, but how else could he gain her confidence? "I didn't mean to say that, and I know you've had it rough, especially with brothers like that. It must be horrible to have to live with such terror."

"It is, it is," she sobbed into his shoulder, hugging him back. "They'se always beatin' me'n sayin' how they'll kill me if I act up. If that happened, it'd be the worse thing in the world, 'cos who'd take care'a my baby? Jory'n Hull hate my l'il girl anyways, an' if I was dead, they'd juss kill her. They'd put her in one'a the drums juss sure as shit."

"The drums?"

"That's how they'se git rid'a folks."

*The drums,* Gray reflected. *Get rid of folks.* He didn't know what the hell the drums were and he didn't want to know. The crucial information had already been relayed—something he could've guessed all along. *They're not just going to let me out of here after they've had their fun. They're going to kill me.*

But when?

"Look—what's your name? Kelly Ann?"

"Kari Ann," she sniffled.

"Your brothers. They're going to get rid of me too, aren't they?"

More sniffling as she nodded, gulped.

"How come they haven't done that already?"

"Oh, they will, just as soon as they're finished."

"Finished with what?"

"Yer car."

So that was it. *Probably stripping the car down, for parts,* Gray calculated. "How much time do I have?"

"'Nuther day, probably. It don't take 'em long. Then they—they'se'll git rid'a ya. But if yer lucky..."

Gray's eyes widened at the suggestion of hope. "What, Kari Ann? If I'm lucky, *what?*"

Her eyes were red from crying. She wiped her nose. "If yer lucky, they won't git rid'a ya right away. They'll keep ya around until they git another car."

Gray thought he got it. Jory and Hull were forcing the girl to bring victims back to the house. Then they'd chain the poor bastard up here and use him for sexual relief for as long as it took them to strip the car down.

"If ya—you know," she began. "If ya do 'em good, then they

probably won't kill ya right away."

The realization, however grim, came as no surprise by now. It made sense. *Homosexual sociopaths. I'm only worth keeping alive for as long as I'm a good fuck and suck. . . .* The more effectively Gray entertained them sexually, the better chance there'd be that they wouldn't kill him until the next abduction.

It looked like Gray would have to be a good bitch.

"Where am I, anyway?" he asked. "Some back room in the house?"

"The attic," she said.

Gray looked at the room's one window, then remembered the single window in the dormer-like room at the back of the house that he'd noticed when they pulled up. *That window must be this window.* As he recalled, it overlooked an area of the backyard surrounded by plank fencing. *I'm upstairs. So how do I get out?* Again, his only hope was the girl.

"Jory and Hull—they've been abusing you, haven't they?" he started. "Incestuously, I mean."

"Oh, no," she answered. "Just blowjobs'n fuckin' me in the ass. Hull says that ain't incest, on account of no come goes in my pussy."

*Oh, so that's how it works.*

"But after they started doin' the car thing, they took ta fellas more, so they'se don't do stuff like that ta me anymore. They just beat me a lot."

"And the father of your daughter," Gray went on. "Didn't you say—"

She looked down in shame. "Well, I'se lied 'bout that. Just said I got raped so's you'd feel sorry for me. He was some fella I been seein', but when I gots knocked up, Jory'n Hull kilt him." Then she broke out into more tears and hugged him. "I'm so sorry. It's juss that I'm so scared all the time, I *have* ta do what they say. I cain't let 'em kill my baby!"

"That's all right," Gray consoled. "I understand. You had no choice. But maybe in some weird way, this is all a good thing—us being brought together."

"What-what'cha mean?"

*Make this good,* Gray warned himself. "I can tell you're a special kind of girl. You're the kind of girl I've been searching for for my whole adult life."

She looked up, teary eyed. "Yuh-yuh-ya really mean that?"

"Of course I do. And I can only imagine what kind of life you have here . . . with your brothers."

"It's pretty bad," she sniffled. "But I gots ta do what they say so's they don't hurt my baby."

Gray took her hand in a performance worthy of an Oscar. "I understand all that, and it's okay. *Any* woman would do the same thing—they'd have no choice. But there's something I've got to tell you, Kari Ann, and I mean this. I think–I think I'm falling in love with you."

Her gazed groped for him, confusion merging with something that had to be hope. "We should be together," Gray continued. "I make a lot of money, Kari Ann. I could take you away from all this. But you have to help me."

"I-I couldn't—"

""You have to unlock this chain from my ankle, and when you go back downstairs, you have to leave the door unlocked. Then I'll get you and take you away from this place, you and your daughter. Then you'll have the kind of life you deserve."

She started with her waterworks again. "My brothers'd whup me! They probably kill me."

Gray whispered soft. "But that won't happen, Kari Ann. Because they'll never know. You won't have to worry about your brothers anymore. I'll take care of you, and your baby. It'll be wonderful."

Her lower lip trembled. Tears welled freely in her caramel-brown eyes. "I cain't! I cain't! I gotta go!"

Flustered, she grabbed the bucket full of pumpkin skins, then she whisked away, closed the door and padded barefoot down the steps.

*Why me, God?* Gray thought. *Why me?*

Gray slept horribly, wakening in the dark from horrific nightmares only to find himself alive in a worse reality. When the moon was high in the room's only window, he rushed to the bucket, voiding his bowels just in time. His pumpkin dinner soared through him; if felt like he was shitting hot broth. The abrupt discharge splattered against the bucket's bottom, and splashed back up to dot his rump. Nothing to wipe with, of course, so he dragged himself back across the wood floor, back into sleep, wet-buttocks'd. Later he rose again, to urinate, and—thanks to the single ceiling light that remained on through the night—had no choice but to watch the hard stream of his pee churn foam into the pale diarrhea. The smell of the room made him recall the outhouse at summer camp when he was a boy.

Birds chirped cheerily at daybreak, sunlight invading Gray's prison. He heard a racket outside, and voices. The chain, he found, was just long enough to let him get to the window.

*Maybe I can see what's going on . . .*

He had to crane his neck but was able to look outside. Down behind the house. From this vantage point he could see into the plank-fence enclosure. There was a garage back there, and a large tarp propped up by tent poles, cover against rain, he supposed. Gray saw several cars within the fencing, including a black-lacquered '68 Camaro and his own Callaway Corvette with the windshield and glass taped over. *What are those assholes doing to my car!* his thoughts screamed. They'd painted it cotton-candy pink. And there was Hull in the background, putting on a coat of lacquer with an air brush. More customization had been previously added; silver cursive letters on the back fender read: KICKIN' ASS, AIN'T TAKEN NO NAMES. *Oh, man,* Gray screamed. *They've turned my beautiful car into a dick-wagon! They didn't even spell 'takin'' right!* It looked like a pimp's car now.

Hull glanced over to Jory. "Come on, Jor. Git that cracker cut up'n outa here."

Gray's eyes moved right. "Shore, Hull. I'se just sharp'nin the blade." There was Jory at a grinding wheel, honing the blade of a frightfully large ax. Then he pulled some more tarp up on the ground.

Beneath the tarp lay a naked corpse.

"Yeah, this here fella weren't much good fer nothin'."

"Ain't kiddin', Jor. Couldn't suck a peter fer shit."

Then came a rubato *thwack-thwack-thwack*

Gray's belly squirmed as the ax rose and fell.

"Not like that city fella we gots upstairs, huh? Ooo-eee!" Hull celebrated. "Like ta suck my dick so hard I felt air goin' in my asshole."

Jory grinned, setting down the dripping ax. "Too bads you ain't inta cornholin', Hull. 'Cos that boy? Like fuckin' a chicken's how tight'a butthole he got. Shee-it!"

Now Jory leaned over, stacking pieces of limbs neatly in the tarp. A forearm here, a shin there. Hands and feet. And finally the head.

And it was a head Gray recognized . . .

*That redneck I saw the other night, picking up the girl. And that's his Camaro there, only they painted it black . . .*

Just then, the girl wandered out of the garage, her halter top off. In her arms she cradled a naked mulatto baby sucking noisily at her nipple.

Hull glared, paint gun in hand. "Git that tar-baby outa here, girl! Cain't'cha see we'se tryin' ta work!"

Gray looked harder at the baby. It squalled, naked, in her arms, less than year old. It looked mostly Negro but . . .

*Jesus . . .*

Closer examination reveled morose defects: a Down's head, one little foot smaller than the other, uneven ears, eyes way too close together. Kari Ann stuck a distended nipple into its drooly mouth, and that quieted it down. But Kari Ann seemed contemplative, her eyes cast to the ground. "But, Hull, I gots ta talk to ya. I means, do we really gots ta kill that city fella? Cain't we just let him go?"

"I've a mind ta slap you upside the head! Gals shore don't come no dumber."

"We gotta kill him, Kari Ann," Jory interjected. "We let him go, he'll tell the cops on us."

The girl's lip quivered. "But what if, ya know, what if he promised not ta?"

"Girl, you musta been standin' in the shit line when they'se was passin' out brains!" Hull roared. "Now git!"

Jory grabbed the severed head by the hair and bolted after the girl. "Hey! Hey, Kari Ann! Come give yer sweetheart a kiss!"

The girl shrieked. "Git that head away from me!"

"Bet if it were some *nigruh's* head, she'd kiss it!" Hull contributed.

Jory chortled, shaking the head. "Come on! Pucker up!" Then he commenced to chasing her around the enclosed yard with it. "Hull!" she screamed. "Make him stop! He's scarin' the baby!"

"Hail," Hull chuckled back. "Ain't nothin' could scare that shit-baby retart critter, but it's shores scarin' the shit outa you!"

"Bet she'se'll poop herself, Hull!"

Her shrieks followed her like a banner until Jory chased her out of the yard. She stormed back into the house, the baby shrieking. Hull honked echoic redneck laughter.

*Yes sir,* Gray thought. *Life's a holiday on Primrose Lane.*

"Hey, Hull! Gander this!" Jory, then, expertly drop-kicked the head across the yard, where it—*thwack!*—bounced off the wood-plank fence and landed on the chopped body parts piled on the tarp.

"Touchdown, Hull!"

"Shee-it, boy," Hull remarked, shaking his head. "You'se shore are somethin'. Come ons, we'se finished fer now. Gotta let this lacquer dry 'fore I'se kin put on the next coat."

"But what about this cracker I done just chopped up? Should I'se put his parts in the drum so's we kin dump it?"

Hull hocked in the dirt. "Naw, it's kin wait. That cracker fella with the Camaro's skinny," he appraised, looking at the chopped body parts. "Wait'll we kill the city fella, that ways we kin stick him in the same drum. Looks ta me they'll both fit. Then we'll dump 'em both the same tam. Tuh-marruh."

*Tuh-marruh,* Gray thought. *Tomorrow.* They were talking about him. He even saw the large metal drum in the yard, easily big enough for two dismembered bodies. Gray's gut quaked.

*They're going chop me up and put me in that drum. Tomorrow.*

But 'tomorrow' lengthened into two more days and nights. Gray supposed the inexplicable reprieve was something he should be grateful for. Hull mentioned that he'd run out of clear lacquer and he wanted ten full coats. This was good.

What *wasn't* so good was how Gray was forced to spend his temporarily extended life. He was promptly sodomized by Jory each night, while having to simultaneously admit Hull's rank penis into his mouth. The brothers were having a hootinnanny, and Gray's mouth and rectum were the party favors. But he took it like a man: on hands and knees, doing the job.

Each night, too, he was forced to eat steamed pumpkin. Gray guessed there was more purpose to it than mere cruelty: it produced bowel movements that were essentially liquefaction, the remnants of which left him slick back there, easier to penetrate. After each violation, he'd sit on the bucket and pour forth more pale diarrhea marbled with Jory's sperm. A terrifying question nagged at him: what would happen when the bucket was full? Would Kari Ann empty it, or would he be dead before that eventuality?

On the second night Gray noticed threads of blood laying in the septic stew. No surprise there, not after the job Jory had done on him just after dark. He'd been really riled, really ready to get it on, and had plungered Gray's asshole like a stopped toilet. Hull's finger-up-the-ass blowjob hadn't been much easier. Hull had been holding back— Gray could tell—staving off his release for as long as possible.

*Probably thinking about goddamn Randy Johnson,* Gray thought. *Works pretty well, huh, Hull?* Fuck. The nail on Gray's index finger remained permanently lined with shit. There was no way for him to sufficiently clean his finger—they wouldn't let him wash (and he wondered if they did themselves), so now the dirty finger haunted him. Any time he'd unconsciously scratch an itch on his nose, that horrible shit-and-spit smell was there. There was no hope.

Or was there?

He'd overheard her, hadn't he? Kari Ann? Trying to talk her brothers into letting him go.

At least that meant she was thinking about it.

The third night, they came up twice. It was hard to concentrate with Hull saying "Wiggle that finger, bitch" and Jory saying "Make that cornhole *tight!*" both at the same time. Jory fondling Gray's testicles didn't help. In time, Gray gulped down another liberal dispensation of Hull's sperm, while Jory came in his ass like a squirt gun.

When Jory inched out, he slapped Gray hard on the ass. "That's a *good* girl!" he celebrated. He reached forward and pinched Gray's nipple. "You're one great fuck. Fuckin' you's like fuckin' a l'il school girl."

Hull bopped Gray's temple with his knuckles. "Say thank ya when my brother comp-ler-ments ya."

Gray rolled his eyes. "Thank you."

"You know, Jory," Hull said. He remained standing, his overalls still down. "I'se *feisty* tonight."

"Yeah?"

Gray felt disconcerted when he saw what Hull was doing. He was tugging on his deflated penis. *What? Again?* Gray thought.

Hull went on, "I don't usually fancy to it but I think, I say, I think I might like ta have me a piece'a his ass, too. Ain't had me a good butt-fuckin' in a while. Now if I kin just get my dog hard again . . ."

Hull kept playing with himself. Gray prayed, *Please, please,*

*DON'T get hard again...*
　　Hull got hard again.
　　"Tear yourself off a piece, brother," Jory said.
　　*For the love of God,* Gray thought. He knew there was no way his rectal cavity could accommodate an erection the size of Hull's. Something would have to give, the same way as if you stuck a cucumber in a donut hole. Gray's *anus* was the donut hole.
　　*I'll bust!* he thought.
　　"Yeah, boy!" Jory rooted. "Git it, brother! Stick that dirty girl!"
　　Hull kneed right up and pushed the baby-apple-sized glans into Gray's asshole. He shoved. Hull's dick went into his colon, and Gray threw up digested pumpkin mush. It felt like Hull had his entire forearm up there. All Gray could do was squeeze tears from his eyes and shudder.
　　"Like that, City?" Hull asked and reached forward to squeeze Gray's "tit."
　　"Bet he does," Jory speculated. "Bet he's gittin' hard hisself."
　　"Naw," Hull confirmed. He grabbed Gray's genitals, which were limp as a handful of Jello.
　　Hull was rocking, driving into him, back and forth. Gray felt skewered. His mind raced against the pain and monumental pressure. "Aw, yeah, aw, yeah . . . ." Gray was nearly unconscious when Hull had his moment. He came like a gila monster vomiting, and when he pulled out, Gray thought he was shitting a coffee can. He collapsed and rolled over, exhausted.
　　"Sleep tight, hon," Jory chuckled.
　　"This'll be yer last nat, boy," Hull informed.
　　"My last. . . . night?" Gray mumbled.
　　"I'll'se be pickin' up the rest'a the clear-coat tuh-marruh. Then we'll be finished with yer car."
　　Jory was rebuckling his overalls. "But don't'cha worry none. We'll be shore ta fuck ya one more tam 'fore we kill ya."
　　The brothers left laughing, slamming the door behind them.

Gray lay paralyzed. Now he knew what women felt like after being raped; it was far more than the physical violation. It was something psychical, too. His soul didn't matter. He was just a body to be utilized for primal pleasure. He was the Kleenex they were using to blow their noses into.

And tomorrow they would throw the Kleenex in the trash.

When they were done "tricking" up his car, they'd simply sell it and would, hence, need a new one. They'd have to get rid of Gray to make room for the next poor sap.

And now he saw the cruellest truth for the first time. Could he really blame Jory and Hull for their crimes? Could he really blame the girl?

In truth, no. He could only blame himself. *I got myself into this nightmare. It's all my fault.* Nobody'd put a gun to his head the night he picked Kari Ann up. He'd done it on his own accord, for lust, for sex. Because she was available to *use.*

*God,* he thought now. Yes, God. Of all things, his thoughts turned again to his Creator. Why shouldn't God be infuriated with him? This was his punishment, the tables turned. Blood and sperm seeping out of his ass, he thought about his life now in an entirely different way. Gray had willingly turned his back on the way life was supposed to be, hadn't he? He hadn't really loved his first two wives, he'd married them for their looks. And his other relationships? Same thing. All the wrong reasons. People were supposed to be together for a reason.

*To be a part of each other's life, to love each other and have kids and raise them to the best of your ability. That's what life's all about, not going to strip joints and picking up hookers.* Gray saw it now: if there really was a God, Gray's entire existence was an offense. He'd chosen irresponsibility over commitment. He'd chosen crude pleasure over morality.

There was a price to pay for that, and right now Gray was paying it.

He clasped his hands together, futilely. He hadn't forgotten about the final strand of possibility. Kari Ann. Maybe she wouldn't abandon him. Maybe—by the grace of God—she'd find a way to get him out of here.

*Please, God,* he prayed. *I know I've been a lousy person and have offended Your laws, but please, PLEASE forgive me. I'm a hypocritical chump, I KNOW that, but I promise if You can find some way to forgive me, I'll make good. I'll change my life, I swear. Let Kari Ann get me out of here and I SWEAR TO YOU, I'll marry her and be the father of her child, and I'll do EVERYTHING IN MY POWER to live a Christian life. I swear . . .*

Gray sat against the wall, fallow in the muddy flavescent light. When he closed his eyes, he saw skiagraphic shapes that all seemed to eventually meld into ax-forms. When he drifted off to sleep, he dreamed of being raped by devils. If he died during the dream, what would happen? Would he just stay there with the devils forever? If so, he knew he'd deserve it.

"Hey." A nudge. "You asleep?"

Did he smell hot pumpkin in the dream?

"Tam fer dinner . . ."

When Gray opened his eyes, Kari Ann was kneeling next to him with the next bucket of pumpkin.

"Oh, Kari Ann . . ." Gray fell apart, hugging her. "I can't take this any more. You've got to help get me out of here. I swear, I'll make you my wife. Everything I do will be for you, and I'll be a father for your baby. I'll never lie to you or cheat on you, I'll devote my entire *life* to you." And it all came pouring out. Gray clung to her, crying. "I promise, I promise–I even promised God. We'll live life the way it's supposed to be lived, and we'll go to church and stuff like that. And as for your baby . . ." *Shit,* he remembered. *The kid's fucked up, got birth defects and a warped head . . .* It didn't matter. It didn't matter to God, so why should it matter to Gray? He took her hand, squeezed it, still sobbing into her lap. "I make great money, Kari Ann. I'll send your baby to the best special schools, I'll get her the best possible care. I'll be the father she never had."

Kari Ann had tears in her eyes too. She stroked Gray's cheek, unmindful of the nearly full bucket of diarrhea, unfazed by his body odor. "I know you'd do all those things, I kin see it in ya."

"Then help me! All you've got to do is call the police!"

"Cain't. Ain't got no phone."

Gray began to tremble.

"But here's what I *can* do," she began. She kissed him on the forehead. "I been thinkin' 'bout it, an' it's real risky . . . but I'm gonna do it . . ."

Gray didn't sleep the rest of the night. He was too excited, he was *pumped.* No, the lack of a phone would prevent Kari Ann from calling the police, but she'd told him what she was going to do. She wouldn't *need* to call them; instead she'd go to them directly. Today, when her brothers thought she was hitchhiking to work, she was going to hitchhike to the police station instead. There was a county sheriff's department only a few miles away.

*Just be ready.*

The way Gray saw it, God was going to give him a break, and Gray would keep his end of the bargain. It was time to give something back.

There was enough chain to let him just get to the window. The window wasn't locked—why should it be? He was chained to the floor. He couldn't climb out, of course, but—

*I can sure as shit open it.*

The wood had part gone to rot; the frame had swollen. It took Gray until a few hours after sun-up to work it free. Huffing and puffing, he kept pushing upward until it began to give. A few times he feared the window might pop out of the frame and land outside in the yard (that would've been the end) but luck—or God—stayed on his side. Gray pried the old window up a few inches, enough to be heard through if he shouted.

He didn't know what time it was but he guessed it must be early afternoon when he heard the crunch of tires rolling over gravel. Earlier, Jory had dropped the dismembered remains of the redneck into the metal drum. Meanwhile Hull had applied the final coat of lacquer to Gray's formerly black Corvette.

Every false hope occurred to Gray: the vehicle he heard coming up the weedy drive would just be the mailman, or some shady business associate of Jory and Hull's. No one on the driveway would be able to see the horrific shenanigans going on in the yard, due to the fence. But Jory and Hull heard the vehicle, too. They both froze at once.

Then Gray's heart sang. A county sheriff's car stopped in front of the house.

A deputy sheriff got out. So did Kari Ann, from the driver's side. Within the fence, Gray saw Jory and Hull peeking through the slats. They looked worried.

"Where?" the sheriff demanded of Kari Ann. "This sounds like a bunch of bull."

"Up there!" Kari Ann wailed. "That's where they'se got him chained up! In the attic! They'se been rapin' him!"

Gray's dream came true. Jory and Hull were scrambling in the fenced yard. And the cop?

He stood with his hands on his hips, staring right up at the window.

"Damn," he said. "I think–I think I see someone there."

"HEEEEEEEEEEEELP!" Gray's throat belted out the plea like a cannon shot. He waved frantically, then rammed his elbow into a glass pane, shattering it. The pieces flew out into the air.

"HELP ME FOR THE LOVE OF GOD PLEASE! I'VE BEEN IMPRISONED UP HERE!"

"I don't believe it," the cop said bewildered to Kari Ann. "Wait here. I'm going up . . ."

Then the cop drew his revolver and entered the house.

Gray's adrenalin was practically dripping off his fingers. He stomped up and down, shouting, when he heard the cop's footsteps racing upward. Gray glanced down in the yard again. There was no sign of the brothers. *They're already heading for the hills!* he thought.

When the door burst open, the deputy sheriff stared, gun poised. "God almighty," he muttered when he saw Gray standing there: chained, filthy, wearing just the soiled t-shirt and black socks. "It's true . . . The girl wasn't bullshitting. Those assholes have got you chained up here."

Gray wanted to rush to the cop and hug him, but the chain wasn't long enough. "Thank you thank you thank you! Jory and Hull—they've been keeping me up here for almost a week! They're stealing cars and repainting them! And they've been . . . abusing me . . ."

"Well don't you worry, fella—" the cop began.

Gray's heart nearly stopped when the shadow entered the room from behind. Over the cop's shoulder, Gray saw—

Hull.

He was grinning through bad teeth, stealthily stepping up from the doorway.

"Look out!" Gray bellowed, spit flying. "Behind you!"

The cop spun. "What the hell are you guys doing? You've got this guy chained up here?"

"That's a fact," Hull replied.

*Shoot him! Shoot him!* Gray thought.

"And you didn't even tell me?" the cop went on. "What a bunch of selfish assholes. Bet you've been stickin' him every night."

"Yes siree, ever nat."

"Hoggin' all the ass for yourselves."

"Well, shee-it, Bobby. We didn't know you was inta boy-cherry. But now that we knows, you's kin help yourself any tam."

"Fuck," the cop grumbled and began to unbuckle his trousers. "I'm so horny I could fuck a hole in the wall."

Hull winked at Gray. "Well that there's yer hole."

Gray's soul felt like a stone transom whose keystone had just been knocked out by a hammer. The rest just crumbled down.

"Belly to wall, bitch," the cop ordered. "I'm in a swivet, I need to come so bad." No time even for hands and knees, the cop shoved Gray against the wall and prepared to fuck him standing up. He rubbed his bare groin against Gray's buttocks, reaching around to pinch his nipples. "Yeah, I'm gettin' hard quick. It's been a while since I've had a good hell-for-leather ass-fuck."

"Well, he's a good 'un. Makes his asshole twitch whiles yer cock's in him. Sucks damn good dick too, Bobby. *Damn* good . . ."

During the preludial molestation, Gray's face was pressed against a window pane, and as his buttocks was thumbed open and spat on, he could see down into the yard.

"Looks like Kari Ann done fell for ya, City," Hull said behind him. "Bet'cha promised to take her aways from here if she helped ya, huh? Jory'll be punishin' the dumb bitch presently. Cain't have no shit like that. It's a sad day whens yer own sister'll betray ya. But how's that fer some luck, City? Of all the cops she could'a ratted us too, she picks the one we'se in business with."

Gray didn't hear anymore, as he was penetrated. Bile raced up his throat, and he bit down on the inside of his cheek so hard, his teeth clicked. One eye seemed to rove independently of the other, as if divorced from the outrage. It looked down into the yard and saw that Jory had already beaten Kari Ann to the ground. She looked up, screaming bloody-mouthed. Jory was chuckling, throwing her baby up into the air, spinning it around like a ball of pizza dough. Eventually, he hooked-shotted it directly into the metal drum, then began to hammer the lid on.

And Gray?

Gray was fucked in grand style. The only difference between being raped by Hull and being raped by this cop was singularly noticeable. The cop's cock was bigger than Hull's.

Gray felt stuffed from both ends. "Sheeeee-it!" Hull whooped, his penis burrowed in Gray's mouth. Jory busied himself at the other end, with deft sodomy. "Gawd-damn, Hull! I'se swears this boy's even tighter'n he was last nat!"

Gray tried to remove his psyche from the scene: it wasn't *his* mouth sucking Hull's penis, nor was it *his* rectum at the receiving end of Jory's. *Pretend it's happening to someone else* . . .

"Aw, yeah! I'se gonna dump me a fuck up this boy's tail! I'se gonna come so much my spunk'll be drippin' out his nose!"

"Here comes supper, City," Hull forewarned. Gray wasn't sure, but the brothers seemed to climax simultaneously. He felt the warm gush deep in his bowel at the same moment Hull released a flabbergastingly large allotment of sperm into his mouth. Gray swallowed it, without hesitation this time. It slid down his belly like a long, hot worm. Then Gray's hands and knees went out, and he collapsed procument to the floor.

*Thanks a lot, God,* he thought. *Thanks a hell of a lot* . . .

"Yeah," Hull guttered. He gave his penis a final squeeze, perhaps for posterity. "I'se said it before'n I'll'se say its again: this fella here is the best cock-suck I'se ever had."

"Best cornhole too." Jory gave a hick giggle, then withdrew his own reproductive architecture from Gray hind quarters. "Hope it don't git worn out, now that Bobby's in on the action."

"Yes sir, Kari Ann shore brung us a winner this time. He sucks dick like a reg-ler champ, and he's got a great car."

Gray slid to the wall and sat up. "And that's the scam, isn't it? You make the girl lure the drivers back here, then you guys take over. You got a remake shop."

Hull scratched his belly, then hitched his overalls up. "That's right, City. We'se paint the cars all diff-urnt colors, then drives 'em up to our fence. And that purdy 'Vette'a yers? It'll fetch us some fine scratch. Three, four grand at least."

Even in his plight, Gray was appalled. "Three or four grand?

That car cost sixty-three thousand dollars! You guys are getting ripped off."

"Aw, we'se ain't greedy here," Hull said. "We likes ta keep things simple'n safe."

Jory, yet again, was wiping his sullied genitals off with Gray's silk shirt. "The fence takes most'a the risk, see. We just delivers the cars. He moves 'em ta buyers."

"So how many have there been?" Gray saw no harm in asking. They were going to kill him anyway, so why wouldn't they tell him? "How many other guys have you pulled this number on?"

Hull stroked his stubbled chin. "Over the years? Shee-it. Probably over a hunnert."

"A hunnert'n fifty's more like it," Jory augmented.

"And way back here in the hills," Gray added, "no one suspects a thing. The cars are repainted and resold. And that county sheriff probably keeps the heat out of here, helps cover your route to your fence. The bodies are never found."

"Right again, City," Hull asserted.

"An' Kari Ann done tolt us 'bout yer little scheme. Promisin' ta marry her, help her raise her kid. Shee-it, what'choo think we is, City. Stupid?"

*Who* was the stupid one?

Gray was dragged by the hair to the corner. Just as he realized what they were going to do, he snatched in a quick breath. Then—

*plup!*

—his head was quickly submerged into the bucket full of his waste.

"Down ya go, City. Blub, blub, blub."

Gray was too exhausted to resist. He had no strength, nothing left in his muscles and nothing left in his heart. Were there bugs in his diarrhea? Little things seemed to be swarming in it, tickling his face, but Gray told himself it was just his imagination. He even came to grips with the circumstance now. They were going to kill him, they were going to drown him in his own diarrhea, but then it would all be over. He felt confident that God wouldn't send him to hell after all of this.

His lungs expanded; soon they would burst. He doubted that he'd pass out before reflex forced him to inhale his first mouthful. But that didn't matter, either. *I'll be dead in another minute, and you know what? I'm ready.*

He sidled over, drenched, and gulped air like a grouper on a pier when they pulled him out. All those liquefied bowel movements dribbled down his face. When he realized that they'd pulled him out one heartbeat short of drowning, he actually yelled up at them: "Come on! Just kill me and get it over with!"

"Kill ya? Kill ya?" Jory said.

"Naw, that were just yer punishment fer fuckin' with us," Hull added, "plottin' behind our backs'n such."

"Yer diff-urnt, City. You's the best we ever had."

"No lie, the *dang* best." Hull gave his crotch a squeeze. "I'll be dagged-damned if I ain't gittin' hard again thinkin' 'bout that sure-fire cock-suck mouth'a yers."

"You knows, Hull?" Jory offered. "You's're right. I'se gittin' hard again too. What say we have ourselfs another nut?"

Hull whipped it out. "Shee-it, yeah. Come on, City. Let's make some more whuppie."

"Aw, Jesus," Gray groaned. His face dripped shit. *Not again!*

Yes. Again. Wearily, Gray crawled forward onto hands and knees, a human coffee table. His mouth engulfed Hull's fattening manhood, and after only a moment of adroit fellatio, it turned hard as a billy club. Behind him, Gray felt the familiar wet splat as Jory expectorated into his buttocks and inserted a billy club of his own.

Hull gripped Gray's ears as though they were handles. "This shore is the life, ain't it, Jor?"

"Dag straight, Hull," Jor agreed, pumping vigorously. He slapped Gray's right buttock. "Come on, City. Squeeze that butthole like you do."

Gray constricted his sphincter—

"Yeah! That's it! Gawd-dag that feels good!"

Gray could only listen with his mouth jam-packed with Hull's cock.

Hull chuckled, patting Gray's head. "Shee-it, City. All them other fellas, we kill 'em lickety-split. But we ain't gonna do that ta you."

"We'se done decided!"

"We'se gonna let you live."

Gray's eyes widened.

Jory stroked away, plunging in an out. "That's right, City. Me'n Hull's already talked it over. We'd be out of our ever-livin' minds ta kill you."

"'Cos yer so good is why."

"It'd be a waste'a good boy-poon."

"An' good mouth-lovin'."

"So's instead'a killin' ya like we done them other fellas, we'se gonna keep ya here."

"But don't's ya worry none. Kari Ann'll bring ya up viddles'n water ever day."

Hull chortled. "An' me'n Jor, we'll'se bring ya up our peters ever nat."

*Ever nat,* Gray thought as he sucked. *Every night.*

"That's right, City," Hull said, caressing the top of Gray's head. It was almost affectionate. "You'se gonna suck my dick. Ever nat."

Then Jory: "And you'se gonna take mine up yer cornhole."

"You hear that, City? Ever nat."

"That's right, City. Ever nat."

"Ever nat."

"Sheeee-it! Ever nat fer the rest'a yer life!"

Gray got the message. He didn't even bother listening any more. He just pinched his sphincter again, and sucked.

# THE SALT-DIVINER

## PROLOGUE

The Onomancers had failed, and so had the Sibyllists. The Haruspicators came next, keen-eyed yet solemn in their blood-red raiments. One of them nodded within his flaplike hood, and then the young girl was stripped naked and lain on the onyx slab.

It was one of the geldings, who'd previously had his eyes sewn shut, that clumsily shoved the ivory rod into the girl's sex. The slim naked thing's hips bucked, and the shriek of pain launched out above the ziggurat as though she were shouting to the gods themselves. Blindly, then, the gelding held up the bloody rod for the Synod to see.

No doubt, a true virgin.

The gelding was summarily beheaded, his body dragged off by silent legionnaires. Next, the highest of the Haruspist's slipped the long sharpened hook deep up into the girl's sex. She flinched and died at once, a tiny river of red pouring forth. But the Haruspic priest was already at work, his holy hand a blur as the hook expertly extracted the girl's warm innards through the opening of her sex. Barehanded, then, he hoisted up the guts and flung them down to the ziggurat's stone floor.

The wind howled, or perhaps it was the breath of Ea himself.

But when the Haruspist gazed intently at the wet splay of innards . . .

He saw nothing.

The King's jaw set; he seemed petrified on his throne. Only one recourse remained, and if it too failed, only doom awaited the King and his domain. He turned his gaze toward the last flank of robed and hooded priests–the alomancers. The King gave a single nod.

One figure stepped forward, face hidden within the hood's roll. From one hand, a thurible swayed, a thurible full of salt.

He depended the thurible over the fire. . . . until the salt began to burn.

Smoke poured from the object's finely crafted apertures, and the figure leaned forth–and inhaled the holy fumes, one deep breath after another, until he collapsed.

The King stiffened in his throne; legionnaires burst forward to render aid. Eventually—thank Ea—the alomancer revived after a distended silence. Even the wind stopped, even the clouds seemed to freeze in the sky.

The alomancer shuddered. Then he gazed at the King with eyes the color of amethyst, and he began to speak...

# I

It started when the salt spilled.

The man looked ludicrous. Black hair hung in a perfect bowlcut, like Moe. He stood at the rail, tubby and tall, with a great, toothy, lunatic grin. "Ald, please," he requested. "It's been eons."

Rudy and Beth nursed cans of Milwaukee's Best down the bar, Rudy pretending to watch the fight on the television. They'd made the rounds downtown, hoping to cop a loan, but to no avail. Then they'd retreated to this dump tavern, The Crossroads, way out off the Route. Rudy didn't want to run into Vito—as in Vito "The Eye"—a minute before he had to. He felt like a man on a stay of execution.

"Are you the vassal of this *taberna*, sir?" the ludicrous man asked the barkeep. "I would like some ald, please." "Never heard of it," swiped the keep, who sported muttonchops and a beer-belly akin to a medicine ball. "No imports here, pal. This is The Crossroads, not the Four Seasons."

"I am becruxed. Have you any mead?"

Rudy could've laughed. Even the man's voice sounded ludicrous: a high nasal warble. *And what the hell is ald?*

"We got Rolling Rock, pal. That fancy enough for ya?"

"I am grateful, sir, for your kind recommendation."

When the keep came down to the Rock tap, Rudy leaned forward. "Hey, man, who *is* this guy?"

*The Salt-Diviner*

The keep shrugged, tufts of hair like steel wool poking out from his collar. "Some weirdo. We get 'em all the time."

Beth, frowning afresh, looked down from the no-name fight on tv. "Rudy, don't you have more to worry about than some eightball who walks into a bar? What if Vito shows up?"

"Vito The Eye? Here?" Rudy replied. "No way." The assurance lapsed. "Hey, maybe Mona could loan us some dough."

"She barely has money for tuition and rent, Rudy. Be real."

*Women*, Rudy thought. *Always negative*. He glanced back up at the fight—Tuttle versus Luce, middleweights—but thoughts of Vito kept haunting him. *What will they do to me?* he wondered.

The keep set down a mug of beer before the ludicrous man, but as he did so, his brawny elbow nicked a salt shaker, which tipped over. A few trace white grains spilled across the bartop.

The odd patron grinned down. Focused. Nodded. He pinched some grains and cast them over his left shoulder. "Blast thee, Nergal and all devils. Keep thee behind, and slithereth back into your evil earthworks."

"We ain't superstitious here, pal," the keep said.

"To blind the sentinels of the nether regions," the man went on, "who stand to our left, behind us. Dear salt, a gift from the holiest Ea, and all gods of good things. To spill the sacred salt is to bid ill fortune from heaven. It was once more valuable than myrrh."

"Who'da hell's Merv?" asked the keep.

"Beware the woman infidel," intoned the patron. "Your paramour—"

"What'da hell's a paramour?"

"A lover," Beth translated, for all the good her education had done. "A girlfriend."

"She is so named," the ludicrous man said, "... Stacy?"

The keep's pug-face tensed up like a pack of corded Suet. "How'da hell you know my girlfriend's name?"

"I am an alomancer," the odd patron replied. "And your lovely paramour, hair like sackcloth and teeth becrook'd, shalt be in a moment's time abed with a man unthus known."

The keep scratched a muttonchop. "What'd'ya mean?"

"He means," Beth said over her beer, "that your girlfriend is cheating on you with a guy she just met."

"A man," the patron continued, "too, of a formidable endowment of the groin."

"'At's a load of shit," the keep said. "You're a nut."

*This guy's something*, Rudy thought. He was about to comment when someone tapped on his shoulder. *Oh. . . . no*. Very slowly, then, he turned to the ruddy and none-too-happy face behind him. "Vito! My man! I was just downtown looking for you."

"Yeah." Vito wore a tan leather jacket and white slacks—*Italian* slacks. They called him The Eye, since only his right eye could be seen. A black patch covered the left. "Your marker's due Friday, paisan. You wouldn't be forgetting that, huh?"

"Oh, hey, Vito," Rudy stammered. "I remember."

"That's six large. The Boss Man ain't happy."

"Barkeep," Rudy changed the subject. "Get my good friend Vito here a beer on my tab, and one for this guy, too," he said, slapping the ludicrous man on the back.

Vito jerked a thumb. "I'll be over at the booth marking my books. Come on over if you got anything you want to talk to me about."

"Actually," Rudy seized the opportunity. "I was wondering if like you could maybe give me a little extra t—"

"I ever tell you how I lost my eye? About ten years ago, I ran up a big marker on the Boss Man's tab, and I made the big mistake of asking him for a little extra time."

Rudy gulped. When Vito disappeared to the back booth, Beth jumped in to complain. "That's great, Rudy. We're nearly broke, you're six thousand in debt to a mob bookie, and now you're buying beers for people. Jesus."

"Guys like Vito like to see generosity. Part of their machismo."

"And now look what you've done!' she whispered.

The insane, toothy grin floated forward; its owner took the stool next to Rudy. "Innumerable thanks, sir. It's not ald; however, I'm grateful to you."

"What the hell is ald?" Rudy asked.

"A high and might liquor indeed, and a favorite of the mashmashus. We invented it, by the way, though your zymurgists of today refuse to acknowledge that. You see, the great grain mounds would accumulate condensation in the sun. The dregs, then, seeped into pools of effluvium, which were squeezed off into the casks." He sipped his beer, crosseyed. I am Gormok. And you are called?"

*Gormok? What kind of fruitloop name is that?* Rudy wondered.

"I'm Rudy. This is Beth, my fiance."

Beth frowned again, and Rudy supposed he could see her point. Nothing he'd promised her had come true. His gambling was like a ritual to him, an obsessive act of something very nearly reverence, and it kept a monkey on their backs the size of King Kong. The stress was starting to show: tiny lines had crept into Beth's pretty face, and a faint veneer of fatigue. She'd lost weight, and the lustrous long caramel-colored hair had begun to take a tint of gray. She worked two jobs while Rudy sweated bullets at the track. And now mob men were calling. *No wonder she's always pissed. I'm gonna get my eye poked out next Friday and here I am buying beers for a shylock and some loose-screw named Gormok.*

"And I affirm," Gormok went on in his creaky, sinitic voice, "that your generosity will not go unrewarded. If I can ever be of service to your benefit, I implore thee, make me aware."

"Forget it," Rudy said. *Nut.* He drained his beer. "Where'd the barkeep go? I could use a refill."

"Our humble servitor, I believe," Gormok offered, "is at this sad moment seeking to contact his unfaithful paramour."

Rudy spied the keep down the other end of the bar, talking on the house phone. Suddenly the guy turned pale and hung up. "I just called the fuckin' trailer," he muttered. "My girlfriend ain't there. Then I ring my buddy down at The Anvil, and he tells me Stacy left after happy hour . . . with some guy."

"A gentleman, too," Gormok reminded, "unthus known and of a formidable endowment of the groin."

"Shadap, ya whack." The keep went back to the phone. Beth maintained her terse silence. But Rudy was thinking

"Gormok. How about doing that salt thing for me."

"An alomance! Yes?" came the grinning reply.

Rudy lowered his voice. "Tell me who's gonna win that fight."

"Alas, the gladiators of the new, dark age," Gormok remarked, and peered up at the boxing bout on the bar television. "But have thee a censer? Clearer visions are always begot by fire."

"What's a censer?"

"It's something you burn things in, during rituals," Beth defined. "And don't be idiotic, Rudy."

Rudy ignored her, glancing about. "How about this?" he ventured, and slid over a big glass ashtray sporting the Swedish Bikini Team.

"It shall suffice," Gormok approved. He sprinkled several shakes of salt into a bar napkin and placed it in the ashtray. "A taper, now, or cresset or flambeau."

*I hope he means a lighter.* Rudy flicked his Bic. He lit the napkin, which strangely puffed into a quick flame and then went out. Gormok's face took on a momentary expression of tranquility as though he were indeed taking part in some ritualistic worship. Then the odd man leaned forward...and inhaled the smoke.

Rudy stared.

"The combatant dark of skin and light of garb," Gormok giddily intoned, "who is called Tuttle, before two minutes have expired, will emerge victorious by a single blow to the skull of his oppressor."

Rudy snatched up Beth's purse.

"Rudy, no!"

*The Salt-Diviner*

"How much money you got?" he asked, rummaging. He fingered through his fiancee's wallet. "*Twenty bucks? That's it?*"

"Damn it, Rudy! Don't you dare—"

Rudy turned toward the mob man's booth. "Hey, Vito? A double sawbuck says Tuttle KO's Luce this round."

Vito didn't even look up. "No more credit, Rudy."

"Cash, man. On the table."

Now Vito raised his smirk to the tv. "Tuttle's getting his ass kicked. Don't make me take your green."

"Come on, Vito!" Rudy barked. "Quit bustin' my balls. Are you a bookie or a book collector?'"

Vito made a shrug. "Awright, Rudy. You're on."

Rudy jerked his gaze to the tv, then drooped. Luce was dancing circles around his man, firing awesome hooks which snapped Tuttle's head back like a ball on a spring.

"You're such a fool," Beth groaned.

"Hark," Gormok whispered, and pointed to the screen.

Tuttle shot a blind jab which sent Luce over the ropes—

"Yeah!" Rudy yelled. Then: 'Yeah, fuckin-A *yeah!*' he yelled louder when the ref counted Luce out and raised Tuttle's arm in victory.

Vito came over. "Good call, Rudy. Just don't forget that six large."

Rudy's smile radiated. "That's five thousand, nine hundred, and eighty, Vito."

"Yeah. See ya next Friday, paisan."

Vito left the smoky bar, while Rudy fidgeted on his stool. Even Beth was rubbing her chin, thinking. And Rudy had a pretty good idea what she was thinking about.

"How'd you do that, man?" he asked aside to Gormok.

"I am an alomancer," Gormok answered through his ludicrous grin. "I am a salt-diviner for the Fourth Cenote of Nergal."

*What you are*, Rudy thought, *is a nut. But I love ya anyway.* He put a comradely arm about Gormok's shoulder. "So, Gormok, my man. How would you like to come and live with us?"

## II

"Who's *that?*" Mona winced when they got home.

*Snooty bitch.* "This is our very good friend, Gormok," he told the blonde coed. Her 38C's pushed against her blouse. "Gormok, this is Mona, our housemate."

Gormok appraised the attractive, tight-jeaned student. "Men have rown leagues for such beauty, priests have scaled ziggurats."

"Uh huh," Rudy said. "Mona, how about going to your room to study, huh? Gormok and I gotta talk."

Mona made no objection, padding off with her English 311 text, *Pound, Eliot, and Seymour: The Great Poets of Our Age.* "Sit down, Gor," Rudy bid. "Make yourself at home." Gormok did so, his lap disappearing when he sat down on the frayed couch.

Rudy nudged Beth into the kitchen. "Get him a beer. He seems to like beer."

"Rudy, this might be a bad idea. I don't know if I—"

"Just shut up and get him a beer," Rudy politely repeated. He went back to the squalid living room, bearing an ashtray and a shaker of salt. "So, Gor. Tell me about yourself."

The lunatic grin roved about. "I am but a lowly salt-diviner, once blessed by the Ea, now curs'd by Nergal."

"Uh . . . huh," Rudy acknowledged.

"I was an Ashipu, a white and goodly acolyte, but, lo, I sold my soul to Nergal, The Wretched God of the Ebon. Pity me, in my sin: my repentance was ignored. Banished from heaven, banished from hell, I am now accursed to trod the earth's foul crust forever, inhabiting random bodies as the vessel for my eternal spirit."

"Uh . . . huh,"

"Jesus," Beth whispered. Disapproval now fully creased her face when she gave Gormok a can of Bud. *Yeah, we've got a live one,* Rudy thought. The next fight—Jenkins versus Clipper—was on the west coast; it would be running late. "That's pretty, uh, interesting, Gormok. You think maybe you feel like doing the salt thing again?"

Beer foam bubbled at Gormok's grin. "The alomance!"

"Uh, yeah, Gor. The . . . alomance. I could really use to know who's gonna win the Jenkins-Clipper bout."

Gormok's grin never fluctuated. He knelt on tacky carpet tiles and went into his arcane ritual of burning salt in a napkin, then inhaling the smoke which wafted up from the ashtray. He seemed to wobble on his knees. "The warrior b'named Clipper, dear friend, in the sixth spell of conflict." Then he collapsed to the floor.

"Holy shit!" Rudy and Beth rushed to help the alomancer up. "Gor! Are you all right?" Rudy asked.

"Too much for one day." Gormok's voice sounded drugged. "Put me abed, dear ones. I'll be better on the morrow."

"The couch," Rudy suggested. "Let's get him on the—"

"Deep and down," Gormok inanely remarked. "I must be deep, as all damned Nashipus are so cursed. Get me near the cenotes."

"A cenote is a hole in the ground," Beth recalled from her college myth classes. "They'd hold rituals in them, sacrifice virgins and things like that."

*A hole in the—*"The basement?" Rudy suggested.

Beth opened the ringed trap-door, then they both lugged the muttering and rubber-kneed Gormok down the wooden steps.

"Better, yes! Sweet, sweet . . . dark."

They lay the bizarre man on an old box-spring next to the washer and drier. Dust eddied up from the dirt floor. "He's heavier than a bag of bricks!" Beth complained.

Rudy draped an old army blanket over him. "There."

"Ea, I heartily do repent," Gormok blabbered incoherently. "Absolve my sins, I beg of Thee!" He began to drool. "And curse thee, Nergal, unclean despoiler! Haunter! Deceiver of *souls!*"

"Uh . . . huh," Rudy remarked, staring down. *Yeah, we've got a live one, all right. A real winner.*

## III

In bed, they bickered rather than slept. "I can't believe you invited that *weirdo* into our house," Beth bellyached.

"I didn't hear you complaining," Rudy refuted.

"Well, you do now. He's . . . scary."

"You don't believe all that mumbo-jumbo, do you? It's just a bunch of schizo crap he made up."

"It's not made up, Rudy. I majored in ancient history, that is, before I had to quit school and go to work to keep you out of cement loafers. Cenotes, ziggurats, alomancy—it's all straight out of Babylonian myth. This guy says he's possessed by the spirit of a Nashipu salt-diviner. That's the same as saying he's a demon."

Rudy chuckled outright. "Somebody hit you in the head with a dumb-stick? He's a flake, Beth. He probably escaped from St. Elizabeth's in the back of a garbage truck and read about all that stuff in some occult paperback. He *thinks* he's possessed by a demon. And so what? Let him think what he wants. What's important to us is the guy's *genuinely psychic*. You heard him, he *predicted* that fat barkeep's squeeze was cheating on him."

"That could be just coincidence, Rudy."

"Coincidence? What about the Tuttle fight? He didn't just pick the winner, Beth, he picked the *round*. He picked a KO by a guy who every bookie in town said was gonna lose."

"I don't care," Beth replied, turning her back to him amid the covers. "He's scary. I don't want him in the house."

"Beth, the guy's a gold mine on two legs. We keep him under our wings, we'll never have to worry about money again. We'll be—"

The scream came down like a guillotine blade. Rudy and Beth went rigid in the bed.

Then another scream tore through the air.

"Thuh-that came from M-Mona's room, didn't it?" Rudy

stammered.

"Yuh-yeah," Beth agreed.

"She's *your* friend. *You* go see what happened."

"Fuck you!" Beth shouted. "Inconsiderate coward son of a—"

"We'll both go, then. Here. I'll protect you." Rudy boldly brandished one of Beth's nail files. Then, disheveled in their underwear, they crept out of the bedroom.

"Aw, Christ," Rudy muttered when he saw the trap-door to the basement standing open.

Then they padded down the hall, and peered into Mona's room...

"Aw, Christ," Rudy muttered again.

But Beth didn't mutter. She screamed.

Gormok, his face smeared scarlet, grinned up at them in the lamplight. And atop the stained bed lay Mona, naked and quite dead.

She was also quite eviscerated.

The student's trim abdomen had been riven open, and from the rive an array of organs had been extracted and arranged about her as if for some macabre inspection. An outline of slowly seeping blood spread about the corpse like a Kirlian aura.

Gormok was eating something dark and wet out of his hands. *Her liver*, Rudy realized. *He's eating Mona's liver.*

"Friends! Hello!" Gormok greeted, chewing. "How art?"

Rudy bellowed, "What in God's name did you do!"

"Not in God's name," Gormok lamented. "In Nergal's. Lo, and to my eternal shame, behold the freight of my curse. I try to fight it, on my heart. But the blasted Nergal has condemned me to such heinous acts whenecerest I breathe on the salt's divine fumes."

'Uh . . . huh." Rudy shuddered, feebly wielding the nail file. *Should I kill him?* he debated. But he thought about that. He'd never much liked Mona anyway. Bitchy, arrogant, and always taking cheap shots. Sure, he'd fucked her a couple times when Beth was at work (—no great shakes in bed, either. Like fucking a starfish—) and since then she'd regularly implied that it wouldn't be a good idea for Rudy to ever raise her rent.

"Gormok, wait here a minute. Beth and I have to talk."

"Of course! Enjoy your discourse, dear friends," Gormok invited. "Whilst I enjoy my meal."

Rudy had to about carry Beth back to their bedroom. She was going pasty-faced, pale. "Rudy," she fretted, "we have to get out of here while we still can! We have to call the police!"

"Don't overreact, honey. He's harmless."

"Harmless!" Beth's eyes came close to jettisoning from her head. "He's eating Mona's *liver!* You call that harmless?"

Rudy had a plan, but he had to play it out right. "Listen, Beth," he said in a consoling, quiet voice. "Mona's got no relatives or friends—hell, she doesn't even have a boyfriend. She'll never be missed. And she wasn't doing well in school, anyway—"

"Rudy! You call the police right now!"

"All right, all right." Rudy held up his hands, his hair sticking up. "I'm calling the police. See?" He picked up the phone and began to dial.

But not the police. Instead, he dialed 1-900 Sportsline. He listened a moment, tapping his foot. Then he hung up and smiled.

"Clipper won the bout in the sixth round."

Beth went into a staccato burst of crying and screaming. "Rudy, you're out of your mind! What is *wrong* with you?"

"Baby, it's only because I love you," Rudy, well, lied. "I'm not doing this for me, I'm doing it for *us*. I want us to be married someday, have kids, and all that."

Beth sniffled, looking up. "Really?"

"Of course, honey," he assured her and gave her a hug. "But I need you to have faith in me, okay? I want you to go to bed now. Just trust me." He lovingly touched her cheek. "I'll take care of everything."

Rudy did exactly that. First, he put Gormok back to bed in the basement. The alomancer, smiling calmly, said, "I'm sated now, dear

Rudy. My curse is relieved, and now I can sleep. And I am heartily sorry for any inconvenience I have caused you."

"Hey, Gor, don't worry about it." Rudy winced a bit, thinking of Mona's liver. "These things happen all the time."

"Until the morrow, then! And for now—sleep. For to sleep is perchance–to dream."

"Uh ... huh," Rudy said.

When he went back up, this time, he locked the trap-door.

Digging graves was hard work, harder than one might expect. Yet dig Rudy did, maniacally in his boxer shorts. He dug deep. Inserting Mona's internal organs back into her opened abdominal vault proved a trying task too, but at least it was unique ...

And later, in the little moonlit backyard, with the crickets trilling and the grass cool under his bare feet, with the scent of the bay in the air, Rudy buried the fickle bitch.

But one more task remained. Gormok said he was cursed to commit murder on any day that he performed a salt-divination. *That's a big problem*, Rudy realized. He couldn't very well have Gormok cutting folks up and eating their livers every time he gave Rudy the read on the next fight or ballgame, now could he?

So ...

He crept quietly back down into the basement.

Gormok slept on, murmuring sweet Babylonian nothings .

*Here goes,* Rudy thought—

—and raised the fire ax.

"Sleep no more!" Gormok quoted Bill Shakespeare as the great blade cut down. "MacRudy doth *murder* sleep!"

Blood flew like spaghetti sauce. Things thunked to the floor. But there was no other way! *Hell, I'm doing him a favor*, Rudy felt convinced as he chopped and chopped.

And chopped some more. Once he'd succeeded in severing

Gormok's limbs, he tied off each stump with twine.

*What a day*, he thought when he was done.

### IV

Beth, shrieking, pummeled up the basement stairs the next afternoon. *"What did you do!"*

"Hey, didn't I say I'd take care of everything?"

"Rudy! You turned him into a . . . a *torso!*"

"Yeah, well, he can't hurt anybody now, can he?" Rudy rationalized. "And he doesn't even care, as long as we keep him happy."

Beth's face crimped. "What do you mean?"

Rudy thought it best to change the topic. "Look!" he celebrated and waved a sheaf of $100 bills. "Our man came through again. Pimlico, baby! Afternoon Tea by a nose in the first! The odds were 32-to-one! Can you believe it?"

Beth, quite reasonably, went nuts. "Rudy! You bet *again?* He's a murderer, for God's sake! We can't keep a murderer in our basement! Much less a murderer who's a *torso!*"

"Sure we can." Rudy placed the stack of bills in her hands.

Beth went lax, astonished. "This looks like about ten-thou—"

"*Eleven* thousand clams," Rudy corrected. "And I already paid off Vito The Eye. We're rolling from here, babe."

Beth's eyes stayed fixed on the money.

"But, uh, you see," Rudy commenced with the bad news. His throat turned dry. "There's a catch. Remember when I told you, 'as long as we keep him happy'?"

"Yeah?" Beth replied.

The catch was this:

That morning, Rudy had shown the head atop Gormok's delimbed body the racing journal as he held the fuming ashtray under the alomancer's nose.

## The Salt-Diviner

"Afternoon Tea, dear Rudy," informed the happy head. "In the first tourney."

Rudy didn't argue, in spite of the odds. But since last night, a question had itched at him like stitches healing.

"Hey, Gor? Yesterday you said something like you had to commit a murder any day you do the salt thing."

"Upon any such day I perform a holy alomance, yes," Gormok affirmed. "Nergal, the abyssal prince, has cursed me as such."

"What happens if you, uh, don't commit a murder?"

"Then the gift of prophesy is lost to me. Forever."

*Balls!* Rudy thought. *Shit! Fuck! Piss!*

"Unless," Gormok's head leaned up and added, "I am, as a substitute, properly relieved of the groin wheneverest such needs of passion call."

Rudy's gaze thinned. "You mean . . ."

"No!" Beth wailed upon the revelation. "No no no!"

"Honey, come on," Rudy urged. "It's the only *way*. If you don't, he can't pick the winners anymore."

"Rudy, read my lips! *I'm not going to have sex with a torso!*"

*Ho boy*, Rudy thought. *Women.* You ask them to do a little something and they get all bent out of shape. *Time to lay on the heavy bullshit*, he decided. "It's for our future, sweetheart. It's for our *children*."

Evidently, *children* was the magic word. Beth pouted a moment more. She looked at him, pink-faced.

"Our . . . children," she whispered. "I- I . . ."

Rudy hugged her, stroked her hair. "It's the only way, honey. I wouldn't ask you to do it, but *it's the only way*. Don't we want our children to have the very best?"

"Our children," she dizzily repeated. "I guess, I guess you're right."

Then she turned for the basement steps, began to descend.

*That's my little trooper*, Rudy approved.

Little trooper was right—and then some. Rudy, being an investigative kind of guy, felt it only fitting and proper to make an observation or two, so he sneaked down a few minutes behind her and peeked through the slight gap in the door...

*Good God!* he thought.

Most would deem this a reasonable thing to think when witnessing one's fiancé engaged in the physical act of love with a living torso. Beth wasted no time in the deletion of her garments, and, despite a rather disconsolate look on her face—just as reasonable—she commenced to her task with something that could only be described as a formidable resolve. She squatted over Gormok, who lay unsurprisingly motionless atop his blanket. This afforded Rudy a front-on view, and though Beth's discomfiture was plain, she soon began to ease into the brass tacks, so to speak, of the project.

In the dim basement light, her face flushed, and her small, pretty breasts began to sway. Meanwhile, her companion gibbered sweet Babylonian gibberish in response to her attentions. *How does she do it?* Rudy wondered. This was, after all, a torso. Moreover, he wondered next: *What is she thinking about?*

Now *there* was a question! What would any woman think about while slamming glands with a dismembered salt-diviner? Perhaps it was brute rationalization, but Rudy came up with the only answer his psyche would allow.

*She's thinking about me—*

Of course. Who else could she be thinking about? Certainly not Gormok. In moments, Rudy became aware of a considerable hardness loitering at his groin. *My girlfriend's humping a torso and I'm getting a woody.* And as he watched further, the image transposed...

He imagined himself in Gormok's place, right there on the basement floor and shuddering in bliss as the slot of Beth's womanhood slid hotly up and down over his cock. His crotch felt smoldering, his heart *raced.* Beth's breasts bobbed vigorously on her chest as she stepped up the momentum. Up and down, up and down, hot and frantic, her hips began to locomote like a machine, until—

*Aw, Christ...*

"Sweet mercy of Ea!" Gormok exclaimed at the obvious brink of his crisis.

Rudy caught his breath, and realized that he'd had a crisis of his own, his libido relieving itself to the sheer exploitation of his underpants...

*I just watched my wife-to-be get it on with a fat torso,* he realized. *And I spunked in my shorts.*

He crept back upstairs, as bewildered as he was disgusted. But he did feel convinced of one thing at least: it was all for a good cause...

## V

No, a great cause, an absolutely big time *wonderful* cause. Within a week, Rudy was something he never recalled being: debt-free. Exit the '76 clunker Malibu, enter his and hers Mustang GT's. The 52" Sony tv was nice too, and so was the Adcom stereo and the $50,000 worth of new furniture.

And the new house. A spacious, skylighted A-frame off Bay Ridge Drive. It was the nicest house in the area that had a basement.

## VI

Gormok remained surprisingly content, considering what Rudy's greed had divorced him of. He jabbered and drank beer through a convalescent straw during the day, propped up behind pillows in bed, while Rudy cashed in at the track. Not once had Gormok's divinations failed, and soon Rudy's biggest problem was what to do with all the money. Beth, of course, had her ups and downs—the freedom to buy anything she ever wanted was a bit spoiled by the constant sexual service she was required to perform upon the libidinous torso in the basement. Eventually, she began to complain...

"That thing downstairs made me give it head today!" she spat at Rudy. "Did you hear me! I had to give *head* to a *torso!*"

*Just like a woman*, Rudy frowned in thought. *You give 'em a good thing and they STILL bellyache.* "Honey, he's not a *thing*. He's not an *it*. You're talking about Gormok—he's our man."

Beth gaped. "*Our man!* Then you go down there and fuck him! See how you like it! You go down there and blow *our man!*"

Rudy thanked the fates Gormok wasn't gay. "Stop being selfish," he told her. "Don't we have everything we want?"

"Yeah, Rudy, we do, and that's my point. We have enough now, so I shouldn't have to do it anymore."

Rudy looked up reprovingly. "Beth, there's never enough."

"Oh, so that's it, huh?" Beth, who rarely wore anything other than panties these days (due to the mounting frequency of Gormok's need), stomped exasperated around the kitchen table. "You think you're going to spend the rest of your life cleaning out the goddamn racetrack while good old Beth fucks and sucks a dismembered Babylonian alomancer!"

"Don't be vulgar, honey. It's not like you."

Beth's little breasts jiggled as she belted out a bitter chortle. "You make me fuck a torso and tell *me* not to be vulgar! I'm sick of it! You hear me! I'm sick of fucking that disgusting, ridiculous, grinning... trunk!"

Rudy brought a finger to his lips. "Keep your voice down. He might hear you. You'll hurt his feelings."

"God," she lapsed, paling. "He takes forever sometimes, and—" she gulped—"he's—he's—he's just so... *huge.*"

*Then quit complaining*, Rudy felt inclined to say. *Women always want the big dick—well, baby, now you got it.* At the table, he weeded out the ones, fives, and tens, into the garbage.

"Beth, oh Bethieeeeeeeeee!" called out the familiar nasal warble from downstairs. "Wither thee, my sweet beatific vision? My lovely, lovely Beth of the light-brown hair?"

"Oh, no," Beth croaked.

"Leave me in turmoil no longer, oh, my wondrous angel, so lovely of countenance and sweet of loins. Come! I beg thee! Come assuage my beckoning fancy."

Rudy cocked a brow. "Assuage my beckoning fancy?"

Beth glared at him. "That means he's *horny* again, Rudy." Her eyes rolled back in despair. "I don't believe this. All I ever wanted was a nice normal average life, and what do I get instead? A torso with a boner."

"Dearest Beth, *please!* Partake of my desire! My loins cry out for thee!"

Beth's disdainful glare focused. "And you, you fucker. You haven't made love to me in months."

Rudy shrugged. It was not an easy thing for a man to rise to the occasion when he knew his squeeze was doing the bop with a naked torso. *Hey, she's got her gig, I've got mine,* he thought. His bevy of call girls at the track wore him out. Some of those girls could suck the paint off a battleship. Not much lead left in the old pencil after when *they* were done. "It's all the stress, honey," he lied through his teeth. "All this betting everyday—it takes a lot out of a guy. And now the IRS is all over me."

"Wondrous Beth!" the torso whined on, "my passion throbs for thee! Oh, let thy lovely loins be wed again to mine! Let your angel's lips give succor to my manly love, and drink of my warm and copious seed!"

"You better get down there," Rudy advised, "unless you want me to lose everything on the next race."

Beth stared at him, her shoulders slumping.

"I hate you," she said.

One thing Rudy had added to the new house, unbeknownst to Beth, of course, was the hidden video camera in the basement. Rudy, after all, was a successful man now, and successful men didn't watch their girlfriends tuck torsos through mere cracks in basement doors. No, they watched with state-of-the-art video equipment. And Rudy had a lot to watch...

*Jesus Christ in a hotdog stand*, he thought, staring at the screen in his den and adjusting the remote, low-light lens.

Despite his arousal, Rudy could no longer deny that watching Beth's sexual feats maintained in him a necessary level of disdain for her. It didn't matter at all that he coerced her to tend to Gormok—that was beside the point. And so was logic. He needed to hate her as much as he could in order to compel her to continue. In truth it was money, not love, that made the world go round, and Rudy liked the world very much.

Sometimes, though, the things he saw on the screen really bothered him. Like right now, for instance. Beth was performing an act of fellatio on Gormok the likes of which would make Linda Lovelace look like Rebecca of Sunnybrook Farm. "Goddamn! can she smoke a pole," he whispered aloud. And he saw with even more distaste that her earlier claim was no bull. To describe Gormok as huge was sheer understatement. Try hung like a fucking Clydesdale stallion. *That fruitloop motherfucker's got more dick than four or five guys,* Rudy grimly realized, and at the same time he stroked his own endowment which, in comparison, more resembled a Jimmy Dean breakfast link than a penis. And what Beth was doing to Gormok more resembled a freak-show sword-swallowing than simple fellatio. Down her assiduous lips went, all the way to the hilt, as Gormok's legless hips squirmed in pleasure. Where did it all go? *Deep throat, my ass,* Rudy thought. *This is deep stomach. She never sucked my cock like that, the dirty bitch.*

And Rudy's hatred did not abate in the least as his hand assuaged his own beckoning fancy. *I'll bet the little whore is enjoying it,* he convinced himself. *I'll bet she's getting off! And, Christ, she's making more noise than a truck-load of hogs at the slop trough!*

As was his habit now, Rudy pretended it was the pillar of his own manhood that was being so fastidiously gobbled up by Beth's suck-to-wake-the-dead yap; it was the only way he could tolerate this—to fantasize. But when he eventually relocated the wares of his prostate gland and balls onto the Scotchguarded carpet, the fantasy shattered. His own release was a mere dribble compared to Gormok's veritable whale blasts of sperm, which Beth allowed her face to be showered with as the alomancer gibbered in glee . . .

## VII

Rudy knew it would happen eventually, but he had a contingency plan for that too. One night he woke to find Beth staring at the big bay window in the bedroom.

"Honey?" he feigned. "What's wrong?"

"I can't even sleep anymore. I can *hear* him down there. He jabbers all night long."

This in fact was true. Even from the basement, Gormok could be heard mattering inanities in arcane languages, and bubbling nasal laughter. *Well, maybe if you fucked him a little better, he'd simmer down*, Rudy thought. *Ain't my fault you're a dull fuck. Suck his big dick harder—try that, bitch. Suck his ass—that'll keep him happy.*

Beth sat on the bed and began to cry.

"Sweetheart," Rudy offered a phony consolation. "Don't cry."

"You said we'd get married," she sobbed. "You said we'd have children."

"Honey, we will."

"When, Rudy? I need to know when."

"Soon, I promise." He stroked her hair, kissed her teary cheeks. "I've got a plan," he whispered. "The race track, the ball games and all that? That's smalltime."

"What are you talking about?" she sniffled.

Rudy reached into the night stand. "See this? It'll set us up for life in no time, honey." What he showed her was the NASDAQ Index of *The Wall Street Journal*. "We'll be *millionaires,* Beth. And then, I promise you, we'll get married and have kids just like we planned."

"Please, Rudy, please," she sobbed, hugging him back.

"I promise," he reasserted. "But you've got to give this just a little more time. Okay?"

Beth's sobs began to abate.

"Honey? Okay?"

"Okay," she croaked.

"Oh, Bethieeeeeeeee!" shot the voice from below. "Come hither, please!"

## VIII

Within a few months they'd moved out of the A-frame in favor of a waterfront estate. The his and hers Mustangs were replaced by his and hers Lamborghini Diablos. Rudy merely had Gormok perform a few divinations, then laid his money down at a broker's. It didn't take long. Blue Chip stocks. Municipal bonds. T-Bills. Not to mention the thirty-million in 6-month CD's Even in the highest federal and state tax-brackets, Rudy had enough to keep them pig-shit rich for life. And that bevy of call-girls? Well, now they were *his* girls. He had thirty of them, one for each day of the month, and he put them all up in luxury condos he paid for in cash. Things weren't bad. No, not bad at all.

And Rudy found a great solace in his calendar-month of bimbos; they provided him the escape his psyche needed, the abstract catharsis which relieved the entails of his complicated, high-stress lifestyle. Plus they fucked good, which furthermore relieved the hatred he now harbored wholesale for Beth. Rudy got lost in his women, and this banished the steady and bothersome awareness that his fiancé was impaling herself on a "bigger" man than he, limblessness notwithstanding. Becky was his favorite, a slim, sultry blonde, whose specialty was tongue-baths, which made Rudy a great adherent of personal hygiene. Then there was Shanna, the full-tilt brunette with a rack of tits you could use to drydock a Los Angeles-class sub, and a welcome propensity for always asking Rudy to enter through the, uh, back door. And we mustn't forget Chrissy—now *there* was a woman! She had looks that would make Jessica Alba seriously consider suicide, not to mention a mouth that could suck-start a Ford Tri-Motor.

Yes, Rudy's buxom recreational brigade all proved quite adroit at helping him cope with his problems, to the extent that his only *real* problem was wondering just how much joy juice his vesicles could manufacture. A man could only put out so much, but lo and behold, his girls were always ready to prove that he was possessed of an endless reservoir of love lava. And on those dread occasions when he felt the old crane simply wouldn't rise, his bevy of beauties were always quick, by their sheer expertise to prove a grand synonymy with Jesus—in that they could raise the dead. Rudy loved his women, he *cherished* them. And whenever he grew sick of one, he simply dumped her and found someone else. Just as there was no shortage of beer in Bavaria, there was no shortage of beautiful women who liked moolah. What a life!

In the meantime, Rudy urged Beth to research, as thoroughly as possible, every aspect of Mesopotamian mythology, ancient ritualism, pre-Christian divination, and the like. She even found one book called *The Synod of the Alomancers*, and learned everything about the Cenotes of Nergal, the Nashipus, the Ashipus, the ziggurats, and all the intricacies of the regalia and the ritual. Rudy felt this necessary in order to make Gormok feel more at home. He had contractors make a mock temple out of the basement. He purchased real censers and thuribles, standards and statues and murals etched with the holy glyphs. He even had a clothier make a special hooded black robe and sash, identical to those worn by the ancient alomancers, which he donned each time he asked Gormok The Talking Torso to perform another divination. Rudy wanted the atmosphere to be right for his dismembered bread-winner; he figured it was the least he could do.

On the other hand, though, Beth grew more and more sullen. She rarely even spoke, not that Rudy was around much to talk to—his harem kept him busy, when he wasn't busy himself wheeling and dealing at the broker's. Beth became stoical, morose. Now, the ludicrous head atop the diviner's torso insisted she service him many times a day, amid an array of kinky twists which were better left undescribed.

But more months went by.

And Rudy's fortune increased exponentially.

## IX

It was funny, sometimes, how the universe worked. Rudy recalled telling Beth once that there was never enough, but actually, now, he found he was wrong. Already he was one of the richest men in the country. What more did he need? So it *was* rather appropriate, in a cosmic way, when Beth walked into his den one evening and dropped the bombshell:

"I'm pregnant," she said.

At first Rudy felt enraged. "Pregnant! You're shitting me! This is a joke, right?"

"It's no joke, Rudy. I'm pregnant."

He gnashed his teeth and jumped up. "You mean you let that goddamn horny torso *knock you up?*"

"I have to fuck him ten times a day," she drily pointed out. "What did you expect?"

"Well—well, goddamn it, Beth! I thought you were on the pill!"

"The pill isn't foolproof, Rudy."

*Calm down, boy,* he induced himself. *Don't panic.* "Yeah? Well, it's no problem. You'll simply get an abortion."

Her face looked carved in granite. "I'm not getting an abortion, Rudy. I'm having this baby."

"No. You're not." He opened and closed his fists, to quell his rage. "You're not going to have a kid by that *thing's* spunk."

"Thing?" Beth chuckled. "I thought he was *our man*. Forget it, Rudy. I'm having this baby. You won't give me one, so I'll settle for Gormok's."

*You evil calculating bitch,* he thought. *You did this on purpose, didn't you? You went off the pill on purpose just to put me on the spot.*

"But I'm willing to make a deal," she went on. "I will get an abortion on two conditions. One, you make me pregnant, and two, you kill Gormok." Then she passed a small box to him. "Open it," she said.

Rudy opened the box to find it occupied by a Smith & Wesson Model 65 .357 Magnum.

"You'll do it right now, Rudy. No more lies. No more false promises. You'll dig a grave in the back yard. Right now. And then you'll take that silly thing outside and you'll kill it. And I mean right *now.*"

Rudy didn't care for being dictated to, especially by a woman. *So she's calling the shots now, huh? Beth the little Torso Fucker. Well . . .* It was all he could do not to smile.

"All right," he told her. "You've got a deal."

Rudy found the shovel. Then he went out back,

He'd been thinking along these lines for a while now anyway, hadn't he? The shovel bit into the soil. He didn't need any more money, which meant he didn't need Gormok, either.

And there was one more thing he didn't need:

*Beth,* he thought, and grinned.

He'd gotten what he wanted out of her. And another point: she was starting to look really beat these days. Skinny, pale, dark circles under her *eyes*. *I'm a high-roller now,* he congratulated himself. *Why's a big time, big-buck guy like me need a little-tit stringbean bitch like her?*

He could move his harem here! Shit, those girls made the Playboy Mansion look like a dog pound. And there were some new ones now too, like Beverly: California tan, waxed pubes, 40 double-D's and nipples sticking out like a pair of golf cleats. *Her tits should hang in The National Gallery!* he reveled as he dug. And Melissa? A cosmetic-surgery paragon; she had a body on her that would put a stiffer on the Pope! Then there was Alicyn, whose vaginal barrel was more dextrous than an olympic gymnast. *Oooo-eeee!* he thought. Not to mention Shelly and Kelly, two brick-shit house redhead twins whose favorite bedroom game was "Sandwich." Rudy never hesitated to play the part of the cheese.

There were so many, an endless Whitman's Sampler of sex!

*Shit yeah! I'll move them all here! The entire bimbo brigade! I'll build a fucking luxury apartment complex in the back yard!* He could picture it. A different chick every day, a mass orgy every night! He'd eat Beluga caviar out of nut-tan bellybuttons, abdomens. Slurp Perrier-Jouet from Tit Valleys. *Blondes on the half-shell, baby! Redheads Au Gratin, and Brunettes Au Jus! I will live like a Renaissance prince!* Yeah. And Gormok? And Beth? Rudy's grin darkened in the moonlight. He rested a moment. Then he began to dig the second grave.

"You come out here with me," he insisted. "I need you to hold the flashlight."

"All right," Beth agreed. "And bring the gun."

Even bereft of arms and legs, Gormok was not easy lugging up the stairs. *The fucker weighs more than a pallet of bricks!* Rudy thought between grunts. Then, as he lowered the torso into the wheelbarrow, Rudy winced as if slapped. Gormok, apparently unable to control his

*The Salt-Diviner*

renal system, urinated quite liberally into Rudy's face.

Beth laughed.

"Dear Rudy, ho!" Gormok exclaimed. "My deepest apologies! Such incontinence, I assure you, is quite a contretemps!"

"Don't worry about it," Rudy forced himself to reply, dripping warmly. "I guess a man's gotta go when he's gotta go."

"And, goodly friend, hast lovely Beth enlightened thee? The wondrous news that the harvest of my loins hast given her a belly large with child?"

"Uh, yeah," Rudy replied. His back strained as he trundled the wheelbarrow along the pool deck. "That's, uh, that's why we're going out back, you know, to have a party, just the three of us."

"Great Ea! My joy comes unbridled!" Gormok exclaimed, close to tears. His stumps roved in glee. "A celebration!"

*There's gonna be a celebration, all right*, Rudy avowed as he grunted onward. *I'm gonna bury both of you whacks, and celebrate by pissing on your graves.*

The great back yard of the estate shimmered in quiet moonlight. It was warm out tonight, and pretty--a great night for burying people. Rudy pushed the laden wheelbarrow to the back of the property. He hefted Gormok's trunk and set it beside the first hole. The mound of freshly turned soil blocked the second hole from Beth's sight.

"But such a strange place for a celebration," Gormok's head remarked, craning atop the torso.

Rudy took the gun from Beth, who stood aside with a smirk. He checked the cylinder, saw that it was loaded, then snapped it shut with a flip of the wrist.

"Do it now," Beth ordered.

Rudy smiled. "What I'm gonna do, you torso-fucking little slut, you Babylonian-cum-swallowing whore, is kill the both of you." Then he aimed the revolver at Beth's stone-cold face.

"Go ahead," she told him. "You think I don't know what you've been planning? Use your brain, Rudy. *Think!* Gormok's an alomancer—he can *foresee* the future. If you think all we've been doing down there is fucking, then you're even dumber than I thought."

"I . . . You . . . ," Rudy said in perplexion. *What the—*

"I had the guy at the gun shop take the powder out of the bullets," Beth next informed him. "It won't fire."

Rudy snapped the trigger a dozen times, each drop of the hammer resounding in a quick metallic *click!*

"But this one will."

Rudy peed his pants when Beth pointed another revolver in his face. "Now . . . kill Gormok," she said.

"With what?"

"I don't care. Just kill him."

The gun barrel steadied on the point between Rudy's eyes. A moment later, he had his foot behind the shovel, the blade at Gormok's throat.

"Have no fear, dear Rudy," the torso strangely commented. The silly face smiled in moonlight. "Fate beckons us all, the joy-filled summons of providence."

Beth kept the gun on him as Rudy bore down. He stomped the back of the shovel until the blade separated Gormok's head from the armless shoulders. Blood pumped from the stump, soaking Kentucky Blue sod. Rudy kicked the head into the grave.

"And now you kill me," he said, turning.

"Oh, no," Beth replied. And before Rudy could turn completely, she brought the gun-butt down hard on his skull.

## EPILOGUE

Rudy would've been wise to read some of the books he'd had Beth get out of the library. Gormok had verified all she'd discovered. The spirit of a condemned salt-diviner could never be killed, only the body it happened to occupy at the time. The spirit merely moved on

*The Salt-Diviner*

to possess the body in closest proximity.

Later, Beth calmly buried Gormok's head and torso. She also buried Rudy's arms and legs. Then she went downstairs, and to the basement's new tenant, she whispered, "Goodnight."

"On the morrow, my sweet beauty!" Rudy's head replied but in the familiar high, nasal warble. "I bid thee the most heavenly dreams!"

Now she could have all the babies she wanted. It wasn't like Rudy was going anywhere. And if she ever ran short of money . . .

There was always the ashtray, and the salt.

# THE REFRIGERATOR FULL OF SPERM

## I

"Hey, Chief?" Hays said. "I ever tell ya about the time I was goin' down on Jinny Jo Carter, then all of a sudden all this gonococcal pus starts runnin' out of her snatch?"

Just as these eloquent words were spoken, Chief Richard Kinion had bitten into a stacked B,L'n T from Ma's Market, heavy on the mayo as usual, and in perfect synchronicity with his deputy's reference to gonococcal pus, a goodly share of that mayo squirted right out onto Chief Kinion's tongue.

"—squirted right out onto my tongue, and I mean a lot of it, Chief, like a big wad of the stuff," PFC Hays calmly continued with his tale. "Shee-it, I'll tell ya, boss. There I was one minute eating the beaver'a one'a the hottest chicks in town, and next minute I got myself a mouthful of venereal discharge, yes sir! God knows how much I swallered 'fore that big wad come out."

Chief Kinion paled, spat out the bite of the B,L'n T, then chucked the rest of it in the wastecan. He gagged at the image.

"Gawd-daggit, Hays!" he eventually was able to object. "You out'chore mind tellin' stories like that when a fella's tryin' ta eat!"

Hays swiveled in his seat behind the booking desk. "Aw, shee-it, Chief. I'se awful sorry, I shorely am. Didn't know you's was havin' yer lunch. But ain't that about the low-downedest thang ya ever heard? Here this gal was knowin' full well she got the clap but she didn't even tell me till afters I got a mouthful. I'm munchin' her carpet fierce, boss'n alls of a sudden start ta taste something *real* bad, and that's when she say 'Oh, Micah, honey, don't mind that, it ain't nothin' but a li'l gonnocacal pus, accordin' to the doctor.' So's then I lookit her cooze and I'se *see* it, Chief. Looked kinda greenish, it did, with a little yeller in it, and—*oooo-ee!*—did it stank fierce—"

Kinion cracked out another gagging cough, his formidable stomach tensing into a knot. "Shut up, Hays, fer Gawd's sake—"

Hays creaked back further in the chair, eyes closed during this recollection of one'a his many exploits. "And . . . you know what it tasted like, Chief? Remember last Fourth of Jew-lye when Pa'n Ima Parker brung that big vat of ranch dip that went bad? Tasted just like that Jinny's twat-pus did. Put my wood down fer a week, Chief—I mean Jinny's pussy, not the ranch dip—and I'se wanted to bitch-slap her so bad fer pullin' that stunt, but, a'corse, I didn't 'cos Micah Hays don't *never* strike a woman."

Kinion sat bent over the wastecan, his mouth cranked open, and sweat breaking on his brow. *No, no, please,* he thought. He didn't want to be vomiting in the station; such an act would not seem becoming of the Luntville Chief of Police. Eventually, though, his stomach settled down and he reclined back, pawing his massive belly.

"Hays, I don't never wanna hear another'a yer dirty stories. *Ever!* Ya hear me?"

"Right, Chief. But I'll tell ya, there weren't nothin' dirty about this—this here were a *disgustin'* story. Dirty's somethin' else, 'cos, see, a dirty story's a story that gits yer wood up. Like . . . I ever tell you 'bout the time I gots together with Mary Beth Banner and her twin sister Alice?"

"Hays, don't—"

"Now *that's* a dirty story, Chief—I'm gettin' lead in my pencil just thankin' about it! I had me one ball in Mary Beth's mouth, the other in Alice's, and one each hadda finger up my ass whiles their pussies're taking turns on my face. And this were *purdy* snatch, Chief, not fulla clap. It were . . . delecterable! Tasted kinda sweet, like the icing on the rum bums they'se make at Fuller's Bakery. Sugary it was, yes sir! And let's just say that later we played a little game called Sandwich . . . and *I* was the cheese."

Chief Kinion shrugged; he had to admit it—the image, that is. It was pretty erotic. *Two beautiful women, identical twins? Neither of 'em stinkers, and both at the same time?* For a moment, the Chief's mind lapsed, and transposed himself into the image.

*I am the cheese,* he thought.

Then the Chief's penis, which hadn't been hard for some time, grew... turgid.

"And what I did next," Hays continued, "was I pumped a big fuck up Mary Beth's ass, and then her sister sucked it out—that's right, Chief, she put her lips right up ta Mary Beth's bunger, she did, and sucked my cum right out of her poop-chute—and then she kissed Mary Beth like somethin' you'd see in Penthouse, only what Alice did, see, was whiles she was kissin', she let my cum fall right into Mary Beth's yap... and then Mary Beth swallered it all like a real trooper! It looked like a mama bird feedin' a baby bird, it did! And she said it tasted better'n the bisuit gravy they serve up at June's. Shee-it, Chief, she even licked her chops afterwards—no lie!"

The image, of course, shattered, and Chief Kinion errped up a great plume of vomit into the wastecan. Well, two, then three, then four plumes, splattering the entirety of the contents of his indisputably large stomach into the Glad Bag-lined can. When he was done the can looked *half full* of his puke.

"Aw, dang, Chief," Micah Hays displayed his earnest consideration. "That's damn shore the biggest upchuck I ever seed. What? Ya et somethin' bad? Like maybe a bad rib or pork-end. Or maybe a undercooked potato at Marley's Hash House?"

When Chief Kinion was finished heaving at the image of Alice Banner sucking semen out of the rectal vault of Mary Beth—and the following oral transference of sperm—he shuddered and wiped his mouth off with a napkin. *Yeah, Hays,* he thought. *A fuckin' undercooked potato at fuckin' Marley's...*

Sometimes, Chief Kinion could just whup Hays right upside the head, and he was even contemplatin' that just this second, but something happened right off that would forestall that possibility.

The phone rang.

"You want me ta git it, Chief?"

"No, Hays, I got puke hangin' off my face, and I just chucked my cookies inta the wastecan," the Chief replied with some sarcasm. "Why should you git it, 'specially since the phone's sittin' right on *yer* fuckin' desk?"

Micah Hays fairly took that ta mean that his boss'n employer would prefer not ta answer the phone hisself. So's he snatched it up, and announced in his clipped, professional southern cop tone: "Luntville Police Department, PFC Micah Hays speakin'. How's kin I help ya?"

Kinion wiped more of the contents of his stomach off his lips with a Stuckey's napkin, half-hearing Hays mutter a series of "Yes, sirs" and "Uh-huhs" into the phone.

"Be right out, sir," the PFC said next and hung up.

"What is it, son?" the Chief asked.

"Best git on up, boss," Hays answered the inquiry. "That there was Doc Willis, and he just tolt me that he been at a medical convention fer the last week. So he come home today and finds all the winders in his house busted, and his wife Jeanne plumb up'n gone."

Kinion stared at this unbelieverble infermation. "His wife . . . gone?"

"That's right, Chief. So's we'se best git out there right now 'cos it looks like the fine town'a Luntville got itself its first kidnappin'!"

## II

"Since we'se got a spell ta drive," Hays said, "I ever tell ya 'bout the time I were shootin' pool up at Our Place, you know, boss, that bar up near the turnoff just left'a the Bon Fire Truck Stop?"

"No, Hays, ya didn't," the Chief was quick ta say. "And I'd like ya ta keep it that ways."

"See, Chief, I were shootin' pool—that is billiards, if yer from the city—against this big fat useless no-account redneck fella named David Wells, and he know damn fine that I'se a more than a fair

## The Refrigerator Full of Sperm

pool shooter so's he challengers me to a game, so I say 'How much ya wanna bet?' and he says 'Well, I ain't got no cash on me, but I'll'se tell ya what, you put up a fifty and I'll'se put up my gal Judy Ann who's sittin' right over there.' And he points over at just about the hottest splittail I done seed that week, boss, sittin' on a bar stool sippin' a Dickel'n water, and she's got these big plump tits stickin' out behind this itty-bitty white-trash halter'n cutoff jeans so short they'se crawlin' so far up her ass she must'a had abrasions, Chief, and she even winks at me! So's I say ta Davie Wells, 'You're on, friend,' and then I'se proceed ta skunk that fat piece'a shit, and nexts thang I know I'se walkin' out that dump with Judy Ann on my arm buts before we kin git in my car, I hear that stuffed porker Davie Wells yuckin' it up out front with his pals Tommy Tresh'n Stevie Hamilton, and he's laughin' like ta shake all the roofs in town clean off."

"Well, uh," the Chief remarked, "what's was he laughin' 'bout?"

"Lemme git t that, boss!" Hays countered. "So's I haul her slim-pixie grandstand ass back ta the Dorr's Motel out on Route 3—you know the place, $14.95 a night, yes sir!—and I'll tell ya, boss, I'se ganderin' this shit whiles we'se are walkin' in, and she had a onion ass if there ever was one."

The Chief's face pinched up. "A *what?* A *onion ass?*"

"Yeah, you know, Chief. Ya take one look at it and ya just wanna cry. Anyways, once we'se git inside, this hot bitch don't waste no time gittin' my clothes of'n givin' me a good dick-lickin, and I'se mean a *really* good dick-lickin', Chief, like she's suckin' the back'a my root'n runnin' her tongue up'n down over my piss-slit, she was, and she even gave my bunghole a coupla licks—oo-yeah!—a real trooper she was, and, Chief, then she pulled down that trashy halter'n shows a pair'a tits pokin' out so plump'n perfect they'se reminderd me'a them sugar-glazed apple dumplings they'se sell at the Grauls Market bakery section fer ninety-nine cents, you know, only *these* apple dumplings had nipples on 'em like red gumdrops stickin' out a good half'a inch! Anyways, so's ingrained I were over her womanly beauty, Chief, I figgert I need ta see more'a it, so's I take ta draggin' her li'l hotpants right off her butt, I did, and then she sits on the bed'n says 'Thank Gawd you won that game, Micah! I ain't been laid fer whiles' so I say, 'Well, what'cha do with yer boyfriend, Judy Ann? Play checkers?' and she says 'Aw, that's just a put-on. That fat pig Davie Wells don't never fuck me, and he ain't even my boyfriend. He just lets me hang around him at the pool hall so's he kin give me ta the winner when he loses,' and then I get ta thinkin', Chief, like what the fuck's wrong with Davie Wells not wantin' ta fuck this dish. What? He ain't got a dick? He's queer? Thems were the only explernations I could think of, 'cos this bitch was hotter than a rock in a campfire, and ain't no red-blooded American fella in his right mind who wouldn't wanna get his pecker in that gorgeous stuff, no sir, and by now my dick's just about as hard'n stiff as a fuckin' phone pole, boss, but Judy Ann's so purdy I knows I gotta have me a taste'a her beautiful poon first, and she must be readin' my mind 'cos just then she shoots that whory grin up at me, then sticks her legs up and spreads 'em so far she looks like a fuckin' wishbone, and I'se eyeballin' that pussy on her, Chief, and—fuck me!—it's shorely the most beautifullest pussy to ever sit 'tween a bitch's gams, not all meaty'n sloppy lookin' like a lotta gals who got pussies on 'em that look more like a pile'a fuckin' cold cuts sittin' in the deli and pussylips hangin' down like rooster wattles, no sir, this here fuck-hole on Judy Ann was somethin' that should'a been hangin' in a museum somewheres, boss, alls rimmed with this soft light-brown hair fine as the hair on a baby's head'n her gash were this luscious soft pink— Box City, boss, that's what she were!—so's then I don't waste no time, I git my mug right down there in the work and git ta munchin' her rug fierce, I did, and she's moanin' and groanin' and flexin' her hips'n runnin' her fingers through my hair, and—shee-it—she tastes just perfect, Chief, just the way a gal should taste, all salty'n slick with plenty'a girl-stank down there, and by now my bone's so hard

I'se nearly drop a big squirt on the fuckin' floor. Blammed best pussy I ever goed down on, yes sir."

Not that Chief Kinion had any desire at all to hear any more'a Hays' stories, even he—the Chief, that is—didn't quite get it. "What? That's it? Ya just done spent ten minutes tellin' me 'bout some hot gal ya went down on, and there's no more?"

"Aw, fuck no, Chief," Hays waved a hand, "that ain't it by a long shot. There's *plenty* more. See, like I just got done sayin', Judy Ann's hole were the best blammed hole I ever had my tongue in . . . or so I thought. See, I'se lappin' away at her poon like a thirsty horse at a trough thinkin' it'll be any second now 'fore she comes after which I'll'se be able ta git down ta the business of humpin' her gash like there's no tomorrah and then fillin' her up with a great big *mess* of my petersnot, boss, but all of a sudden she pushes my face away from her hole'n says all hot'n breathy, she says 'Oh, Micah, honey, you are shorely the *best* pussy-eater in this here fine state!' and I say 'Yeah, I know, so why's did ya push my face off?' and she says 'Cos I need ya to do the rest, honey, I'se mean I need it *bad!*' and then I scratch my haid'n say 'Judy Ann, what'ja mean you need me ta *do the rest?* You mean, like, hose ya down, right? Hump ya ta high heaven?' 'No, no,' she said back, 'I'se'll show ya. See, I'se a little differnt from most girls, but it ain't no big deal, so don't'cha go freak out on me like most fellas . . .' And a'corse I'm thinkin' like what the fuck is this white-trash ditz talkin' 'bout, but then, boss, she shows me. What she does, see, is she sticks her fingers in her poon and kind'a digs around in there like maybe she lost a ring're somethin', and then eventually she . . . well, she pulls somethin' out, and what it was she done pulled out was . . ."

Hays glanced dramatically at the Chief.

"Was *what!*" the Chief barked back, seein' his own irate face in his deputy's mirrored sunglasses.

Micah Hays grinned. "I'se glad ya asked that, Chief, 'cos what she pulled out'a her gash was . . . a little peter!"

Kinion winced in confusion. "You mean like . . . a *dick?*"

"That's a fact, boss, it was a *dick* she flipped up out'a her pussy—no lie!—only this dick was, like, real little, like no bigger than a cigarette butt, and it had a shaft and veins and a little knob on the end, and it even had a teeny little pair'a balls at the bottom!"

Kinion smirked. "Yer fulla shit, Hays."

"I swear on the Bible, Chief, 's'true! And then I say ta her—or him—or whatever—I say, 'Judy Ann! How's it come ta be that the gal with the purdiest pussy I ever seen's got a little dick stickin' out of it!' and she says 'It's some fancy thing that they calls congenital zygotic hermaphroditism'n bi-gonadal embryotic syndrome're some such. See, I'se mostly a gal, but when I was still in my mama's womb somethin' happened and I started growin' a peter to be a boy but then my cells, like, changed their mind'n made me a girl but the little peter stayed anyway. There's like four or five gals like me born ever year, Micah, my mama showed me where it said so in *Life* magerzine, and what I really need fer ya to do, Micah, is, well, you know, I want ya to suck my little peter!' and then, Chief, I swear, she starts jackin' it, that's right, she starts jackin' her tiny dick 'tween her index finger'n thumb. I kid you not, boss, this gal had a little *boner!* So ya know what I do then?"

No, Kinion didn't know and he didn't *wanna* know, not really, but he asked anyways. "Yer tellin' me that ya . . . well, that ya sucked this little peter'a hers?"

"*Fuuuuuuuck* no! Shee-it, boss, I didn't suck her peter! I flipped the bitch over, fucked her ass till she squealed, spewed in her shit, and left, but a'corse that fatboy redneck Davie Wells and his pals was all standin' outside bent over laughin' like fuckin' hyenas and by then a'corse I knowed what they was laughin' about. But you gotta admit, Chief, it shore is an interestin' story, ain't it?"

Chief Kinion groaned. "Hays, just shut up and drive."

Doc Willis's house sat out offa County Road 3, the only thang on that road as a matter'a fact, and it were a big two-story ramshackle place with a wraparound porch, a lotta trees, and a coupla what the city folk might call "garden gnomes," in other words a coupla them 'dickerluss li'l statues'a black fellas dressed up like fuckin' horse jockeys holding lanterns. Chief Kinion never quite could figger that shit out.

But Doc Willis—he were another story. Well respectered in town. Distinguishered. And as fine a doctor as you'd ever wanna meet . . . well, not that he did any doctorin'—never had in the ten years he'd lived here. Merely enjoyin' his retirement, and that brung up another point, bein' the Doc had hisself one fine-lookin' wife with whom to enjoy that retirement, yes sir. Doc was about sixty, Chief Kinion reckoned, and down here in Russell County no one raised much of a flap 'bout a sixty-year-old man marryin' a gal who was now in her thirties. A'corse, he married her ten years ago, he claimed—just before he'd bought the house—so's she were in her twenties at the time but . . . hail. A successful fella like the Doc kin do whatsever he wants, right? His wife Jeanne was one right looker—no surprise there either as the Doc were shorely the wealthiest fella in Luntville. Nothin' down here were deemed societally amiss 'bout a good-lookin' gal hitchin' up with a older fella with bucks. It were the lay'a the land, and—as PFC Micah Hays had said once, this here looked like some pretty good land to lay.

"You think she maybe run off?" the Chief ventured to his assistant whiles he were parkin' the town cruiser in front'a the Willis place.

"Shee-it, Chief, if she run off, why's all the winders busted?"

A right fine point, the Chief supposed. They got out'n loped up to the house, spyin' the Doc's fancy kraut Mercedes. Shiny red. Looked brand new'n not a speck on it.

"Shee-it, Chief," Hays admired. "Shore is purdy. Man, I could bust me some poon in that there set'a wheels, ya thank?"

"Hays, from what I kin see, you don't need no kraut Mercedes to pick up tail. You could be drivin' the town garbage truck'n ever gal this side'a the county line'd be follerin' ya down the street."

Hays' cut his famous Elvis-like sneer'n clapped his hands together once. "Yes sir! I'se the Pied Piper of Love! That's what they call me!"

"Yeah? But a selfish cockhound's what I call ya. Now git'cher mind off splittail. We got's police work afoot."

"Selfish? Me?" Hays seemed took aback. "Aw, Chief, you're settin' me ta tears! I ain't selfish! I'se kind, considerate, passionerate, always concerned with the gal's needs. They all tell me so, I swear. I mean, just last night, I had me a date with Janey Jo McCrone, bought her a Big Mac'n a shake at Mack-Donald's, then we goes back ta her place—"

"Hays! Can it," Chief Kinion insisted. "I done tolt ya back at the station—no more dirty stories."

"Aw, Chief, it ain't dirty, I'se just tryin' relate somethin' to ya that'll change yer opin-yer-un that I is selfish. Cain't have my fine boss thinkin' somethin' so neggertive, ya know."

Kinion sputtered. "All right, Hays. Long as it ain't dirty, go ahead'n run yer yap."

"So's me'n Janey Jo—not ta be confused with Jinny Jo—we git back ta her l'il crackerbox in Trailertown, Chief, and I hump the dogshit outa her. Shee-it, I hump her so hard the bed broke all the whiles as I'se humpin' her she's squealin' 'Oh, Micah Hays, I love you!' and ya know what I'se say back, Chief? I say, 'Shee-it, Janey Jo, I don't love you but I shore's hell love fuckin' yer dirty cracker hole,' and I'se say shore'n I'se mean shore as a shiny new dime at the bottom of a well! So's then I pump a big 'un in her, boss, like—*ooooo-eee!*—I socked me so much peckersnot up that snatch she won't have to git fucked again fer a year! So's next I pull out, shake the last'a my nut off in her face, wipe my dick off in her hair, then I go pee in her toilet, don't flush, leave the seat up, haul my duds back on, wipe a booger off on the curtains, crack a fart, grab me a beer outa her fridge, and leave without even sayin' goodbye to the slut!"

Chief Kinion stared crosseyed at the young deputy. "Hays! I

thought you was tryin' ta convince me you ain't a selfish cockhound!"

Hays cracked his hands together'n laughed a mite loud. "Aw, shee-it, Chief! I were just pullin' yer leg, havin' one on ya! S'true, I think the world'a women but only what's 'tween their gams. They ain't good fer nothin' but ta drop a load in, and afters I drop mine, boss, I is outa there! I ain't got time to buy roses on fuckin' Valurntine's Day'n hold hands in the park! Fuck that shit, man!"

"Ya know somethin', Hays?" the Chief grumbled. "You is one shore-fire fucked up young man."

"Dang straight, Chief!" Hays guffawed. "And lovin' ever minute of it!"

By now they'd made their way to Doc Willis' front door, and found it strange that Doc Willis hisself weren't waitin' for 'em considerin' the urgency of his call. "Shee-it," the Chief muttered under his breath. "If I thought my wife had been kidnapped I'd shore's hail be waitin' outside . . ."

"You gots that right, Chief."

But when the Chief thought about his half-hearted statement fer a speck, he realized it weren't true at all. *Kee-rist, I wish someone'd kidnap my wife 'cos she ain't nothin' but a 260-pound Trailer Cow who eats more than a road crew, snores louder than a fuckin' gorilla, and ain't let me fuck her in problee five years, not that I'd wanna fuck her fat sloppy self. Shee-it, come ta thank of it . . . I thank I'd rather fuck the gorilla . . .* But all stray ruminations aside—and certainly none, of course, that he could relate to his deputy—the Chief raised his big ol' hand and rapped loud on the door but as he done so, the door swung open, provin' that it was ajar.

"Doc?" the Chief called out into the doorway. "Doc Willis? It's the poe-leece!"

But no reply were forthcoming.

"Guess we better go in, huh?" Hays speculated.

"Guess so."

And that's just what they did, all right, and the inside'a Doc

Willis' digs were right nice. All fancy carpet'n fine wood panelin', not to mention a shitload of antique furniture which all looked mighty pricey.

Big country kitchen too, all fixed up with the most 'spensive appliances like a big six-burner range, four differnt sizes'a T-fal skillets, a dishwarsher, a Cuisernart, one'a them fancy citified 'frigerators with a ice-maker even. The Chief were fairly impressed, he was, and thought that with a kitchen like this he could *fix* hisself some viddles, yes sir.

"Hey, Chief. Take a looky here."

Kinion moseyed on over and saw what Hays meant. "Why, if that ain't the weirdest thing . . ."

What Hays had noticed were a good half dozen 2-liter Coke bottles upended in the big stainless-steel sink.

"Cain't make jack crap outa that, boss," the deputy postulated. Six little white bottle caps sat in a line beside the sink rim. "Empty Coke bottles, all turnt upside down. Looks ta me like someone purposerly emptied 'em."

"Yeah, son, shore does but why in tarnations would someone do that?"

"A cabaleristic purpose unbeknowst ta us, I'd say, Chief—"

Kinion stalled for a frown.

"—or I guess the guy either don't like Coke or he needed the bottles fer somethin' else." Seemed a damn shame ta waste all that Coke just fer the bottles, but that weren't exactly what was paramount on the Chief's mind just then. Findin' Doc Willis was.

Cabalistic empty Coke bottles aside, they searched the rest of the lower-level. Nice house, shore, but no Doc Willis nowhere at all on the first floor. Every window downstairs, however, had been shattered from the outside in, and this fact struck both the Chief and Micah Hays as plenty strange.

"I kin see some fella bustin' a winder ta git into the place," the Chief observed. "But—"

"What sense is there'n bustin' *all* the winders?" Hays finished. This was aggravatin' and then some. "Doc Willis! Where the hail are ya?" the Chief's voice echoed up the fancy windin' staircase. But again, no response.

"Come on, Hays, lets up'n check the rester the house."

They tromped up in their shiny police boots, passin' 'spensive lookin' pitchers hangin' along the way. Upstairs were dark'n quiet jess like downstairs. Hays'n Kinion peeked in a coupla rooms but still was not able to locate Doc Willis.

"Hey, Hays? You thankin' what I'se thankin'?"

"What's that, Chief?"

"That maybe the Doc's wife weren't the only one kidnapped?"

Micah Hays frowned. "Why'd anyone wanna kidnap Doc Willis?"

"Why'd anyone wanna kidnap his wife?" the Chief countered.

"Well, 'cos, fer one, kidnappin' is often a sexually motervated crime, and the few times I seen Jeanne Willis I pulled wood so fast I plumb near busted my pants."

"Hays!" the Chief objected to his deputy's unending insertion of dirty references into everthang to come out his mouth. "Stick to the point!"

"But that is my point, Chief. You asked why'd someone wanna kidnap Jeanne Willis and that there is my answer. Some pree-vert might'a snatched her fer, you know, hobknobbin' of the sort without consent. Where as it's a tad unlikely that anyone would wanna kidnap Doc Willis hisself because, well, most kidnappers problee wouldn't wanna fuck him, and secondly, the prosperect makes even less sense since most kidnappings also involve ransom, and we all's know the Doc's richer'n shit."

"Well, yeah," the Chief bumbled.

"And futhersmore, Chief, don't you thank it's really strange now, about the winders? Ever last one of 'em, broke from the inside out'n not just the downstairs winders but the ones up here too? I guess you hadn't yet hadda chance to notice that, huh, Chief?"

*What the* . . . No, the Chief hadn't noticed, and Hays were right. All these upstairs windows were shattered too, from the outside in, bits of glass all over the floor. "Of course I noticed it, Hays. I didn't say nothin' yet 'cos I wanted to see if you did. Which brings me to my next question. How in—"

"—holy hail could somebody bust all the upstairs winders from the outside in unless they walked a ladder 'round the whole fuckin' place?"

"And why?"

"Thems some dandy questions, Chief, and I reckon we won't find no answers 'least till we search the rest of the joint."

Several spare bedrooms and a den, all well-kempt and nicely appointed, and all devoid of Doc Willis. "Chrast, this place is big," the Chief complained once they got to the master bedroom at the end of the hall. "I need ta take me a breather, son."

Hays poked around while Kinion set aspell on the big four-poster bed. "Jiminee, Chief, a fella could have hisself a whole lotta fuckin' on a bed that big—" Then a chuckle. "—and I 'spect ol' Doc Willis had hisself just that with that big brick shit-house wife'a his. Don't care how old the ol' fella is—a wife with a rack'a tits and set's curves like Jeanne Willis could put a hard one on a Kansas City faggot."

"Stop that disrespectful talk, Hays!" the Chief took exception, still huffin' and puffin' from the laborious search'a the house. "Talkin' 'bout a man's wife like that—shee-it, Hays! What if the Doc overheard ya!"

Hay flipped a hand in disregard, mulling around the dresser. "Aw, shee-it, Chief, he cain't overhear nothin' 'cos he ain't here." Then Hays slid open a dresser drawer, his face lighting up. "Ooo-eee, Chief! Take a looky! Pitchers!"

"Daggit, Hays, don't'choo be rummagin' 'round in there! Ya got no right to be invadin' the Willis' priversy!"

But the brash constable had already removed the stack'a pitchers—er, pictures, that is—and held 'em up. Vacation snapshots of Doc and Mrs. Willis at Cancun. The first was a long shot of Mrs. Willis in a skimpy red bikini by a swimmin' pool. "Holy moly, Chief, would'ja gander that body! Fuck, I could jerk me off a big dicksnot just lookin' at it!"

"Watch yer dirty mouth, boy! That's a man's wife yer talkin' 'bout!" But the Chief, even in his protest, hadda admit, Jeanne Willis was one walkin' beautiful hunka-hunka woman. He tried not to look at the photo but failed fer the most part. Yes sir, there she was, all fine womanly lines'n curves, smooth white skin goin' tan, and a class rack'a hooters all wrapped up in that there l'il bikini. Indeedy, this photergraphic image'a Mrs. Willis seemed ta grin right out at the Chief from the pitcher, a right seducterive kinda grin, and big noon-blue eyes'n cute short coiffered hair. Morosely, the Chief thought, *Why cain't my wife look like that . . .*

"Shit, boss, I'd haul them l'il bottoms right off her behind and use 'em fer dental floss," Hays articulated. "I means, just lookit at there berkeenee, just like what the splittails wear'n Calerforna, yes sir!" After which, the deputy flipped through some more pitchers and then fairly whooped: "Hot damn, boss! Is that a glimpse of a valley in Heaven're what!"

*Ho boy!* the Chief couldn't help but think spyin' this next pitcher. Here was a frontal from the chest up in that high Cancun sunlight, wherever the fuck Cancun was (he figgered it was problee in Maryland). That same foxy grin'n twinkle in the eye, that purdy face alls wet from the ocean, and best of all them big firm hooters satchled up in the red bikini top, filled out quite well, yes sir. The wet fabric made no secret'a the half-collar-sized nipples underneath, and they'se was stickin' out more'n a tad.

Hays cut his ever-familiar grin. "Is that a rack'a chest fruit or what, boss. I say *fuuuuuh*-uuuuck *me!* Ask me thems the *best* kind'a rib melons, not too big, not too small, just like the tomaters at Grimaldi's Market, you know, the big 'uns he sells fer a little extra." Hays gave his crotch an acknowledgin' squeeze. "Hey, Chief, would ya like haul that Calerforna berkeenee top off and just lay yer pole 'ween that meat? Bet'cha would, huh? Just squeeze them there two tits together'n give her a good ol' fashoin tittie-fuck, huh? Then pull a good long spooge right inta her chin—"

"Daggit, Hays, put them pitchers up!" the Chief shouted now but a'corse deep down at the core'a hisself, he couldn't deny the delecturbility of the image, and for the second time today, he felt an inklin' of a boner comin' on.

"Bet that puts some kick in yer joint, huh, Chief?"

Oh, yes, but the Chief, even in this luxurious distraction, could admit no such thing. He had a responserbility, as Chief'a Police. "Put them pitchers back, boy, or I'll put my foot upside yer head! Ya got no right to be goin' through folks personal belongin's!"

"Well, hail, Chief, you'se the one who said we should search the house—"

"That's right, Hays, search the house ta see if we could find Doc Willis and ya shore's hail not gonna find him in the fuckin' dresser drawer!"

Hays gave the pitcher a last look and his crotch a last rub, then he replaced the vacation photos'n closed the drawer.

"Now check the rest'a the room!" Kinion ordered. "I gotta tell you everthang? Check the bathroom!"

Hays turned to do so, and as he did, the Chief, still a mite worked up over that pitcher'a Jeanne Willis in her bikini top, gave his own crotch a rub when Hays weren't lookin'.

"You just give yerself a crotch-rub, Chief?" Hays queried with his back turned.

"No! Shut up! Check the bathroom like I tolt ya!"

Hays shuffled over to the bathroom, looked in, shrugged. "Well, I'm checkin' it, Chief. So what about it?"

"What's in it!"

"Well, a sink, a toilet, a bathtub, a mirror. But ya know what's not in there, Chief?"

"What!"

"Doc Willis."

"Don't git smart, boy!"

"Oh, wait'cha just one sec, Chief. Look whats we got here." Hays disappeared momentarily into the bathroom, then re-emerged, holdin' up a pair of corn-blue frilly panties. "Looky there, Chief. They gots themselfs a laundry hamper in there'n I just dug me out a pair'a Mrs. Willis' purdy panties—"

"Damn it, Hays! Put that back! Only a pree-vert digs around in a lady's dirty laundry—"

Hays showed his standard shit-eatin' grin, then lifted them soiled panties to his nose and took a long, deep sniff. "Yow! Now that there's a right ripe hash mark, boss. Ooo-eee! This gal's got some flavor for shore!" Then Hays offered the bunched panties to the Chief. "Go on, Chief, I won't tell no one. Hard-workin' man like you deserves a treat. Take yerself a sniff'a that—"

"Hays! Put it back!"

"Aw, come on, boss. Ain't nothin' like the smell of a gal's crack to get a fella's blood goin'."

Chief Kinion's voice rocketed about the room. "Put it back and go check the closet, or by God I'll—"

"Relax, Chief, all right already." Hays gave the panties back from whence they came, then did as ordered. He opened the closet door and looked in.

"What's in it!"

"Clothes, coat hangers, shoes," Hays replied.

"Fine! Go check the other closet!"

Once again, Hays did as ordered, peeked into the second closet. "I'm checkin' this one too, Chief. Wanna know what's in it?"

"Yes!"

"Clothes, coat hangers, shoes, and—well—Doc Willis. He's in there too."

"Uh . . . what?" the Chief asked, hopin' he hadn't heard it right.

"Doc Willis hisself, Chief." Hays pointed. "Layin' right here in the closet lookin' 'bout as dead as a pile'a rocks, yes sir."

Chief Kinion's face drew up into squeezed lines. "Yer jokin', right, Hays? Doc Willis ain't really in that closet, is he? And dead, you say?

Hays fully faced the Chief'n shrugged. "Well, Chief, I can say that Doc Willis is layin' in this here closet, but I cain't say fer absolute fact that he's dead, on account I ain't a doctor myself, and I ain't got no stetherscope're EKG machine on me. But I thank I can say that he's *problee* dead 'cos, see, his throat's cut right through his aderm's apple, and I'll'se tell ya something else, Chief. Not only is Doc Willis layin' here in the closet, there's a red-hairt gal in a Army uniform standin' right behind ya holdin' a gun."

This was ridiculous, just more'a Hays' fuckin' 'round. The Chief was too old for shennanergins such as this, and he shorely felt that a man'a his position was deservin' of far more respect than havin' his leg yanked by his deputy. *Maybe if I fired his wise ass, he'd get the message that police work is serious business. Fer Chast's sake! Doc Willis with his throat cut in the fuckin' closet and a gal in a Army uniform standin' behind me with a gun?* "Hays, I've had enough'a yer foolin' around. How'd you like me ta—"

But the Chief, before he could complete the fair warning, heard a click. He snapped his gaze around from where he sat on the bed, and what he saw was this:

A gal in a Army uniform standin' right behind him holdin' a gun.

"Freeze," the woman said in low, stern tone, "or I'll blow your head off."

The Chief peed his pants.

### III

It took awhile ta straighten things out. Fer one, Doc Willis was indeed layin' there dead in the closet, his throat cut clean through; secondly, there was indeed an Army gal with her gun drawn, and thirdly, it seemed that this Army gal with her gun drawn suspectered that Hays and Chief Kinion might have somethin' to do with the Doc Willis layin' there dead in the closet.

"Chief Kinion, I apologize for startling you to the extent that you . . . urinated in your trousers," the woman said, and put her Colt .45 back in her black Army-issue holster. She was dressed smartly in summer Army khakis, wore a pair of neat brass pins on her collar along with twin silver bars indicatin' the rank of captain.

"I, uh, well, it weren't startlement, Miss," the Chief excused, keepin' the front of his pants covered with a pink terry-cloth towel from the Willis' bathroom. "See, I gots me some bladder problems is all."

"Really, Chief?" Hays asked. "You never said nothin' 'bout that ta me. I—"

"Shut up, Hays . . . Anyway, Miss, I'm shore you can see that my deputy and I ain't got nothin' ta do with Doc Willis' murder. We'se was just—"

"I understand, Chief," the gal said, and, well, she were right fine lookin': shiny red hair almost to her shoulders, nice figger undersneath that tan, tailored Army tunic, and a kind of cool, very businesslike tone to her voice which was somethin' the Chief immediately found ta be very attracterive. "Pardon my initial response," she went on to further her explanation. "I heard voices in here so I came in with my gun drawn as a logical precaution."

"A'course, a'course."

"Oh, and forgive my lack of manners, Chief. I've neglected to introduce myself. I'm Captain Dana Majora—"

But then Hays stepped in to quite oddly interrupt. "Well tells me this, Captain Minora—"

"That's Majora, PFC." She turned her purdy eyes—jade-green eyes—to the Chief, and the Chief quite liked the way that whenever she were gonna say somethin' of import, she would always address

*Edward Lee*

him directly, makin' a clear acknowledgerment of his authority. And though he couldn't quite say fer shore, he thought that ever so often, on such occasions, that the fine, upstandin' and downright cute-enough-like-ta-make-the-Chief-cream-the-trapdoor-in-his-jockies Captain Majora shot him a coupla looks that might indercate a tad of attraction on *her* part too.

"So now ya kin see," the Chief augmented, "that me'n my deputy is here solely in response to the call we received from Doc Willis hisself 'bout his suspicion that his wife'd been kidnapped —"

"Chief, you ain't gots ta 'splain yerself ta her," Hays suddenly burst in. "If anythang, she's the one who needs ta do some 'splainin'."

Chief Kinion glared up. "Hays, what'choo harpin' about now, boy?"

"This gal here's obveruslee in the military poe-leece, and, accordin' to a piece'a paper called the Consterturion'a the United States, the military is always ta be controlled by a civilian government, which means they ain't got not law enforcement powers whatso's ever in civilian jurisdictions like what we'se all standin' in the middle of right now. So's how 'bout you start 'splainin', Miss. And ya kin start by authentercatin' yer identity by showin' me yer proper military I.D card."

The Chief couldn't believe his deputy's sudden outburst of ill manners. "Hays, that ain't no way to speak to a lady so pipe down!"

But the woman didn't hezzertate to reply, quite to the contrary, "Chief, your deputy's observations are duly astute, and here, PFC, is my U.S. Army identification card." She passed Hays the white plastic card for his perusal. Hays examined it, shrugged, then gave it back. "Hmmm, looks all right, I guess . . ."

After which she continued, "However, I'm not a military policewoman, I'm a field operative with INSCOM."

"INSCOM?" the Chief blinked up. "What's that?"

"The U.S. Army Intelligence and Security Command, Stolen Property Detachment," she said quickly and very curtly.

*Gawd,* Kinion thought. *She is one attracterive gal fer shore!* "That's mighty impresserive, Miss-er, uh, 'scuse me, I'se mean Captain Majora," he bumbled. "And I'se shore sorry for my assistant's surly tone. But I do got a question myself. Like . . . what the hail is the U.S. Army doin' out here?"

Majora stood smartly in her crisp, starched government-issue duds. It might also be worth mentionin' that her tits stuck out quite amply behind that khaki tunic, yes sir! "What I'm about to tell you gentlemen is classified, but since it is the Army's duty to cooperate fully with civilian law enforcement, and since you, Chief, are the senior law enforcement official in this jurisdiction, I'm obliged to be forthcoming. I'm here to investigate a possible conspiracy to perpetuate the theft of specialized ordnance from the nearby military reservation, thirty miles due south, known as Fort Paduanna."

"Ordnance?" Hays butt in. "That means ammernition, don't it?"

"Yes, PFC, it does," Captain Majora tersely answered.

"Fort Paduanna's been closed fer three years!"

Majora nodded. "That's quite correct, PFC, and that's the classified part. Fort Paduanna is indeed officially closed as an active military operations base. However, it still retains a redeposition function."

The Chief scratched his chin. "A—"

"What that means, Chief, is that active Army personnel are still on duty there in order to maintain the security of stored binary chemical weapons awaiting destruction in accordance with the SALT II Treaty."

"Uh . . . Oh," the Chief replied.

"And the reason I'm here, to specify, is to investigate the possible involvement, and now"—she glanced coldly at Willis' dead body—"the obvious murder of Doctor Willis."

The Chief was duped. "Didn't you just say somethin' 'bout the theft of ammernition? What's a country doctor got ta do with that?"

"He was no country doctor, Chief. Instead, he earned a doctorate in applied plasma physics from MIT, whereupon he joined the U.S. Army Science and Research Command. He spent twenty years in the Army, working on classified primer technologies. Ten years ago, however, after having risen to the rank of colonel, he retired. Then he moved here to presumably enjoy his retirement."

"Captain Majora," the Chief couldn't help but pipe up. "I gotta admit, I'se at a loss ta foller anythang you're sayin'."

But Hays, once again, interrupted. "Look here, lady. We'se here makin' the proper investergation of the killin' of Doc Willis and the disappearance'a his wife, and I don't see that that's got anything to do with this jive conspiracy yer spoutin' about."

"Hays, don't be so rude ta the Captain!" Kinion loudly insisted.

But Majora remained poker-faced. "I'm investigating the same thing, PFC. What you need to understand is that just before he retired, Willis was in the process of designing a new series of high-technology proximity fuses for the Army's W-79 warheads. Recently our D.I.A. intelligence surveys have been reporting the same fuse mechanisms being discovered in the armories of such countries as Iraq, North Korea, and Red China."

Kinion's big face remained in its state of perplexion, but Hays seemed to get it: "So what'cher sayin' is that your bein' here is only a coincerdence ta our bein' here. We'se investergatin' a missin' persons whiles yer investergatin' Willis as a suspect fer sellin' military technolergy ta the commies."

Majora raised a stiff brow. "Well, I myself would phrase it a bit differently but, yes, PFC, in essence you're correct. We've been maintaining surveillance on the Willis residence for quite some time."

"Well," the Chief posed finally seein' through the fog, "if you've been maintainin' surveillance on the property, did you happen to see anything unusual within the last hour? 'Cos 'bout an hour ago's when Doc Willis called us."

"No, Chief, I didn't. No activity at all on the premise."

They all set on that a spell, thinkin' 'bout it. Chief Kinion felt a right amiss, he did. Proxerimity fuses? Sellin' technolergy ta the commies? Army surveillance on a house in the sticks?

It was like a story that didn't make no sense!

Hays, as might be expected, were standin' aside with his arms crossed, but ever so often he'd sneak a glance at the Captain, eyeballin' the impresserive femerine shape'a her and no doubt pitcherin' in his mind all the hobknobbin' he'd like ta lay on her, and this, well, this kinda caused a spark of displeasure in the Chief 'cos he just knowed, on account'a the way Major a'd look at him ever so often, that if she hadda choice between either him're Hays to take to bed—

*It'd be me,* the Chief thought. "Hays!" he blurted. "What'choo eyeballin' boy?"

"Uh, nothin', boss. I were just contemplatin' the incongruenties of the case."

"Yeah, well why don't you lead the way whiles we incongruenty ourselfs back on downstairs and call the county rescue squad—"

"Good idea, Chief," Hays remarked, "so's we can git the Doc's body out here 'fore it starts to stink worse than the fat pile at Burt's Meat Market."

Kinion just shook his head as the three of 'em filed out the room 'n headed back downstairs. But as they did so, this absolutely loverly scent'a perfume floated offa Captain Majora and drifted right smack-dab inta the Chief's face. He nearly swooned, he did, at that luxurious scent, and, shee-it, he didn't even know what swoon meant! And just as he were startin' to picture the good Captain in more provocative apparel, rangin' anywhere from tight purdy evenin' dresses to her birthday suit, Hays obnoxerous voice burst forth:

"So's tell me this, Captain, what'cha make of all them empty Coke bottles in the sink?"

The Captain's pause seemed to float in the stairwell. "The . . . what?"

"Shee-it," Hays hacked. "Big fancy Army investergator and ya didn't even notice that?"

"Why, no, I didn't."

"And I suppose ya didn't notice how alls the winders been broken from the outside in, huh?"

"I did notice that, PFC. But I'm afraid I haven't yet been able to deduce a serviceable explanation."

"Yeah, well I got somethin' for ya to deduce, and—"

"Hays!" the Chief bellowed on the steps. "Put a lid on it!"

Back downstairs, Hays led the way to the kitchen, figurin' that would be the location of the nearest phone. He found it, all right, next to the fridge, and it was one'a them fancified 'lectric-type phones that didn't have no wire. Hays picked it with a gape, but before he could even attempt to dial the county ambulance, Captain Majora said, "PFC? Did you say something about empty Coke bottles in the sink?"

Both Kinion'n Hays turnt 'round and saw the fine-lookin' captain standing in front of the sink . . .

The empty sink.

"Why, ain't that befuddlin'," Hays remarked.

Chrast. Kinion saw fer hisself. The big fancy stainless-steel kitchen sink had not a thing in it when just awhile ago he was fer certain it had been filled with a bunch'a upended 2-liter Coke bottles. Also missin' were the six li'l white bottle caps that were previously lined up along the rim'a the sink.

"Don't that beat all," the Chief muttered.

"Ain't nothin' else it can mean, boss," Hays offered. "We'se both seed 'em. And if they ain't here now, that means someone must've took 'em outa here whiles we was all upstairs."

Before any further speculation could be made, then, they all three of 'em jerked their gazes up at a sudden sound.

"Holy—" the Chief exclaimed.

"—shit!" Hays finished.

But Majora was already dashing out the side door, her pistol drawn, because, see, the sound they alls heard was that of a car startin' and pullin' off at a accelerated speed. At once the thought exploded in the Chief's mind: *Somebody's drivin' away in my patrol car! If blammed Hays left the keys in it again, why I'll'se have him spendin' the rest'a his career cleanin' the public toilet at the town square!* Hays dashed after Captain Majora, and the Chief, well, since it was not possible for him to really *dash* anywhere, he hoofed it out behind the others as fast as his 260 pounds could take him.

And once they'se was out front, Kinion saw that it was not the Luntville police cruiser that had been made off with, it was Doc Willis' shiny red Mercedes, whose dust they'd all been left to stand in.

"Damn," Majora said beneath her breath.

"Shee-it!" Hays riled. "Someone plumb up'n stolt the Doc's car! Shouldn't we chase 'em?"

"There'd be little productive point in that, PFC," Captain Majora answered, reholstering her .45. "That was a Mercedes 560SL with a 5.6-liter overhead cam V-8. Our vehicles wouldn't stand a chance of catching him."

"Shee-it," the Chief said. "I wonder who took it."

With a chuckle, Hays made his own venture. "Well, Chief, at least we know who didn't take it. Doc Willis, 'n'less 'acorse a dead man can drive."

"Hays, don't run yer yap unless ya got somethin' helpful to say," Kinion complained, and all this confusion'n stress'n activity suddenly set his belly to burnin' up fierce with gas. But it was quite queer just then, because immediately after Hays had made the useless comment that Captain Majora took a few slow steps backwards, and she was looking up at the house.

"What'cha ganderin', Captain?" the Chief asked.

"Second floor, Chief," she replied, shielding her eyes with her hand. The sun blazed high, and as she continued lookin' up with her arm raised so to keep her hand over her brow, the Chief, fer only a second, mind you, 'cos he weren't no pree-vert like Hays, the Chief could see right down that gap below her short sleeve khaki Army shirt and could see her soft, purdy, shaved underarm, and he had to admit it was the finest armpit he'd ever imagined much less seed. It were the armpit of an angel, yes sir! And just past it, he caught a sideshot of the snow-white cup of her bra, and when he tried to picture the tit that filled it . . .well, the Chief dang near had to give hisself a crotch rub.

"—that window right there," she was continuin' in that stern, cool, businesslike voice'a hers, 'that's the window in the master bedroom. Not five minutes ago, the three of us were standing in the master bedroom, and I am certain beyond all doubt—"

"That winder was closed!" Hays observed.

Yes, it shore was, and now the Chief made his own observation. *And now it's standin' wide open...*

Majora and Hays dashed back into the house, while the Chief—well, we've already been through that. Least ta say, he lumbered on up behind 'em, humpin' up them stairs again and thumpin' right back into the master bedroom but by the time he got there, Hays and Majora had long since arrived and had made their astonishing discovery which the Chief, only now, could see with his own two eyes.

Doc Willis' body no longer lay in that there closet, no sir. 'N fact, it didn't lay nowheres in the room at all. It was gone.

### IV

A right quick, a'corse, the Chief put out a state-wide APB on Doc Willis' fancy red kraut Mercedes, and a missin' persons on his wife. What he kept under his lid, however, was the disappearance'a the Doc's body which, though theoretically explainable, might sound at least a smidgen ridiculous and no doubt aim a few critical chuckles in the Chief's direction. What was he to say? What? *'Tween the time I walked downstairs 'n heard the sound of a motor startin', Doc Willis' body disappeared? And so did six empty 2-liter bottles'a Coke? And, no, I'm not implyin' fer a second that I think Doc Willis' CORPSE dropped out the winder 'n stolt those bottles 'n then drove off in that fancy nazi car...*

Shee-it. It were tough bein' Chief!

The lovely Captain Majora had departed in her drab government car, but promised to git back in touch soon. Since she anticerpated an investigation that might be on the lengthy side, she needed to get situated at some local accommodations, and the Chief helpfully suggested the White Horse Motel right off'a Main Street, across from the stationhouse. Doc Willis bein' kilt and havin' his body stole, and a'corse his wife disappearin'—these were certainly grave matters in a town like Luntville, but the Chief did recognize one good point: the beautiful Captain Majora workin' with 'em on the case. *Yes sir,* he mused. *She shore is one fine-lookin' and soffistercated gal, all class*—And then he pictured her in his mind--a rather sensual image: Waking up to chirping sparrows, fresh morning air billowing in through the open windows of his double-wide, turning in the warm bed beckoned by her lovely scent and then seeing her there asleep at his side, one pretty arm draped lovingly across his large chest, and then her big green eyes flutter open and she looks at him and smiles and whispers "I love you, sweetheart . . ."

Here here.

## KINION AWAKES FROM DAY DREAM at DINER

"That bad news Army bitch oughta take the poker out of her ass fer starts, Chief," Hays then duly interrupted the fantasy. "I'll bet she's got hair up her buttcrack, like a big plot of it, ya know?"

The Chief just sputtered. Right this minute, he and Hays was sittin' at the back booth'a June's Diner because, see, after the delectible Captain Majora had parted their company, Kinion realized that this case were in need of some serious rumination, and since June were runnin' a pig's feet special fer $1.09 a plate, the Chief reasoned they could do some'a that ruminatin' right here.

"What'choo got against the Captin, Hays?" Kinion inquired. "All day you been lookin' at the gal like you got a mouthful'a sour milk."

Hays pinched his chin, thinned his eyes as if speculatin'. "It ain't nothin' I gots against her, boss. Just that there's somethin' fishy about her—and I don't mean her pussy. I'se mean, the whole thang's a crock, you ask me."

"What'cha mean, the whole thang, boy?"

Hays sucked on a pig foot, then leaned back far in the booth as if he'd just heard a bad joke. "Come on, Chief! All that bulljive 'bout Doc Willis sellin' classerfied technolergy to the commies! Doc Willis? Cut my John Henry some slack, huh? We both knows Doc Willis just fine. And here comes this stiff'n starch brass-ass Army splittail tellin' us he's some kinda traitor."

"Chrast, Hays, she's a commisherioned officer with the U.S. Armed Forces! You sayin' you don't believe what she say?"

Hays' lips pursed right up; his whole face was a crease of incredulity. "Aw, come on, Chief. She's got more bullshit than Old Man McClucky's manure pile out past the Old Post Road."

Chief Kinion leaned forward over the table, his face set with a fat grin. "I ain't dumb, Hays—I know what'chore problem is..."

Hays appeared without a clue. "Ain't got no problem, Chief, 'least none that I'se aware of, unless ya call it a problem ta have a ten-inch crotch-serpent that's hard all'a the time. What problem you talkin' 'bout?"

The Chief knew his game. "Don't bullshit me, boy. You's just all bent outa shape over Majora on account she ain't interested in you in the least. It's a right clear, instead, son, that she's got her purdy sights set on me."

"Aw, Chief, I hadn't noticed," Hays said, "but that's mighty fine! I'd never wanna think'a myself in compertition with my upstandin' boss, and if you thank she wants some'a your pants-pork, then more power to ya! Shee-it, Chief. Go fer it. Split her poon with yer hog till she squeals, 'cos that's all women want anyhows. They want that lumber up their snatch and ta feel yer hot squirt'a cocksnot, yes sir! And I hopes you git'cher tool so far up her ya bust her cervix! Hail, fuck her five're six times, git her really spunked up good so's she'll have yer juice squishin' up her hole fer awhiles. I ever tell ya 'bout the time I balled Chissy Ann Clanner nine times? No lie, Chief, I fucked her stanky gash *nine times*—all in one night. A'corse I didn't call her afterwards—to hail with that shit, boss—feel 'em, fuck 'em and fergit 'em's what I say—but anyways, 'bout a week later I walk into Dipietro's Tavern and, shore 'nuff—"

"Hays, Hays, please," Kinion griped. "Ya don't need ta tells me the whole story . . ."

"'Corse I do, Chief, and likes I were sayin', shore 'nuff there she is waiting tables and naturally she remembert the hail-fer-leather fuckin' I give her a week before, so's she's all over me, boss, yappin' 'bout how much she misses me'n wants to see me again, so's I just say 'Chrissy Ann, yer pussy stink so bad it'd kill a possum eatin' a pile'a roadkill, and I wouldn't fuck you agin with a toilet-plunger handle on account it wouldn't be fair to the handle.' So a'corse she huffs off in a swivet, goes down to the booths by the pool tables'n then she leans over to pick up the empty Bud bottles'n—damn!— if I didn't see coupla lines'a my babyjuice runnin' down her leg! Riverlets, I guess it's called if yer a college feller. Yes sir, she had riverlets'a my cock-hock runnin' right outa her hole'n goin' down her leg! A blammed *week* after I put it there!"

Well, the Chief had some doubts 'bout that but didn't care ta give it voice. Instead, he pushed the rest'a his pig's feet away, no longer feelin' terribly hungry after listenin' to all this talk 'bout weekold cum runnin' out a gal's dirty pussy down her leg. All's he did instead was pinch the bridge'a his nose like he always do when he's digustered, like earlier today when Hay's tolt him 'bout the time he were inadvertantly lickin' gonococcal discharge outa some gal's hole. "Hays," he grumbled, his belly a mite sour now, "do ya always hafta be so descripterive?"

"Oh, shee-it, Chief, I ain't tryin' ta be decripterive, I'se just tryin' ta convey my happiness for ya in that this slim red-hairt Army jizz-deposit's got a likin' fer ya." Hays sucked the last of the meat off the next pig foot. "Just make shore ya go down on her first 'cos that's what gits 'em to love ya. Lick that stanky meat hard'n fast, boss, and it helps ta work yer finger in'n out ats the same time 'cos that really gits 'em hot, and once ya git ta cornholin' her, boss, just make shore ya reach around'n keep a finger up that stanky slit 'cos—"

"Hays! That's enough!" the Chief cracked loud enough ta turn some heads in the place. Hearin' the dirty talk 'bout town gals were bad enough, but it were reglar blassfermee ta hear the same talk 'bout the luscious Captain Majora. Just . . . shut . . . up!"

"Sorry, Chief, I were just tryin' ta give ya some pointers, on account—and I means no disrespect, sir—but on acount I reckon ya ain't had many occasions ta lay some peter on some strange, if ya know what I mean, what with you bein' married to that fat cracker cow of a wife ya been married to fer the last twennie some-odd years . . . Oh, and I'se mean no disrespect by referrin' to your betrothed as a fat cracker cow. That's just Guy Talk, ya know. Fer instance, if'n I was married, I'd take no offense if you was ta refer to my wife as a fat cracker cow 'cos, in a sense, alls women is. None of 'em ain't nothin' but a bunch'a dirty fuck-dumps, boss, ain't nothin' but a bunch'a stanky fun-holes on two legs. Aw, yeah, they tell ya they love ya, they'll take care'a ya and be faithful to ya forever, but they ain't nothin' but a bunch'a lyin' truckstop whores, all of 'em, ya thank? Greedy, selfish, cocksuckin', cum-eatin', leg-spreadin', take-it-up-the-ass-fer-two-bits, pussy-reekin' trailer-park jizz-buckets . . ."

The Chief were too distracered by the oncoming flow'a imagery to take exception to this tirade'a misogerny to reply right off, but once he calmed hisself down and got a grip on hisself, he opened his mouth to do just that: unload on Hays in the big way 'bout havin' such'a low opinion'a of the fine things that God put on this earth called gals. "Hays!" he bellowed like to shake the roof'a June's Diner, "if you so much as ever, and I'se mean ever, say one more derogeratory thang 'bout gals, I'll—"

And it was at this precise time that Hays' Motorola portable radio squawked off in the crackly voice'a the sector's dispatcher who, by the way, was a woman: "Unit Two-Zero-Eight, this is County Dispatch."

"Go ahead there, County Dispatch," Hays replied into the mic. "This here's Luntville Unit Two-Zero-Eight'n PFC Micah Hays, rip-roarin' and ready to tackle some serous poe-leece work. And let's me tell ya, County Dispatch, you are one hot-soundin' chick, so what say we go out sometime?"

A static pause, then: "Two-Zero-Eight, please conform to proper radio-traffic conduct as outlined in the County Manual for Interagency Communications Protocol. Violations of such protocol may be punishable by reprimand and a $1000 fine."

"Shee-it," Hays whispered to the Chief. "She problee ain't had no cock in about ten or twenty years, got a pussy on her dry as a pile'a pretzels. That's why she's actin' like such a frigid post-mentalpausal bitch—"

"Two-Zero-Eight," the dispatcher proceeded, "respond to citizen complaint of a possible Signal 9N at 861 Mount Airy Road."

"Roger that," Hays dutifully replied. "Unit Two-Zero-Eight is on the way! Over'n out, sweetheart!" The PFC hooked the radio back on his belt. "Git them viddles down, boss. Time to go check out this Signal 9."

Chief Kinion made a quick nod, wiping his lips with a napkin. Signal 9? He didn't quite recall that one, did he? Nevertheless, they pushed off from the table.

"My treat, boss," Hays insisted, whippin' out his billfold. "I'll even leave Martha the Tail a good tip, yes sir."

Matha the Tail, now that was another the Chief didn't quite get. She'd been runnin' the counter at June's for long as he could remember. A sassy, skinny ol' gray-hairt woman probably pushin' the shit outa seventy by now. Had no teeth in her yap'n never wore dentures, and here she was right now smilin' toothless at Micah Hays as they lumbered up to the register ta pay.

"Well, hey there, Martha," Hays greeted. "How's my favorite gal in the whole blammed town?"

The woman's smile pulled her weathered face up into somethin' that had more lines than a state road map. "Why if it ain't Micah Hays, every woman's southern dream. When you gonna come by and see me again, hon?"

"You'd be too much fer me, Marth," Hays complimented. "Some gals are just too hot, ya know. 'Sides, me'n the Chief here got an urgent call out on Mount Airy Road, and when duty calls, we'se there."

"Just you be careful, Micah Hays," the old woman urged. "Anything ever happen to you and ever single gal in county'd be at a loss."

"You got that right, Martha." Hays slapped down a five. "Keep the change, darlin', 'cos you're worth it!"

Martha the Tail shot him a lascivious wink. "You tryin' to buy my affections, honey?"

"Martha, your affections is worth millions!"

"Oh, ain't you just the sweetest thang," Martha gushed.

The Chief's frown sharpened once they was back out in the sun. "What's that shit all about, Hays? She acts like she got a thing fer you."

Hays whipped out the keys as they approached the Luntville cruiser. "A'corse she does, boss. All women got a thing fer me, 'specially after they had me."

Kinion stopped in the dusty parkin' lot. "Now hold on there, boy. You ain't tellin' me that you . . . well, you know—"

"Fucked her?" Hays interpreted his supervisor's curiosity. "Hail yes I fucked her, Chief."

"But . . . she's—" How could he say this without soundin' disrespectful to the elderly? "She's, uh--"

"A busted, toothless, seventy-year-old hag?" came the PFC's next interpretation. Then he shrugged. "Pussy's pussy, boss. Just 'cos it's old don't mean it shouldn't be fulla cock. Ya know how cheese is better after it's been aged? Twat's the same. Or let me put it this way, sometimes I like my meat seasoned. Yes sir, 'bout a year or two ago, I done fucked the giblets'n gravy outa that old bitch, and I ain't just talkin' 'bout her snatch. Ooo-yeah, boss, she kin fuck'n suck with the best, ol' Martha the Tail."

Holy hail. The Chief were absolutely flabbergastered, but then . . . *What can I expect from Hays?* he realized. But then that brought up the next topic of inquiry. "You are one irredeemerble male slut, boy, such that I cain't hardly believe it. But tell me this, somethin' I'se always wondered—"

"You wanna know why she got that nickname, huh, boss? You wanna know why they'se call her Martha the Tail?"

"Well, yeah. It's always been somethin' I never could quite figgure."

Hays opened the driver's door and slid in. The car started right up, and Hays pulled out, snappin' on his sharp-lookin' mirrored sunglasses. "Shee-it, Chief. I never told you 'bout the time I fucked Martha the Tail? Well that's just dandy 'cos it's one'a my best stories and we gots ourselves a good twenty-minute drive—plenty'a time to tell ya . . ."

Chief Kinion sighed in his seat, knowing that he had it comin' for asking in the first place. *Me'n my big chow-hole,* he thought.

"It was one night, like I said, a year or so ago," Hays began his tale of Martha the Tail. "I'd been up the bowlin' alley with the boys and had me like eight or ten beers, but it was men's league and there weren't splittails around fer me to pick up and fuck till their cracker brains rattle in their heads so I decide to hail with it and go on home but it were just my luck I weren't a mile out on the Route before my left rear tire blows'n *worse* luck still that my spare was flatter than Dolly Carrigan's chest after her masterectermee, so I ain't got no other choice but to hoof it. So I'se walkin' along the Route, and it's a nice hot night, Chief, the crickets chirpin' and the moon out and I got me a belly fulla good brew so I'se start ta thinkin' wouldn't it be just dandy if some dog-horny young bar-bitch droved by'n picked me up, but what happened instead, see, was some dog-horny *old* bar-bitch picks me up and it's Martha the Tail drivin' that big piece'a shit Chevy jalopy'a hers that looked like it were probably old as she was, and anyway, she's drunker'n a truck-stop tramp she is and my dog's up'n barkin' so fuck it, right? Old tramps need love too, so I figger it'd be selfish fer me not to give her some. So she drives us back to that old shit-box of a house her pa left her way back when, 'member? He was all stewed on shine and falled into his thresher? And once we git inside, she's all business, boss. She's got my pants down to my socks and she's suckin' my dick like it's a meal--as fine a cocksuck as I ever had, and I've had me more than a few, and lemme tell ya somethin', Chief, you ain't HAD head till you've had it from a toothless gal, and I swear I got my peter shoved so far down her throat I thought maybe I was about to come on her gall bladder're somethin', but I decide to do the old bitch a favor so I hold off'n tell the hag to git outa her clothes so's I can fuck her hard'n proper like the way all gals need ta be fucked, and once she got outa them duds—shee-it, boss—I thought I was lookin' at somethin' on one'a the slabs down at the county morgue. Her tits hung down so far it looked like maybe gorillas had been swingin' from 'em, and she got big gnarly nipples on her that looked like a coupla loogies like you spit out when ya got a chest cold, only they got hairs stickin' out of 'em and she got a bellybutton on her like someone shot her with a pumpkinball, Chief. All in all, this old cracker weren't nothin' but a bag'a bones—"

Chief Kinion brought a hand to his forehead, as if overtaxed by exertion. "Hays, please, ya ain't gotta tell me the whole thang, just why folks call her Martha the Tail."

"And I'll be gettin' to that in a minute, Chief," Hays assured him, steering now through the long sunny bends of Route 154, "and like I was saying, this old cracker weren't nothin' but a bag'a bones but a'corse this particular bag'a bones had a coupla holes in it that my dick was very interested in. And she's lyin' there on the dirty floor pantin' like mutt in heat and her skin all saggin' and then she spreads her legs—and I might add that her legs looked like a coupla broomsticks painted white—and her pussy looks like a ground-pork sandwich, boss, except that ground-pork sandwiches don't generally got a big pile'a hair at the top, and I figger that just 'cos it's been around since probably like before the Battle'a the Marne ain't no reason why I cain't put a big petersnot in it, right? So's I push that old bitch's knees back into her mummy face and get the pipe right up there, yes sir, right into that ground-pork sandwich and I get to humpin' her so hard I figgure her old bones might break, but what the hail? A nut's a nut, right, and I figgure I'm doin' a kindness to her since the last time she had a good hard fuckin' like this was probably like back before Harding was in office, but ya know what, boss?"

Kinion's face felt puffy and hot, and them pig's feet weren't settlin' too well now. "What, Hays?" was the only reply he could make.

"I start to notice somethin'…well…Kinda funny. Like somethin' felt not exactly ordinary on my ten inches'a pecker, sorta reminded me'a what it might feel like to have my wood in a bag'a raw chicken gizzards, and then she looks up all gustin' breath and sweaty and she says, 'Don't stop, honeybunch! Keep stratchin' 'em! It feels so good to git 'em scratched by a nice big pecker like what you got!' So I say, 'Scratchin' 'em? What'choo talkin' 'bout? Scratchin' *what?*' and she says 'My vagernul polyps, that's what the doctor called 'em. See, Micah, I got these growths in my pussy called polyps, and the doc says they'se harmless and I'se too old to have 'em removed anyhow. But, holy hamhocks, they itch! I pick up young fellas all the time and they scratch 'em for me with their peters but-but-but *nothin'* like you, Micah! That big dick on you scratches 'em deep! Deeper than they ever been scratched! Look, I'll show 'em to ya.' Fuck, Chief, I didn't really wanna see no growths in this old dust-bag's cunt but-- hail. I pulled my willy out and Mathra jacks her skinny legs back as far as they'se'll go and then pulls her old pussy open with her fingers and shows me. A right gross it was at first but then as I got ta lookin' I found 'em downright *interestin'*, I did. She kinda like flipped back her pussylips and folded 'em out and I could see 'em, I could *see* them there polyps! Looked like her pussy was fulla *meatballs!* And I figger what the hail—she wants me to scratch them meatballs with my dick, then I'll do it. So I park my peter right back in there and git back fuckin' her good'n hard like the old bitch that she is and shore enough, boss, I come *all over* them polyps, yes sir! I done flooded the Valley of the Meatballs, I did, and while I'se comin' she's havin' a nut herself, friggin' her clit with her finger—looked like Dash Woolley's nose her clit did, right before he keeled over from drinkin' hisself to death—and my dick can *feel* my come slickin' up all them polyps in there, oh yeah! It were an absolutely new kinda pussy experience, boss, yes sir, fuckin' a pussy full'a *polyps*."

    The dissertation ended, or at least it seemed to then, as Micah Hays properly decelerated and veered right onto the spur of Mount Airy Road. *Thanks God it's over,* the Chief thought, a paw to his belly, but then another thought dragged back. *Wait a minute . . . Polyps? Vagernul growths?* "Hays," he couldn't help but ask. "What's all that got to do with folks givin' her the nickname'a Martha the Tail?"

    "Nothin'," Hays answered. "'Least not yet 'cos, see, the story ain't over. After I hosed down her polyps with my spunk, next thing I know, ol' Martha's back to doin' a *fierce* suck job on me—she got both my nuts in her mouth at the same time—no lie—and she's suckin' on 'em like they're hard candy, and a'corse my dick's still hard anyways on account I *never* lose my wood, 'least not after the first jackerlation're two, and she's suckin' my balls'n strokin' my pole with her spitty hand and I'se thinkin': hail, I'se gonna have ta give this old biddy another load for history, and she says 'Micah Hays, not only are you the most handsomest man in town but God hung a pecker on you that is posertively the most beautifullest. I seen a lotta peckers in my time, but I ain't never seen one as gorgerous as this,' and I imagine she *has* seen a lotta peckers in her time, Chief, probably been seein' 'em since like back before the Boer War, and a'corse I trully did appreciate the complermint, not that it weren't somethin' I already knowed, which is not to sound eagertistical, Chief, but I gotta admit ever splittail I ever dumped a fuck in has tolt me the same thing, that my Johnson is the best they ever seed—"

"Just tell me why they call her Martha the Tail!" the Chief nearly exploded.

"Oh, right, boss, I'se gittin' right to it like I'se promised. After that dandy suckjob on my nuts, they'se feel like they got enough sperm in 'em to like knock up every splittail in China and my dick's so hard it looks like it's gonna split open like when ya leave a hotdog in the microwave too long, so what happens next, see, is Martha flips over'n gits up on her skinny hands and knees'n says 'Now put that great big beautiferal peter right up Martha's ass, honey, 'cos I need a cornholin' like I ain't had in a coon's age,' and I figure it's probably quite a spell *longer* than a coon's age since she had a love-stick big as mine up her backside, like maybe not since before Schylar Colfax were Secretery'a War, and since I'se never one to refuse a gal what she needs, I pop my peckerwood right in there'n get to givin' her the backdoor hump somethin' fierce. Now a'corse I'se always preferred a somewhat *tighter* asshole on a gal I'm cornholin' but, hail, this old bag cain't help it. A fella's only right to figger that an asshole's gonna lose some'a its elasterticity after it's been gettin' poked and takin' shits since back before the internal combustern engine was invented, and ever fella knows that second nut'a night's always the best, I figgure the best place at the time ta *have* that nut is right up into the middle'a what she et yesterday, yes sir. Some gravy for her poop, ya know? So I grab onta her bony old hips and really give it to her'n them empty sacks for tits she's got're swingin' back'n forth like a coupla pieces'a flat pasta, and she's reachin' back friggin' that big nose-sized clit'n startin' comin' again'n shriekin' 'bout how I'se the best fuck she ever had in her life and then—wham-o, boss!—I have myself a *dandy* nut'n pump so much jizz up her ass I wonder when it's gonna start fallin' out her nose, but when my nut's done, I figger I done my duty fer the elderly so's I best wipe my dick off in her crack'n git on home, so's I'm about ta pull my stick out but she says 'No, no, ya cain't go yet, Micah! Please! Ya see, there's still one more thang I need'ja to do fer me!' and I'se thinkin' shee-it, she wants me to fuck her a *third* time? Shore, I could do it, I can fuck all night, just ask any gal in town, but I ain't really up to it, ya know? Might even have a tough time keepin' wood after for so long lookin' at the way her skin's hangin' off her and them empty tits swingin', but I decided to give her a more gentlemanly let down rather than sayin' the truth that might, you know, hurt her feelings, like sayin' her ancient pussy ain't worth another stiffer from the Great Micah Hays or I wouldn't fuck an old whore like you with Dash Woolley's cock'n the only reason I done so the first two times is 'cos I'm drunk or somethin' like that, no, so I say 'Jiminee, Martha, a fine hot gal like you just up'n wore me out! You done took it all from me, darlin', I'se so wore out it'll be a day 'fore I can get it up again.' But then she looks back over her bony shoulder'n says "No, no, I don't need ya to fuck me again but, see, when a gal gets up in her years like me, we start gettin' problems, ya know, like them polyps in my pussy I was tellin' ya about that you were so kind enough ta scratch for me,' and then I say, 'What'cha mean, Martha? Don't tell me ya got polyps up yer ass too!' and she says back, 'No, no, I ain't got no polyps up my ass but I *do* got me a problem back there. It's what the doc calls Inflamed-Bowel Syndrome—see, I got these sores up there'n I can only eat certain foods'n gotta take special medercation'n such. And another thang I gotta do is have me an enema every day—that's what the doc said—so what I want'cha ta do, honey, since yer pecker's still up my ass, is pee,' and I say 'What! You want me ta *pee* up yer ass?' and she says 'That's right, sweetheart. See, I got so many medercal problems in my old age, more than a few n'fact with my backworks, if ya know what I mean, and I just *hate* stickin' that enema nozzle up my rear 'cos it *hurts,* but since your *own* nozzle's already up there, how 'bout savin' me a step? Just be a dear and give me a nice warm piss-enema, will ya, honey?' Well, shee-it, Chief, I've had gals ask some pretty dang strange things of me in the past but *never* has *no* gal ever asked me to pee up her ass, and just then it hits me, and it hits me hard—like just how *bad* I do n'fact have to pee 'cos like I tolt ya I'd chugged me eight or ten beers back at the bowlin' alley and alls of a sudden all eight or ten or 'em had snuck up on me a right fierce, so I figer what the hail? Kill two birds with one stone, right, Chief? She needed an enema and I needed to pee so—fuck it—I just leaned back and let 'er rip. I musta put the biggest beer-piss in history right up Martha's backside, yes sir. I guess she didn't quite count on so much not knowin' how many beers I'd drunk back at the bowlin' alley but—hail—she wanted it so she got it. I swear, boss, I musta been peein' in her a good five're six minutes—no lie—dang near thought it would take the rest'a the night! But finally I finished'n popped my pecker out' started to get ready ta leave, but when ol' Martha stands up, I nearly bust out laughin'! and I guess you're thinkin' what the fuck's so funny 'bout peein' up a gal's ass, huh, Chief? Well, I'll tell ya, dang straight. Ol' Martha stands up and I guess she's fixin' ta walk inta the bathroom'n push all my piss out her ass, but you shoulda *seen* her, boss! I peed so much inta her that her belly was stickin' out like she was eight months pregnant! It were hilarious, it was! And ever time she took a step, I could hear all that hot piss sloshin' around in her gut like if ya got a gallon jug'a milk but it's only half full and ya shake it around? *That's* what she sounded like!"

*Hot piss sloshin',* the Chief thought. Indergestion was now creepin' up his throat, and all he could do was blame hisself for askin' 'bout this in the first place. Not that his question had been answered, but he weren't about to remind Hays'a that. Best to just let it lie'n get on with their business. Kinion cleared his throat. "Fine, Hays. So what's this we'se goin' to? A Signal 9—"

"A Signal 9*N,* Chief," the PFC responded. "And you know what *that* means."

"Uh . . ." Well, actually and as were previously notated, the Chief couldn't recall his county signals. "Uh, right, that's a, a . . . Disabled vehicle, ain't it?"

"Naw, Chief, come on. Haven't ya memorized yer county code sheet? A Signal 9 is a suspicious person—"

"Oh, 'acorse!" the Chief affirmed. "I was thinkin' of the *old* county sheet, back 'fore you came on."

"Uh-huh, so then I'se guess ya also know what a Signal 9*N* is, right, Chief?"

*Shee-it!* "How's am I supposed ta remember stuff like that what with all my complercated duties as chief!"

"Oh, well I shorely understand, boss, so's I'll refresh yer noggin. See, the *N* in Signal 9*N* stand fer *nekit.*"

The Chief gawped. "Nekit? As in buck nekit?"

"That's a fact, Chief. Not just a suspicious person but a *nekit* suspicious person but judgin' from the address, Chief, that is 861 Mount Airy, that sounds like Claude Gullard's place, huh? And— shee-it, Chief—I'se shore as hail hope *he* ain't the suspicous nekit person 'cos I gotta tell ya, the last thang I need to see is that fat cracker buck nekit, no sir, ain't no way I wanna gander Claude Gullard's cock'n nutsack'n hairy ass. Uh-*uh!*"

Them polyps was bad enough'a image, the thought'a Claude Gullard nekit didn't help. The Chief's mind groped for distraction. "Ain't there that candyass liberal whatchamacallit house out there? You know, that county thang—"

"Danged if you ain't right, Chief!" Hays exclaimed slappin' the steerin' wheel. "The County Watch-House fer Boys! Bet that's what it was. One'a the punks inside probably got a girlfriend sneakin' in and then when they'se was hobknobbin' maybe one'a detent staff come along so this gal hot-foots it outa there'n didn't have no time ta git her clothes back on 'fore she done so . . ."

The institution that PFC Hays referred to was a Russell County "cooperative": a medium-security halfway house for teenage boys who'd committed felonies but were too young to be prosecuted. So they stuck 'em here for six-months at a clip ta teach 'em a lesson. A'corse, purdy much, the only lessons they'se learnt was how to commit crimes better from what'cha might thank of as the aggregation'a criminal knowledge, but that were fairly besides the point.

And when they pulled up at 861 Mount Airy Road, it were indeed Claude Gullard who come out his front porch, only he weren't nekit thank God, but he did indeed prove ta be the complaintant.

He was fat and stank, and wore overalls whiles he were scratchin' his ass'n tellin' Hays and the Chief 'bout what he seed, and he didn't have no t-shirt on under them overalls which afforded an unwelcome view'a his upper chest which actually looked like a pair'a tits only with hair on 'em. "That's right, Chief, I shore 'nuff saw it with my own eyes I did. It were a gal, a right fine lookin' one if ya ask me—"

"Did'ja get wood?" Hays asked with a note of sudden interest.

"Hays!" the Chief bellowed. "That ain't relervant at all, so what'cha doin' askin' somethin' so blammed dickerluss!"

But Hays defended his inquest a right quick. "Chief, I hate ta disagree with ya, but I'se gotta say that my question were *perfectly* releverant on account it clarifies a subjecterive point in our interview with Mr. Gullard here. I mean when Mr. Gullard says this nekit gal was a right fine-lookin', we need ta establish just *how* fine-lookin' she was. And if we knowed if she were fine-lookin' enough to pop wood on Mr. Gullard here then we'd know she were more than likely *very* fine-lookin', now wouldn't we? And such knowledge would only increase the effercacy of our investergation'a the complaint, now wouldn't it?"

But before the Chief could slap Hays upside the head fer proposin' somethin' so nonsensical, Claude Gullard stepped right up with his opinion: "Dang, Officer Hays, I say that's a mite downright percepterive of ya. You musta gone to collerge to have yerself a set'a smarts like that."

"Dang shore did, Mr. Gullard," Hays was proud to say. "Got me a degree in Criminal Justerce from Ball U., and I'se grad'jer'ated top'a my class."

Claude Gullard's eyes went wide with undilutered awe. "I say *wow*, Officer Hays, that shore is somethin'. Chief, where'd you go ta collerge?"

"I didn't go to no dag hippie collerge!" the Chief kindly replied. "I don't need ta go to no dag hippie collerge to run my police department!"

Claude Gullard scratched his hairy tits through his overall top. "Well, then . . . how come it wer PFC Hays who thought to ask me if I got wood and not you?"

By now, Chief Kinion wanted to pull his hair out at the frustration'a this situation but a'corse that wouldn't've been too easy, see, on account the Chief didn't have much hair left ta pull out. And then Claude Gullard, he said, "And ta answer yer question, Officer Hays, yes indeedy, when I saw this very fine-lookin' gal runnin' buck nekit across my yard, I shore as hail got wood right quick, like alls of a sudden I were raisin' a flag pole down there in my overalls, n'fact, I had me wood so hard I gots to admit, fellas, I had whip it out real quick'n jack me off a fast one, I did."

Hays nodded, eyin' the Chief. "See that, boss. Now we'se *know* that this here weren't just yer *average* nekit gal runnin' across the yard but a *real wood-popper,* Chief. Which leads me ta my next speculation."

Kinion wearily rubbed his face; it was getting to be a habit. "And what might that be, Hays? Really. I'm dyin' ta know."

"Well, Chief, right off hand I can only think'a one gal in particular that could put instant wood on me at the mere thought, and that would be Jeanne Willis, yes sir."

"Aw fer Gawd's sake, Hays!" Kinion lost control. "What the *hail* would Jeanne Willis be doin' runnin' round out here buck *nekit!*"

Hays answered the question with a question, this one bein' directed at Claude Gullard. "Mr. Gullard, could'ya be so kind ta tell me if this nekit gal had short brownish hair that might be called coiffered, if, like, you was from the city?"

"Why . . . why yes, she did!" Claude verified.

"And did she have, like, a set'a tits on her that was not too big, not too small, just like the tomaters at Grimaldi's Market, you know, the big 'uns he sells fer a little extra?"

Claude Gullard slapped his thigh. "*Dang* if you ain't 'zactly right, Officer Hays. This gal hadda set's tits on her *just* like what you described! And I'll'se tell ya somethin' else. She had—what they call it, you know, like them fucked-up folks from Calerforna . . . I know! She had *tan lines,* Officer, like what gals git on their skin when they'se out in the sun a lot'n wearin' them berkeeneree thangs!"

Hays fired a subdued grin to the Chief but the Chief weren't buyin' none'a this malarky, and he said so: "Hays' that don't mean nothin'! It weren't Jeanne Willis runnin' round out here with no clothes on. Shee-it, it coulda been *any* gal with short brown hair'n nice tits'n them citified tan lines!"

"Well, shore, Chief, you're right," Hays backstepped. "You're the boss'n I goes with what you say ever time."

"Fine," Kinion agreed, "so keep it shut and let *me!* ask the questions." The Chief turned his gaze to Claude Gullard, and then the Chief opened his mouth ta speak but—dang!—he shore couldn't think of a single thang ta ask. "Well, Hays, I'se a little tired today, so's why don't you ask some more questions."

"Shore, boss," Hays said, and asked, "Okay, Mr. Gullard, so's when you seen this nekit gal who wasn't Jeanne Willlis runnin' across yer yard, where 'zactly was she runnin' from?"

Claude didn't waste no time in answerin'. "Right back there," he said'n pointed to the back'a the pile of rotten boards that were his abode, "from the woods behind my house, you know, that blammed—"

"County Watch-House fer Boys, huh?" Hays deductered.

"That's absolutely right, Officer! That dag liberal Demercrat place they stuff fulla punks'n treat 'em real cushy instead'a throwin' 'em inta the real county clink where they'd learn the error of their ways a mite fast," Claude Gullard expressed his rather conservative opinion, "on account after just a coupla nights of gettin' butt-fucked by a bunch'a big shines with cocks big 'round as coffee cans—yes sir, they'd learn *real fast* not ta go breakin' the law when some fella named Toby's got his hog stuck up in there to the balls."

Well, the Chief didn't really know what he thought 'bout such things that were dependent on societal demergraphics'n such but none'a that was what this were about, right? And though he didn't believe fer a second that this nekit gal was Jeanne Willis, he did recognize that the fulcrum'a this call should take them up to the County Watch-House fer Boys lickety split. But just as the Chief were gonna thank Claude fer his time and head on up to the House, the overalled man with hairy tits added a final observance, well, two actually. "Oh, and somethin' I fergot, Chief. When this nekit gal run off across my yard she disappeart just past them trees out yonder and then a coupla seconds go by'n I hear a car drive off. Couldn't see it, but I shore's hail heard it."

"Maybe a red Mercedes," Hays offered.

"Bull*shee-it*," the Chief replied.

"Oh, oh, and one more thang," Claude remembert, "though I'se not quite shore what it were but . . . she seemed to be holdin' somethin' as she were runnin' but . . . fer the life'a me, I cain't figger what it could'a been. Somethin' she seemed to be carryin' under her arm . . ."

"One'a them big plastic Coke bottles?" Hays proposed, "like one'a them 2-liter ones?"

Claude slapped his thigh again. "Yeah! Yeah! How'd you know that, Officer?"

"Never mind—thanks fer your time, Claude." Kinion grabbed Hays by the arm and hauled him off around the back of the house. "We've dicked around long enough here, Hays, with you askin' Claude Gullard if he got a hard-on. And that bull-hockey 'bout the Coke bottles'n coiffered hair'n tits the size'a Grimaldi's tomaters—that weren't nothin' but the power'a suggestion."

"Well, I don't know 'bout that, Chief, 'cos see—"

"Just shut up'n come on!"

They tromped back through the weeds until they come to the front side'a the County Watch-House, and first thang the Chief noticed was . . . well . . . *Sounds awful quiet fer a halfway house fulla teenage wahoos'n rowdy punks.* Indeed, it sounded *real* quiet, and there weren't no sign of any manner'a activerty no wheres.

"This is a mite weird, don't ya think, Chief?" Hays asked.

"Dag right. Let's go on in'n see what's goin' on . . ."

The big steel front door stood wide open. Not good. Nor was it good when they found no sign of a guard or reception officer inside.

Er, at least not *immediately* inside . . .

Their boots clicked down the shiny tile floor. It was dark inside; small barred windows high along the main corridor leaked in light. A sign on the wall read: WELCOME NEW RESIDENTS!

"Aw, shee-it, Chief," Hays complained without haste. "They don't even call 'em inmates or convicts—they call 'em *residents.* Guess they don't wanna offend their young senserbilerties, huh? What a bunch'a Clinton-Gore, Janet Reno, left-wing, grab-ass, ass-kissin', pinko, bleedin'-heart liberal *poop!*"

"Keep it shut, Hays."

Another sign around the corner read: PLEASE, NO LOUD TALKING.

"Oh, these poor fellas," Hays made some sarcasm. "Cain't even talk loud. Sounds like cruel'n unusual punishment ta me, like we'se fuckin' with their civil rights! Dang, Chief, ya thank we oughta call the ACLU?"

"No, I thank ya should *shut up!*"

Past the main halls were dormitories, not cells, and a number of classrooms. A college-like cafeteria came next, nice tables'n chairs. "Shee-it, Chief," Micah Hays vented more opinion. "I gotta agree with Claude. This ain't no way to deal with a bunch'a wiseass undiscerplined punks. Our tax dollars goin' into footsie joints like this so's a bunch'a criminals can have fancy dorm rooms with TVs and nice beds and a blammed cafferteria! They oughta be sleepin' on wire bunks and eatin' cold beans off a tin plate! Work 'em 16 hours a day on a chaingang, I say. That'd show 'em not ta break the law."

"They're just teenagers, Hays, they're kids," the Chief said. "Ya don't *punish* kids nowadays, ya rehabileritate 'em."

"Shee-it," Hays smirked. "Ya ask me, turn this place into a county butt-whuppin' house, that's the way. First offense, give 'em a two-by-four shampoo, second offense bust some bones. They'll get the message. Or like Claude said, throw 'em in the county slam, let 'em git their butts plumbed raw fer a couple weeks straight. Cain't sell drugs or rob folks when you're walkin' funny. Yeah, Chief, ya ask me—"

"Well, I *didn't* ask ya so *shut up!*" The Chief's booming drawl rocketed down the hallway. "We'se gotta find a detention officer, find out what's goin' on."

The end of the next hall took 'em to a big set of double doors and a sign: GYMNASIUM. "Shee-it, Chief, I shore hope we'se ain't interruptin' their volleyball game, 'cos these poor boys have the right ta rehabileritation." Hays chuckled. "Yes sir, sounds like a suppression of Constitutional rights fer a bunch'a little robbers'n rapists ta not git their proper exercise'n fun." But when Hays pushed open them double doors, he just stood'n stared, and the Chief did likewise.

"Well shit my shorts," Hays uttered.

"Fuck," Kinion responded.

What faced them was no doubt the bizarrest thang either of 'em had ever saw. Each and every single teenage resident of the County Watch-House fer Boys—all thirty of 'em mind you—lay side by side on the gym floor in a single line, and the three staff detention officers lay right along with 'em. Yes sir, a line of fellas from one end'a the gym to the other.

And if that weren't odd enough, this next fact might shorely be. Each and every one of 'em had their pants pulled down to their ankles 'n odder still was that their peckers was all stickin' up hard as rocks. That's right, what Hays'n the Chief stood starin' at was a row of exactly thirty-three hard dicks, all shapes 'n sizes.

But not one of these fellas was movin', not at all, like they was all lyin' there on the floor next ta each other and were asleep or—

"Shee-it, Hays," Kinion fretted. "Are they—are they *dead?*"

"Not unless the dead can have wood, Chief. I mean, look! They alls got boners!"

"I can see that, Hays . . . Go check."

Hays looked at his boss. "Check what? Their boners?"

"NO NOT THEIR BONERS GOD DAGGIT! CHECK TO SEE IF THEY'RE ALIVE!"

With a tremor from the Chief's explodin' voice, Hays set out ta do as instructed, leanin' over each kid'n checkin' fer pulse. "They'se all alive, boss. Somethin' musta knocked 'em all unconscious."

"Slap one around, wake him up."

Hays grabbed one pimply faced kid by the collar'n shook him, then laid a few backhands across the kisser. *Slap! Slap! Slap!*

Nothin'.

"These kids is all out stone cold, Chief, and the detent officers too! And, come on over here. There's somethin' else . . ."

*Something else? Thirty kids'n three adults lyin' unconscious in a row with their hard-ons out? What else* could *there be?* Kinion walked behind the row of unconscious boys where he could now see their faces.

Hays was right. Another oddity remained.

They all had great big smiles on their faces.

And in less than a second later, them double doors *barged* open. Hays and the Chief instinctively grabbed fer their sidearms but stopped when they saw—

"State Health Department!" some fella in a crewcut and ambuhlance suit barked out. "Make way!"

At least two dozen more fellas, then, trotted into the gym, bearin' stretchers which they'se quickly dropped, rolled a kid on, then carried back out.

The Chief scratched his bald head. "State Health Department?"

"How in the hail did they even know to come here?"

They followed the line of stretcher-bearing men, back out to the front'a the facilerty, and that's where they saw two bigass buses with the State Health Department logo on 'em. All them fellas was quickly loadin' them unconscious boys unto the buses.

"This don't make no sense, Hays." Kinion's head flashed in the sun.

"Somebody must've seen that gym before we did, Chief, and then called these state health fellas."

"Yeah, but who?"

A slim shadow crossed their backs. "It was me."

Kinion and Hays jerked around at the voice—

"*I* called them, Chief Kinion," Captain Majora informed them.

## V

To commit what might be deemed an incongruenty within the parameters of structural and/or editorial protocol, here we now discover a violation in the standard and accepted acknowledgement that when an author composes, say, 16,000 words of a novella told entirely from a third-person-limited point of view . . .

Art Koll pushed himself up from the meeting table, a formidable feat being that he weighed a solid 300 pounds. He wore the buzzcut and chiseled face quite appropriately as perhaps the most outspoken member of VFW Post 3063, outspoken in that he eagerly spoke out against homos, lesbos, freakos, pervertos, pinkos, druggos, and any other denomination that sought to undermine the moral fabric of this grand country. And the kids, Jesus! Look at the kids these days! Devil tattoos'n all these metal gewgaws in their faces and t-shirts with serial-killers on 'em or pictures'a Jesus shootin' up drugs. Just last year he'd flown all the way out to Frisco to attend the 30th reunion of Alpha Company, 2/81st, 1st Armored Division, of which he'd been a proud Sheridan M551 loader during the Big One: Viet Nam, and he'd stood right up in front of all surviving 16 members and proclaimed into the microphone: "Like the great Mac said, 'Old soldiers never die!' Shee-it, men, thirty years ago we was fightin' fer the freedom of our children, and look what our children become! Boys wearin' lipstick'n dresses, gals shavin' their heads! Fer lunch today I walked just downtown in this fucked-up freako city and I'se swear I couldn't tell the boys from the girls. All freako tattoos with upside-down sataneric crosses on 'em, rivets in their tongues'n nails'n fish hooks in their faces, and hair stickin' out the color'a Kool-Aid! And I'se wearin', quite proudly, my M551 shirt which reads HANOI OR BUST, and some boy with yellow hair'n blue lipstick'n what looked like shower curtain rings in his ears walks up ta me in a black dress'n says, 'Guess you went bust, huh, baby-killer!' so's instead'a cleanin' his fruito perverto clock, I said, 'We shorely *would'a* made it ta Hanoi if we'd had a coupla you fellas in the field with us 'cos then Charlie Com would take one look at'cha and they'd be bent over laughin' so hard we could'a benchmarked all their dink asses and won the fuckin' war in one day!' So then this thing in the dress kinda goes *hummph* the way a gal does when she knows she's wrong, and then it says 'Yeah but you baby-killers *didn't* win the war,' and then he whips out his compact and starts fixin' his lipstick, so's I say 'Listen, sister, we may've failed in achievin' our primary objecterive of keepin' the good people of South Vietnam out'a the clutchers of Commurnism only because we had a bunch'a pinkos in the White House'n fuckin' Congress, but we shore as *hail* didn't lose that war. The dinks killed 58,000 of us but we scratched *two million* of their gook asses and we blowed the arms or legs of half a million more and turned their entire road system into craters that they *still* ain't been able ta fix and we defolierated half their farmland with good 'ol Agent Orange and they *still* cain't grow nothin' there, so you tell me we *lost?* We kicked the rice out'a those dink motherfuckers so hard they'se *still* seein' stars, and you know why, girlie? To show the world that the United States of America will challenge any diabolical plot to spread Commernism inta the free world and looks what happens, Susy, like right now there ain't no Commernism at all 'cept in fuckin' China'n North fuckin' Korea and a coupla other dink hell-holes, and the whole lot of 'em cain't even make it no more without the financial investerments from *us!* And it's a dang good thang we fought that war 'cos if we hadn't, Betty, you shore as shit wouldn't be standin' here with hair the color of a fuckin' canary'n wearin' lipstick and a fuckin' dress'n havin' enough metal in yer face to fill a tacklebox, nor would you even be able to exercise yer freedom'a speech 'cos there wouldn't *be* none, Harriet! You'd be in some fruit camp somewhere eatin' tree bark and shit'n bent over plantin' rice fer the Commissar!'"

And with that diatribe, the rest of the members of Alpha 2/81 jumped to their feet and applauded, much in the same way that the members of VFW Post 3063 applauded him every week right here at their HQ in Luntville, after which they all sat around drinking beer and telling neat war stories so they wouldn't have to go home while their wives were still up. Yes, it was a grand country, and Art reasoned that every time back in the Nam when he'd slammed a 155 full of APERS or white phosphorous into that big Sheridan breach, he'd helped make it a little greater. And, no, he'd never killed any babies—well, there was that pack of 10-year-olds on Highway 13 and Art had chopped them up with the coax but, hell, the kids were all sappers anyway. If someone was trying to kill you, what difference did it make how old they were? Just another lesbo homo freako perverto pinko druggo sensibility. So, anyway, right now Art lumbered back up and said "Jimmy fix me up with another Dixie, will ya?" and then he excused himself to the rear of the meeting hall and slipped into the bathroom.

He urinated with gusto, relishing the fine life God had given him, the nice doublewide he fully owned now, the nice truck (not one of those Jap jobs, a *Ford*), and a fine job at the mill. And just as he would damn near *fill* that urinal with the wares of his bladder—

"Daggit!"

—all the lights went off.

An unconscious change in his position caused the remaining stream of his kidney juice to buffet against the side of the urinal and splashed back onto his slacks.

"Daggit!"

But what happened to the lights? At first he suspected that maybe someone had turned them off as a joke but then no one was in here but him, and if anyone else had entered he'd have certainly seen them since he was standing right next to the fucking door. *Power failure?* he considered. Sure, it happened sometimes during storms but tonight there wasn't a cloud in the sky. Just the moon, the stars, and the twilight heavens.

"What'n dang tarnations!" he exclaimed. "A blammed fuse must'a blowed!" He zipped back up and turned, feeling for the door handle, but when he pulled that door open—

"Hoooooly—"

Art stuck his big face in the door gap, peering out into the meeting hall. No lights out there, either, at least not the white overhead fluorescent lights he would expect.

It was blue light he saw now. A dark, fluttering blue light that barely offered any illumination at all. Kind of reminded him of those hippie blacklights they had in the sixties, that'd light up pinko peacenick hippie peace posters.

And then—

The windows began to explode—

And he saw—

## VI

"Simple, Chief Kinion," the salubrious Captain Majora explained once they got back to the station. "Pure coincidence, yes, but I merely overheard your dispatch to 861 Mount Airy Road over my police scanner. I happened to be in the area—that's why I got there first and was able to call the State Health Department and apprise them of status at the County Watch-House for Boys. Then they deployed the EMT buses."

"*Now* I get'cha, Captain," the Chief confessed, perfectly satisfied with the shapely woman's account. "You Army folks shore are thorough. Who'd have thunk'a that: monitorin' the police radio band."

Hays smirked, pluggin' the coffee pot in across the booking room. "One question, though, Captain. You say you just 'happened' to be in the area. Well what did you just 'happen' ta be doin', huh?"

"Hays, how the Captain spends her time ain't none'a yer business," Kinion said through a smrik of his own.

"Yeah, but Chief, I just thank it's a mite—"

"Just shut up and fetch the coffee like I tolt ya!" Then the Chief turned his jowls to the lovely Captain who sat across from him at the desk. "I'se shorely apolergize fer the sassy tone my deputy's taken of late."

"No apology necessary, Chief," Majora replied, and it might

be worth noting that, now, she was not dressed in her official Army summer khakis but instead a real purdy burgundy blouse and a pair'a black denim jeans that, well, accentuated her southerly regions quite nicely. "I was just out for a drive, familiarizing myself with the locale, and I might add, Chief, this is a beautiful town you have here."

"Why . . . thank you, Captain—"

"Please, Chief, call me Dana," she invited. "It's perfectly appropriate when I'm off duty and not in standard duty uniform."

The Chief about crapped his size 54 trousers. *Gawd in Heaven! She just asked me ta call her by her first name! Maybe . . . maybe she really has taken a likin' to me!*

"And I must say," she continued, leveling those cool, clear eyes, "I really am honored to be able to work with a man so professional and perceptive."

The Chief about crapped again.

But it was back to business right quick, it was, as the indefectible Captain Majora went on further: "It's so anomalous, though, don't you think, Chief? Thirty teenage boys and three detention officers, all rendered simultaneously unconscious—"

The Chief nodded. "And at the same time too."

"All in the same position, and with their genitals exposed."

"They was exposed all right," Hays cut in, "and hard as rocks and throbbin'."

"Hays!" Kinion yelled. "Weren't you supposed ta be makin' coffee?"

"It's comin', boss. Got the filter in alls loaded up with yer favorite."

"Fine!" The Chief caught himself; he didn't want to seem brusk in front of the Captain, and he certainly wanted her to get a full gander at his professional side. "But ta respond ta yer question, Captain—er, I'se mean *Dana* . . . I cain't think of a much in the way of a crederable reason that would explain how all them fellas come ta be knocked out. Maybe bad venterlation, or, well, come ta thank of it, I'se remember quite a ways back when Fort Paduanna was still open and they'se was doin' some field exercises and happened to be usin' tear-gas, so's all that tear gas blowed up near town and had our Boy Scout Troop 469 pitchin' a fit out in the woods during their annual Camporee."

Captain Majora's pretty eyes opened right up. "What a brilliant conjecture of feasibility, Chief! It never occurred to me!"

Kinion's jaw dropped. It were wonderful that she referred to somethin' ta come out his mouth as brilliant, but . . . *What the hail's she mean?* "What? You mean like tear-gas could do somethin' like that?"

"No, Chief, not tear gas, but what if there was an accidental leak of some Army incapacitant, like carbon trioxide or DBN? Those gasses can render human beings unconscious for protracted periods, Chief. And, as I mentioned yesterday, Fort Paduanna is no longer on active operational status but it still is utilized as a redeposition vault for binary chemical weapons awaiting destruction. I'd say it's more than reasonably likely that they have some incapacitating agents stored there too, and it's a good bet that some of it leaked out into the air."

Naturally, the Chief nodded in full agreement. "Well, Dana, that's 'zactly what I was gettin' at."

More boos, then, fron the peanuts gallery. "Aw, shee-it, Chief. Fort Paduanna's an easy 30 miles away. What, you's sayin' some milertary *gas* blowed *thirty miles* across the boondocks and wound up in the dang County Watch-House fer Boys? Less chance'a that than the Saints winnin' the Super Bowl—"

"Hays! You leave the calculatin' ta the Captain'n me!" the Chief advised rather loudly. "And how long's it take you to pour coffee?"

Hays winked discreetly at the Chief. "Shouldn't take too long now fer this baby ta get drippin', boss."

"Actually, Chief," the exquisite Captain Majora announced, glancing at her milspec wristwatch, "it's gaining on twenty-two hundred hours. I need to contact my brigade commander to begin an investigation on the ensiled inventory at Fort Paduanna. Then I need to turn in. Early to bed, early to rise—that's the Army."

"Oh, why, a'corse," Kinion said.

Captain Majora stood up, wafting her delectible perfume scent, and when the Chief stood up hisself, as was polite to do when a lady were leavin' the room, he glanced down quite accidently and caught a quick glimpse of her soft white cleavage showin' in the top'a her blouse.

The Chief suddenly felt like he had a live frog in his pants.

"I'll see you in the morning, Chief. Goonight," she bid. Then a fast glance to Hays. "Goodnight, PFC."

"Guh-guh-goodnight, Captain—er, Dana," Kinion bumbled.

Then Captain Majora exited the station, leaving the lovely perfume scent in her wake.

"Looks like ya got some lumber in her pants, Chief," Hays snickered from the coffee pot.

Kinion sat down right quick. "Dag it, Hays! She left! If you'd've got that coffee made in a little less time than it takes to change a transmission, she might'a stayed longer!"

"Sorry, boss, the machine only works so fast." Hays set a fresh cup before the Chief. "And gimme a break, Chief. Early ta bed, early ta rise? More like *horny* ta bed, *horny* ta rise. Chrast, that ice-queen bad-news stick-in-the-mud's got it somethin' fierce fer you."

The Chief looked up at his deputy. "Ya . . . ya thank so, Hays?"

"Well, boss, I cain't thank'a any other reason why ever time she looks at you she looks like a fuckin' jackal bitch in heat with a belly fulla spanish fly. See the wet spot in her pants when she left?"

"Come on, Hays! She didn't have no wet spot in her—"

"Chief, either that Army whore had a pussy drippin' like a broke faucet when she left, or someone done dumped a bucket'a water in her lap."

*Fuck,* the Chief aptly thought. Could it be true? What could a fine, upstandin' and a'corse sheer fuckin' beauterful gal like Captain Dana Majora see in fella like the Chief?" "Well, she did ask me to call her by her first name," he voiced.

"Chief, take it from me—I'se an expert on splittail. When the stuck-up ones act like that, they might as well be wearin' a sign that says FUCK ME LIKE THE SPERM HOLE THAT I AM. So's when you gonna go fer it?"

The Chief were absolutely taken aback. "What'cho sayin', Hays? You sayin' I'se oughta ask her out?"

PFC Micah Hays erupted laughter. "Ask her out? Shee-it, Chief, why do that 'cos ya gotta spend money on her. Don't *ever* spend more'n, say, five or six bucks on a gal, just enough ta git her drunk. It's the gals who oughta be payin' *us*, you ask me, 'cos men is the ones who got the only thangs that give their lives meanin', and that's cock. So ta hail with all this *datin'* shit, boss, just pick up a 12-rack'a Keystone, git her shit-faced in yer car, then cream in her slit'n wipe yer dick off on her fancy blouse. That's the way *all* gals wanna be treated, and that's alls they *deserve* anyway on account'a Eve bit into that apple in paradise and since then they ain't nothin' but God's cursed--that's why He made their pussies smell worse than a pile'a catfish guts settin' in the sun on a hunnert-year-old wharf. Only reason gals walk the earth is to have fellas use 'em fer fuck-dumps. So do it 'nless ya wanna miss out. Be like a chef, Chief, and baste her Pussy Souffle with your Hot Southern Pecker Sauce. She's a mutt in heat, boss. She wants ta git it till her cunt and her cornhole's big around as a manhole. If *you* don't fuck the poop out'a her, some other dog'll come around who will."

The Chief was mortified, not just from the blazin' misogerny that Hays piped but 'cos the last thang he said. *If she wants me, I better do somethin' 'bout it. 'Cos if I don't, some other fella will...*

"But, Hays, I cain't just go snufflin' around the Captain—shee-it!—I'se a married man."

Hays shook a forgiving head. "Don't get me wrong, Chief. I'se have the highest respect fer your fine wife Carleen, and I don't care that she weighs more than flatbed full'a cinderblocks on their way ta build a fuckin' dam, boss, 'cos I'm shore she's a wonderful wife who gives ya all the thangs in life ya want—"

"Get to the point, Hays," the Chief shot out with more venom than a poisernous snake. Fuck. *My wife? Given me all the thangs in life I want? Only thang she gives me is a blammed headache and a bed full'a fart-stink . . .*

"Shore, Chief, and on ta back ta what you was implyin' 'bout how you're hessertant 'bout how's you cain't be unfaithful on account'a you're married. Well, what I say ta that is, just 'cos ya done made the biggest mistake of yer life, that ain't no reason ta make the second biggest. Look at it this way, boss. Women are ashtrays and yer dick is the Marlboro. Better git in there 'fore the ashtray gets too full up with other fellas' butts. Gals ain't nothin' but spunk-buckets, well . . . fill that there bucket up ta the rim'n boogie. Besides, Captain Majora ain't nothing but a liar anyways."

A liar? The Chief were outright offended. "What'choo talkin' 'bout?"

"Aw, come on, Chief. That's gal's got more horseshit than Churchhill Downs. Tryin' ta tell us she *intercepted* our call over some blammed *police scanner?* Some funky *gas* leakin' out some closed fuckin' Army Fort thirty fuckin' miles away? Doc Willis bein' kilt 'cos he was sellin' *bomb fuses* or some shit ta the commies? The only thang harder ta swaller than all'a that is maybe one'a Grimaldi's watermelons. What'cha need ta do is fuck her hard, drop yer snot, then kick her outa town 'cos she ain't nothin' but a phony. Shee-it, Chief, she ain't even in the fuckin' Army."

*Say what?* Kinion objected, "Hays, you're plumb et up with a case of the dumbass, boy! What'choo mean she ain't in the Army?"

Hays poured his own self a cup'a java, plopped in a coupla cubes'a sugar, and stirred. "I don't know what she is, boss. Maybe one'a them state IAD investergators or one'a them silly tabloid reporters're somethin', but she ain't in the *Army,* boss. I *know* me that."

"Oh, yeah, smart boy?"

"That's a fact, Chief, on account'a my Uncle Sandy. He just done got out the Army last year'n yesterday when we seed that redhairt cooze in her uniform at Doc Willis' place, she were carryin' a Colt .45, right?"

The Chief scratched his chin, thankin'. "Well, yeah—"

"My Uncle Sandy tolt me that the Army uses them fucked-up Eye-tal-yun Beretta 9-mills now. The Army ain't had the Colt .45 in their inventory fer over ten years . . ."

## VII

*Fuckin' Hays . . .* Kinion lumbered outa the station house towards his personal vehicle which, by the way, was a close-ta-mint '72 ragtop El Dorado. Heather gray, nice set'a wheels, yes sir, and that big 460 V-8 *kicked.* But the Chief were in a swivet, he was. Partly because he'd like to knock Hays upside the head like real hard fer all'a his pessermism'n bad talk about the comely Captain Dana Majora, but also because . . .

*Shee-it . . .*

Somethin' picked at him, see? Like sugar pickin' at a bad filling, or a woodpecker pickin' at bark. The Chief knowed a number'a fellas who was in the Army'n recently got discharged, lifers a lot of 'em and one in particular, J. Lee Pierce, shee-it, he were a firearms instructor in the Army at Fort McClellen fer thirty years. And every other Thursday since he gots out, the Chief'n J. Lee went down to the Pontiac Brothers Gun Club off'a Powers Road, and they popped caps at the paper men, see, and they even had other nifty targets for fifty cents of Jane Fonda, Saddam Hussein, Janice Joplin, and that triangulatin',coke-snortin', medercal-records-hidin-on-account he-don't-want-no-one-ta know-'bout-his-drug-rehab'n-herpes-treatment, back-stabbiin', chicken-company-kickback-takin'-in-

## The Refrigerator Full of Sperm

exchange-fer-campaign-funds'n further tradin'-U.S.-computer-technology-to-the-blammed-slave-drivin' Communist-Chinese-in-exchange-fer-still-*more*-campaign-funds, adulterizin', whuppin'-his-dick-out-in-front-of-20-year-olds-while-big-bad-govenrnor, sendin'-his-deputy-counsel-twelve-times-to-Swiss-banks-with-fuckin'-carry-on-luggage'n-soon-after-the-fuckin'-Secretery-of-Commerce-cannot-account-for-$800,000-verifiably-paid-by-the-government-of-Vietnam, three-former-girlfriends-all-found-dead-from-suicide-with-pistols-in-their-right-hands-even-though-they-were-*left*-handed, same as-the-self-same-deputy-council-was-found-dead-in-some-Civil-War-Park-in-Virginia--that's right folks, a left-handed man found dead by suicide with THE FUCKIN' GUN LEFT IN HIS RIGHT GODDAMN HAND AND HIS FUCKIN' FINGER-PRINTS WEREN'T EVEN ON THE GODDAMN GUN BUT SOMEONE ELSE'S FINGERPRINTS *WERE* found on the goddamn gun but the goddamn Special Prosecutor whose name was Fis—oh, fuck it! THE GODDAMN SPECIAL PROSECUTOR DIDN'T DEEM THIS FACT TO BE SIGNIFICANT! But let's get back to the individual we're referring to whose face adorns the paper targets along with all them others, yes, that lowdown, spineless, lyin'-ta-millions motherfucker whose name is—

Aw, shee-it. That ain't what this story's about, so we'll'se git back to the narrative: Each'n every time the Chief and J. Lee Pierce gone target-shootin' at the gun club, J. Lee was firin' his pride'n joy which happened ta be a Governement Model Colt 1911A1 .45, and every dang time he finished firin' that big bull, he'd always say the same thang. He'd say, "Shee-it, that there is the finest dang pistol ta ever be made on God's killin' earth. Beats the shit out'a me why the goddamn Army'd dump it fer that fucked-up Beretta 92F piece'a shit stove-pipin', breech-jammin', pin-snappin' Eye-tal-yun 9 millimeter . . ."

Hmmm. At the very least, it were . . . curious.

So the bug were planted, and the Chief didn't really even know it yet. His keys on that nifty NRA keychain jingled when he whupped 'em out his pocket, and he were just about ta slide his humongous butt inta that there leather front seat'n start up that big 460—

*Dag it!*

But he didn't. What he did instead was look straight across Main Street, and you know what he was lookin' at?

The White Horse Inn which, ta remind those who might'a fergot, was the same motel that the stimulating Captain Majora were stayin' at . . .

Then . . .

*Dag it, Kinion! What the hail are you doin'?*

What he was doin' was this: he was walkin' right across Main Street, and it might be fittin' ta describe the way he was walkin' as *stealthy.* Weren't nothing goin' on in the center of town this late; Main Street, ta either side, stretched on in hazy darkness, the moon hangin' low over the hills yonder. A quiet, lazy night like most; things generally only got rowdy down near the south town limits where they had all the bars and a'corse the truck stop off'a the Route. The Chief were mighty grateful, he was, to be blessed with a town that weren't chock-full'a criminals'n other scummy sorts of characters, and since there were no signs of traffic or pedestrians out along Main, well, that made it even better fer what the Chief had in mind.

*If anyone sees me,* he reckoned, *I'll just say I heard me a funny noise, or I can say I thought I seed somethin', like maybe a suspicous person!*

Of course, the only suspicous person on the street right now was Chief Kinion hisself, but the way he figgered, it was all in the line'a duty, right?

The neon sign buzzed with its glowin' tubes: WHITE HORSE MOTEL, ONLY $25.99 PER NIGHT! VACANCY! It weren't nothin' fancy, just a narrow, one-story job with a nice white paint job. They had ten decent rooms in a row, and the Chief could see a few lights on, and he could also see Captain Majora's drab government

*The Refrigerator Full of Sperm*

sedan parked in front'a the second unit from the end . . .

He crossed Main Street and traipsed around that same end—er, leave it to say he did his best to move around the back'a that motel as inconspicurissly as was humanly possible. He was surpised that his big size-13 footfalls didn't make much in the way'a sound as he walked over the high weeds in back, and a'corse the deep and steady chirruppin' of crickets hid the noises of his progress all the better. He stopped a moment, let his eyes git adjustered to the dark, then recommenced. The back winder of the last unit was still lit, and the Chief were happy the blinds was closed 'cos he shore didn't wanna have to hunker down and crawl beneath it. There was only the tiniest gap in that set'a blinds, and Kinion couldn't help but steal a quick peek: some short tubby fella on the bed in a sleeveless t-shirt and shorts and black socks, and he had this big burst'a kinky hair growin' around a bald spot and a face that looked like maybe a clay mask squeezed down in a cheese press. *Jiminy!* the Chief thought. *That there is about the ugliest fella I ever done seen!* This fella had a full dark beard but it really looked like shit, it did, more like a bunch'a dick hair on his face than a proper beard, and he was sitting there on the bed pickin' boogers out his nose'n wipin' 'em underneath the bed frame whiles watchin' Gomer Pyle on the TV. *Ugh,* the Chief thought and moved on past. But next came the second winder, and them blinds was open a bit more. Kinion stood back, then ever-so-slowly leaned his kisser mug forward to catch the light between them slats, and—

*Ho-boy!*

The beauteous Captain Majora was in there all right, sittin' at the little writin' desk that came with the room, the big bright floorlamp shinin' down on her. She looked engrossed, she did, tappin' away at one'a them new-fangled little computers that folds up to the size'a somethin' you can put in a briefcase, and in fact there *were* a briefcase layin' open on the bed. In the closet he could see her khaki Army uniform hangin' and also the black leather holster containin' the questionable Colt .45 which was the blammed thang that'd caused the Chief to undertake such an extreme measure of inquest in the first dagged place. But it weren't none'a that which set paramount in his power'a observation, it were instead the fact that as Captain Majora sat there tappin' at that little computer, she was doin' so with no clothes on!

That straight silky red hair just *shined* in the lamp light, it did, and then there was that plush, ample rack'a hooters on her standin' right out as she typed, with nipples of the softest pink Chief Kinion could imagine. It were a view of paradise, it were'n better yet, almost as if God had answered a unspoken prayer, the Captain pushed away from the desk just then and stood up and stretched!

*Aw, fuck...*

The Chief's dick jiggled in his shorts just from this first sight'a her. She was the incarnation'a the word purdy: slim'n trim'n shapely covered by all that perfect white skin, and she was just standin' there still stretchin', reachin' fer the ceiling on her cute li'l tiptoes with her head back'n eyes closed'n them angel tits protrudin'. . . *Aw, fuck!* the Chief thought again as he could now see that dainty little plot'a soft red hair 'tween her legs, stickin' out, it was, a little tuft, and he could even see that adorable little womanly groove behind the hair, and with that came a foreknowledge in the Chief's mind as he knew, unethercal as it might be, 'specially fer the chief of police, but, yeah, he knew he was gonna have ta do somethin' he ain't done in years—

*Aw, fuck! I'se gonna have ta beat off!*

It wouldn't take long—not lookin' at that! And, hail, weren't no one around who might see him, right? Right now his peter felt like a ear'corn in his pants, and that corn damn shore needed ta be shucked. The Chief's hands, very slowly then, began to lower to his zipper—

"Dang!" came a fierce whisper. "Would'ja look at the milkcans on that bitch!"

Chief Kinion nearly shit his pants and puked on the winder at the same time, and his heart stopped and didn't seem to start back up again till he was about one second away from a coronary. Of course it was Hays who'd whispered the crass comment, sneakin' up behind the Chief's back.

It was all Kinion could do to suppress his bellow to a whisper. "Hays! What'n Gawd's name are you doin'—"

But Hays was still peeping in the winder. "Shee-it, boss. She's shore got a cute l'il cut 'tween her gams, huh? Ooo-ee, and gander that red pussy hair! Dang, Chief, you shore got yerself more restraint than me 'cos, see, if it was me standin' here peepin' in on that bucknekit tramp, I'd be jackin' me off a hard snot right on the winder..."

The Chief, in spite of his obvious outrage, did feel a tad'a relief in that he hadn't quite yet gotten around ta pullin' out his dick when Hays made his surprise appearance.

"Aw, looky, boss... She's done turnt around so's ya kin see her butt!"

First impulse was to slap Hays silly, but that might not be too wise on account even though the winder was closed, the Captain'd probably hear a ruckus takin' place, and that would not be a good thing. So, the second impulse was ta—

*Fuck it,* the Chief thought, and looked back in the winder.

And gulped.

Captain Majora, still nekit, mind you, was now standin' with her back to the winder, and what a back it was ta gander. And she were still stretchin' too and then got ta doin' exercises like bendin' over'n touchin' her toes and ever time she bend over, that gorgeous angel's ass on her were shown ta every detail.

"Yeah, I'd be jackin', boss," Hays whispered.

*I'd be jackin' too, Hays, if you hadn't showed up!* the Chief could not help but remind himself. The unallayed boner in his pants only served as a *further* reminder. But the Chief's eyes stayed fixed on them open winder slats nevertheless and it occurred ta him then fast as a sock in the eye what a beautiful thang a gal's ass could be, and this ass in particular, this ass on the wondrous Captain Majora...

well, it defied bein' mere beautiful. It transendered human language n'fact. Tight but so well-shaped, perfect creamy white, yes sir, and not a pimple on it nowheres, and each time she bent over, the Chief's willy did a flex. It were almost like that paragon of a butt on her were winkin' at him! And it were teasin' him too, the way the butterks parted ever-so-diminurtively—he could almost see her brown-eye, he could! And what with the way her legs were spread, this gave him a backshot'a that delecterble li'l tuft'a red fur 'round front, and then the Chief's muse sailed away'n he thought, *If my wife had a butt like that, why, I'd be the happiest man ta ever trod the earth,* but the truth socked home with a fair amount'a immederacy . . .

*Shore, Kinion, but it just so happens that your wife* don't *got a butt like that. What she got instead is somethin' that looks like a couple'a hunnert-pound bags of pigfeed throwed together . . .*

Hays grinned devilishly, and whispered, "Wouldn't it be dandy, Chief? I mean, shove her face-first against that there wall, jack off a giant petersnot on her back, and watch all that cum just run right on down inta her ass-crack? Then give her a good ol' dick-spankin', yes sir, that's what she needs—Aw, shee-it, guess the butt-show's over."

Majora had ceased with the nekit exercisin', and seemed very concerned suddenly lookin' at somethin' on the li'l flipped-up computer screen. Then, in haste, she hauled her Army clothes back on, grabbed her .45'n holster, and left the motel room, and a second later, the Chief'n Hays could hear her drive off in her government sedan.

"Where's she off to in such a hurry?" Hays wondered.

"I don't know, but I'll tell ya where *you're* off to!" Kinion grabbed his deputy by the collar and quickly walked the two of 'em back out ta Main Street. "You're off to the Land of Whup-Ass!" The Chief were pissed-off, all right, but he did his best to keep his piss-off buttoned up till they gots back across the street in front of the station but once they got there . . .

"I oughtas ta ring yer neck, boy!" the Chief exploded.

"Hey, Chief! What's got yer dander up?"

"You, that's what! What'choo doin' sneakin' up behind me like that!"

Hays shrugged. "Hail, Chief, how was I supposed ta know you be peepin' in her winder whiles she were nekit?"

"I wasn't *peepin'* ta see her *nekit!* I ain't no pree-vert!"

"Well, Chief, I weren't implyin' that there's anythin' wrong with peepin' on a bitch. Hail, that's what winders are for. Ain't nothin' that any other red-blooded American fella wouldn't do."

"I weren't *peepin',* Hays! I was merely employin' a little investigative surveillance on her!"

"Why?"

"Why! Because you're the one who's tellin' me she ain't really in the Army so's I was merely checkin' her out ta see if she was doin' anythang suspicious!"

"Look more ta me like you was checkin' out her ass-crack, boss—"

Yeah, the Chief felt like beltin' Hays a good one, he did. "Just tell me what the holy *hail* you was doin' follerin' me!"

"Weren't follerin' ya, Chief," Hays explained. "I came back to the station but seen you weren't there but yer car still was. Then I seen ya walkin' back behind the motel, so I come ta git ya."

"Come ta git me fer what!"

"We got ourselves another call," the deputy informed. "And it sounds a right serious. See, we'se got a couple dozen housewives just called the dispatcher all sayin' that their hubbies are missin'."

A call? At this hour? "A bunch'a fellas *missin',* you say?"

"That's a fact, boss. Ain't none of 'em come home tonight, and they'se all got one thang in common. They'se all was supposed ta be havin' a meetin' out at the VFW hall."

## VIII

"Dispatch, this here's Unit Two-Zero-Eight, and I'm callin' to properly noterfy ya that we is 10-6 to VFW Post 3063."

"Roger, Two-Zero-Eight."

"Oh, and if I'se happen ta git back before you're off duty, honeybunch, how's about I come over there and—"

Kinion grabbed the mic from Hays and hung it up with a curse on his lips. "Knock that shit off and drive!"

"That's a big 10-4, boss."

So here's they was again, out on a call with Hays drivin' the town cruiser and the Chief ridin' shotgun. Chrast, it was gettiin' late; maybe one day the blammed mayor would allercate enough funds to hire a night cop. *Yeah,* Kinion thought, *and if I had a square asshole, I could shit a television.* But what could *this* be? Bunch'a VFW fellas not turnin' up? "Shee-it, Hays, they'se probably all went off to a bar or somethin'."

"Naw, Chief," Hays countered. "See, one'a the ladies who called—that would be Glenda Rawner, you know, Chief, that big fat sloppy woman with the underbite who looks like someone knocked her in the jaw with, like, a barn rafter? She's married ta Conner Rawson, you know that pissy fella who got one'a his legs blowed off in some war'n rumor has it his leg weren't the only thang blowed off 'cos—"

"I know who the Rawsons are, dag-blammit, Hays! Git to the point!"

"Well, what I was sayin' was I was sayin' that Glenda Rawson found the doors to the VFW hall locked but *swears* she heard someone walkin' 'round in there'n not only that, she says she saw a some fella look out the winder at her but he didn't answer the door. Says all the lights was out, too, even the parkin' lot lights. Sounds kinda screwy, huh, Chief?"

*Kinda screwy . . .* What with Doc Willis bein' kilt'n his wife disappearin' and then all them boys at the Watch-House goin' unconscious with their pants down, yes sir, that shore made this a fucked-up day, and it were quickly turnin' into a fucked-up night with this VFW bullshit. But Kinion looked at the bright side: at least now he wouldn't be gettin' home till way after his blubber-factory of a wife would be asleep so's he wouldn't have ta listen to her bitch. Boy'o boy, when Carleen got to bitchin', the Chief'd sooner hit hisself in the haid with one'a the big ball-peens they sell down at Hodge's Hardware.

And then a'corse there was this business with the radiant Captain Majora. Why were she packin' a gun the Army no longer used? How'd she git ta the County Watch-House fer Boys faster'n he and Hays did? And where she run off to so quick just a little while ago when she doin' the nekit version of the Denise Austin Aerobics Show?

"Aw, shee-it, Chief," Hays remembert. "Now that I thank of it, I never did finish my story 'bout Martha, did I?"

"Yes," the Chief asserted, his belly hitchin' at the thought. "You did."

"Naw, naw, boss, I never did get to the end and told ya why it is they call her Martha the Tail."

Well, as a matter'a fact, that were true, but right now the Chief shore didn't want to hear no more disgusterin' stories from Hays, 'specially after that double pork burger he'd picked up at R.A.'s Barbeque Stand. "Fergit it, Hays. I don't wanna hear."

"Shore ya do, Chief—"

"No, Hays. Just shut up and drive!"

"That's a big negatory, boss, 'cos it ain't right fer a fella to start a story but not finish it proper. So's I'se gonna tell whether ya like it're not."

"Hays, if ya so much as—"

"See, boss, like I tolt ya, after I put that big ten-beer piss up her ass, she gits ups ta go to the bathroom, right—and, shee-it—*I* shore as *hail* didn't have to go to the bathroom myself, no sir, not after drainin' my bladder up that old cumbucket's brownhole. Anyways, like I were tryin' ta tell ya, she gits up, and—Chrast, Chief!—I'se can hear all my piss just *sloshin'* in her'n her belly's stickin' out like a sack'a grain I peed so much in her, and then, Chief, then—"

But Hays stopped just then, and began to slow down. "Dang, Chief, looks like I'se'll have ta tell ya later 'cos we'se here."

Kinion thanked the Lord for that, and so did Kinion's breadbasket. Shore enough, Hays had just pulled into the parkin' lot'a VWF Post 3063, and he were correct in what he'd previously related: all the lights were out: the buildin', the lot, even the big VFW sign out front. But—

*VVVVVROOM!*

The sound jolted 'em, and suddenly there were a bunch'a dust fillin' up the lot, and then the Chief jumped out the car'n looked behind him, he saw—

"You gotta be shittin' me!"

—a great big long bus roarin' away, and before it roared away completely, Chief Kinion could see the stenciled letters on the back of it, letters which read—

"State Health Department!" Hays jumped out and read out loud.

"Those fuckers *again?*"

Kinion and Hays stood in the dust. The bus, now, was long gone down the road. The two men approached the VFW hall, and at once Hays noticed something.

"Looky, Chief. See that?"

"See what?" Kinion answered.

Hays pointed to the front winders of the hall—

*No glass,* the Chief realized.

"No glass, see that, boss. All them winders've been busted from the outside in, just like Doc Willis' place."

"Well ain't this just a dandy kick in the ass!" the Chief complained.

"Yeah, and there goes a dandier one . . ."

At the other end of the darkened lot, *another* vehicle was pullin' out and stompin' off like real fast: Captain Majora's government sedan.

"Still think she's legit, boss?" Hays goaded. "Second time today she done beat us to our own calls."

The Chief stroked his gibbous chin. Shore, it was a great big heap of strange that seemed to be pilin' up 'round the luscious Captain Majora, but—

"Now wait a mintue, Hays, only reason she got out here before we did is 'cos we was delayed on account of, uh, well . . ."

"On account'a you wanted to peep in her winder whiles she were nekit so's ya could gander that tight l'il butt'n red gash on her—"

"I was doin' no such thang, I'se already tolt ya!" Kinion hollered, "I was merely investergatin' a suspicious situation!"

"Well, whatever, boss, and you can waste the rest of the little time you got tryin' ta 'splain yerself, or you can git on after her, see where she goes."

"Uh, what?"

"Foller the dirty, lyin' bitch in the town car. You still got time ta catch up."

Kinion considered this suggestion and—dang—it seemed like a purdy good one. Then he snapped to, lumbered toward the car. "Come on, Hays, git in!"

Hays threw Kinion the keys. "You go on yerself, boss. See, I gots some investergatin' of my own ta do back at the station."

Kinion looked back, duped. "Well, how the hail are ya gonna git back to the station without a car?"

Hays turned up a subtle smile. "Leave it ta me, Chief, and you best git rollin' n'less ya wanna lose her."

Hays was right—there weren't no time ta argue. So's he jumped on in the Luntville patrol car and spun wheels outa that VFW lot fast as if he were persuin' a moonshine run, follerin' the same direction that Majora had left.

And when the Chief were well on his way, PFC Micah whipped out his set'a lockpicks and begun ta look for a car ta steal . . .

## IX

As Chief Kinion drove with the pedal to the metal, cruisin' a mite quick down Old Harley Road, he did n'fact wonder what Hays had on his mind but he were quite a bit more intensely concerned about what Majora might be up to. Not only was it funny 'bout her Colt .45 not bein' in the Army inventory no more, but it were even more so funny 'bout how she coulda got noterfied 'bout whatever went on back at the VFW Post. She couldn't possibly have heard it on a police scanner as she'd said she had earlier 'bout the County Watch-House fer Boys 'cos the Chief seed fer hisself when he was ganderin' her bare ass that she didn't have no such scanner in her room, and nor had she picked up a phone, and nor had her phone rang, so... *How in the hail did she know ta come out to the VFW Post and call them dang State Health Department folks again?*

It weren't too long, however, before the Chief caught a glimpse of her tail lights up ahead, and so's he let off the speed a tad. He didn't wanna catch her, he just wanted ta see what she were up to now, and she shore as heck weren't goin' back ta her motel room 'cos this were the blammed oppersit direction. So he just set ta follerin' her, discretely like so's she wouldn't suspect she were indeed bein' follered. And in the meantimes, he got hisself an idea...

"Dispatch, this is Luntville Unit Two-Zero-Eight, ID-1," the Chief said into his portable Motorola. "I need me a 10-17."

"Go ahead, Two-Zero-Eight," came the static response of the county dispatcher.

See, the Chief weren't as dumb as some would think, and he knowed full well that any emergency transport call would be logged with State MAC computer no matter if it were local, county, or state, and he also knowed that the county-band dispatcher had access to that infermation, and what he knowed thirdly was that any medical transport responderred to by the State Health Department would have a status-tag on that there log!

"I need arrival'n desternation status of the State Health Department's response to the Luntville VFW Post 3063, please," he said into the mic.

"Standby, Two-Zero-Eight."

Over the line, the Chief heard the dispatcher tappin' them computer keys. But then there came a pause, and she got back: "Two-Zero-Eight, the State MAC log reports no transport dispatch of any Health Department vehicles to that location."

*The fuck?* "Well I just seen 'em myself, leavin' the post not five minutes ago!" Kinion complained to his radio. "What about earlier today? Check fer a State Health Department dispatch to the County Watch-House fer Boys out on Mount Airy Road."

More static, more keys tappin', then: "Sorry, Two-Zero-Eight, State Health Department reports no dispatches of any of their vehicles today, not to the locations you mentioned, and not anywhere."

At first the Chief was fixin' to pitch a fit on account he'd seen these vehicle with his own eyes both times but then . . . *Hmmm,* he thought. "Thank you kindly," he said in the mic. "I must'a had me some faulty infermation. Two-Zero-Eight out."

Yes, sir, that heap'a strange was just gettin' higher'n higher it was. Not just from what the dispatcher had just tolt him, but from what he noticed this here instant.

See, way up on ahead'a him, he could still see Majora's tail lights on that government sedan, and what that sedan done next, see, was it turnt left offa Old Harley Road and right smack-dab onto County Road 3, and if there was one thang Chief Kinion knowed was that there weren't nothin' at all on County Road 3 but one single house . . .

Doc'n Jeanne Willis' house.

# X

Micah had hisself a fair choice'a cars in the lot, all of 'em a'corse belongin' to them old VFW geezers, so he picked a nice Olds 4-door with some room and used his HPC-brand lockpicks to git in 'er'n git her started. See, the PFC didn't see no harm 'cos he weren't really *stealin'* the car; he was instead *appropriatin'* it fer urgent police business which it said you could do right there in black'n white in the State Annotated Code, it did, and besides, the owner shore didn't need it right this second since he was in the back'a that great big State Health Department medercal transport bus'n probably was unconcious anyhows with his pants down and his old peter hard just the same as all'a them boys at the County Watch-House. So's Micah hopped right in'n drove off he did, headin' back fer the station just like he done tolt the Chief. A'corse it were at least a *little bit* of a white lie since although he were *headin'* fer the station it weren't the station he was plannin' on immediately *returnin'* to.

It were the White Horse Motel.

Yeah, he knowed, all right, he knowed the Chief—fine man that he was—weren't seein' thangs quite as clearly as he should be on account he had eyes fer that red-hairt cum-trap Majora. Funny what pussy could do to a fella, 'specially a fella like the Chief since he problee ain't had hisself a good lay since back before we put fellas up on the moon. But Hays knew a lyin' fur-pie when he saw one, and that's just what Majora was. Shore, she was a looker, and Hays wouldn't mind blowin' a big dick-loogie right up any or all'a her holes 'cos that's all gals were foremost: 3-holes for fellas ta put their peters in'n have a good come. A looker, yeah, but Hays weren't nearly so as impressed as the Chief was. A little too prim'n proper she seemed, and a little too sqweaky clean. What a gal like that *really* needed was to first have her starch broke and git dirtied up some the ways women should be. *Yes sir, git ten good, hard fellas together and treat her to a All-Night Pool-Table Special. Ooo-eee, that'd break her down'n git the sass out of her a right quick. Lay her smart ass down and put a fuckin' on her from dusk till dawn, put so much cum in her she wouldn't be able to git no more in, and she'd shorely be grateful fer it after.* See, what Hays—in his incontrovertible experience—reasoned was that the more ya treated a gal like a lowdown dog-dirty whore, the more they liked it 'cos it fulfilled some inner need they alls had to be treated like spunk-drains. Personally, Hays couldn't figger it fer the life'a him, but after treatin' well over 700 gals like just that, he were posertively convinced. That's right— no lie—n'fact the PFC's tally were done up to 'zactly 721—that's *721 different gals* he'd had his trouser-meat in, and a fair share'a them he fucked more times than he could count! And it weren't no lie either that well over a hunnert of 'em he fucked the dogshit outa 'fore he was 16 years of age! Shee-it, when Micah Hays were but 7 years old, he was ballin' the stuffin' out of his babysitters, and he shore as shit were ass-fuckin' by 10. In junior high school he wasn't just fuckin' all them l'il 7th-grade gals but he was also fuckin' the daylights outa bunch'a his teachers. Shee-it, he remembert one time when he weren't but 13'n didn't even have all his dick hair yet and though he could shore as shit get wood'n come, his nuts weren't yet makin' no spunk, but anyway, he remembert this one big chunky science teacher he had named Mrs. Christian who had like kind of a dumpy bod but a primo set'a tits and one day Micah was sittin' in class lookin' at those big rib-melons and thinkin' how great it'd be ta see 'em in the buff and—shore 'nuff!—he popped hisself a huge boner right there in his pants and since he were sittin' in the front row, see, Mrs. Christian got a good look at it, no doubt thinkin' to herself: *What in tarnations? That there 13-year-old little boy's got a dick that's three-times bigger than my husbands!* so 'acorse she asked Micah to stay after class and let's just say he put more than his pencil in her school box. Wound up fuckin' that bitch coupla times a week till he got on to high school. Word travels fast, see, and when a fella's hung like Micah Hays (not ta mention when a fella's so good a lover'n can git a gal's pussy off so fine), it might as well'a been broadcast over the blammed intercom. By 9th grade, n'fact, he was not only fuckin' a coupla different girls ever week but more'n a handful'a teachers, like Miss Brill—she were one'a the gal phys. ed. teachers, and she was skinny'n tall and didn't have hardly no tits on her at all but that didn't matter to Micah Hays, no sir—she might not'a had no tits but he shore as hail knew she had a beaver 'tween her legs, but anyways one day outa the blue Micah were on his way out to little league practice but Miss Brill just up'n grabbed him'n hauled him back into her little office'n locked the door. See, she'd heard all about how good Micah Hays was, and she shore's shit wanted in on some'a *that* action herself so she just hauls off her sweat pants'n hauls Micah's pants down'n a'corse he's hard already so's then she eyeballs it'n about shrieks, sayin' "Good Gawd, Micah Hays, that is the biggest tallywacker I ever done seen!" (and keep in mind, he were still just a kid back then!) so Micah, bein' the dillergent student he was'n always wantin' to exceed the expectations'a his teachers, he got to layin' some serious dick on Miss Brill humpin' her hard'n fast just like women wanted, and she just kept squealin' "Harder, Micah! Harder!" so harder it was till it got to the point that she might as well'a had a jackhammer up her twat, and, shee-it, this scrawny bitch just couldn't git enough so's she pulls her knees back to her ears and just keeps shriekin' "Harder!" but then somethin' happened, see, and at the time, bein' so young'n all, Micah couldn't quite reckon what it was but he heard a wet poppin' noise and alls of a sudden Miss Brill's shrieks of whore-heaven bliss turnt inta screams and all this blood starts pourin' out her snatch like tappin' a keg'a cherry wine and, well, ta make a long story short what happened was that Micah had fucked this woman so hard he transectered her blammed cervix, he did! and she wound up havin' ta go to the harspital! He felt a mite guilty 'bout it at first—*Holy shee-it!* he'd thought. *I done busted Miss Brill's hole!*—but, hail, he was only givin' her what she were askin' fer, right? So it weren't his fault, not really, and since he popped her cunt *before* he came hisself, he didn't feel guilty neither 'bout jackin' it off the rest'a the way. So's, anyway, that there is the story'a the very first poon ta be broke wide open by Micah Hays, but little did he know back then that there'd be many more ta foller.

Well, er, dang! It seems that this here narrative has become a tad sidetracked what with the preverus passerge'a redneck smut, but what Micah Hays were doin' right now, see, is he were drivin' back ta town in a big plush Oldsmobile he just up'n stolt—er, not stolt but *appropriated* via the proper provisions'a state law—from the VFW lot and then he pulled right on in to one'a the parkin' spaces out front of the White Horse Motel, and it weren't but a coupla seconds later, he was walkin' 'round back'a the motel to where's he earlier found the Chief winder-peepin' on that squeaky-clean, red-hairt, needs-ta-have-her-hole-busted-fierce, lyin' white-trash whore and problee fixin' ta jack hisself off whiles lookin' at it. That would be the second winder along back but a'corse before Hays could git to the second winder he hadda pass the first winder but there weren't no one in there 'cept some short, fat fella with fucked-up hair and a beard that looked more like he'd smeared peat moss on his face, and—Chrast!—this here fella had ta be 'bout the ugliest fella in all'a northern America, like he had a face that could not only stop a fuckin' train but maybe even cause that train ta turn full around on its track'n go back the way it came, yes sir, that's how ugly he was; in fact this fella's face looked more like the bottom of a lame foot than it looked like a face, but that all was besides the point. This fella—quite chunky he was—was sittin' there on the bed in his scivvies, see, watchin' the television'n he was pickin' boogers out his nose one after another'n wipin' under the bed'n on the nightstand, but what he was doin' with his other hand was he was givin' his crotch a good feel-up he was like he was maybe milkin' a cow rather'n takin' a dick-squeeze, and then this fella pulls his shorts down'n starts jackin'! A'corse it looked like Mother Nature had taken a giant shit on this poor fella 'cos not only was he problee the ugliest fella on Gawd's Green Earth but he had hisself a boner that looked about maybe three inchers—and that were a generous estermation. Then Hays spied what had gotten this fella's wood up—er, not wood, really, but maybe Tinker Toy—and that would be some silly show on the television with a bunch'n hot Calerforna-lookin' bimbos runnin' around on a beach wearin' red swimsuits and, like, savin' people's lives who was drowin' in the water. The chicks, shore, they was fine-lookin', yes sir, fine-lookin' enough ta fill a seminary with hard dick, but the last thang Micah Hays wanted ta do was stand here watchin' what might well've been the ugliest livin' member of the human species beat his meat, so Micah went on ta the second winder'n, well, committed an act that might be described as, well, breakin' and enterin'.

*Fuck it,* he thought. *I ain't no burglar. Burgarly, as defined by the State Annotated Code, is the unlawful violation of a physercal perimeter with the premeditered intent'a theft.* Well, hail, he weren't gonna steal nothin', he was just fixin' ta have hisself a look-see. That weren't no crime, were it?

He popped the brass lock with his pocketknife, he did, then slid that winder right open and come on in. First thang, he made a spontaneous visual assessment of this here perimeter, and noticed a closet with some clothes in hangin' in it, some more clothes on the floor, a black briefcase on the bed, and one'a them new-fangled laptop computers settin' on the desk with its top flipped up. Naturally, Hays went to the area of most paramount importance: the clothes on the floor, 'cos he noticed a pair'a frilly light-blue panties lyin' there so a'corse he snatched 'em right up'n gave 'em a good hard sniff.

*Aw, what a abserlutely USELESS splittail,* he thought 'cos, see, them panties didn't hardly have no odor at all! No hashmarks, no pee-stains, no nothin'. Hays were of the opinion that if a gal's pussy didn't stank, it weren't worth his time. Girl-stank, that were the ticket! A fella's gotta know what he's doin' while he's doin' it, and if that girl-stank don't waft up 'tween humps like ta bite yer face off then, well, where were the pleasure in that? Shee-it, Micah Hays *loved* the stink of a gal's hole; he loved it almost as much as the hole itself and, dang it, if he was gonna do a gal the charitable service'a treatin' her to the gift of his pre-emmernint hard cock then her pussy better *stink,* blammit. *Pussy that don't stank is like hooch with no alkerhol,* he constructed a wholly appropriate simmerlee, *or like puttin' a lawn mower engine in a fuckin' Corvette. No kick, no juice.* Not much more point in fuckin' clean pussy than there was in eatin' pizza with all the cheese pulled off! But enough'a pussystank and the lack there of in Majora's dirty panties—Hays was here on serious business so he figgert he better get to it, so what he did next was turn on the TV 'n fiddled with the dial until he found that show that that fella in the next room who might well'a been the ugliest fella in the entire history of civilization, and—"Dang!" Hays exclaimed aloud—now there were some bodacious blondie in the same red swim suit with a pair'a packed-to-the-max tits'n a mouth made fer cocksuckin' if there ever was one, and she also had this real whory-lookin' vine-tattoo on her arm which Hays thought looked like shit, he did but, fuck, this slim nut-brown bitch was doin' mouth-ta-mouth recessertation on some guy, and all Hays could think was *How's about some mouth-ta-COCK recessertation right here, ya jizz-eater!* Chrast, Micah, even in that he knowed he was here on serious police business, he could not help but form a muse're two 'bout this splittail on TV, like he knew just what she needed, he did, like what she needed was ta have some'a that bigtime Hollywood ego taken outa her prudy sails, yeah! *Like maybe drag her bigshot, 50-grand-per-epersode, TV-Star tush out ta Cotter's Field some night 'n haul that silly red swim suit off her bones 'n then get down ta some righteous cornholin', yes sir. Stick my dick so far up her bung she'd be able ta taste her shit on my knob, then pump enough cum up her ass, she'd have Shit Babies. Yes sir, that's what she needs and she'd thank me fer it!* Hays stared ever more attentively at the pitcher on the screen and it occurred ta him then that this was shorely the first time in his life he ever wanted ta fuck a television, and as hard as he were gittin' lookin' at this purdy Calerforna hosebag, he thought he just might do that, yes sir, just drop his pants and jack off a great big cock-hock right on the screen, hopefully when Blondie's yap was open and then fantersize that his spunk was runnin' down her throat 'fer real right down inta her belly which was problee full fancy pink champagne'n sushi'n kiesch'n plantain chips and all that other fancified Hollywood shit they eat out in Calerforna. But a'corse now that he thunk of it, that weren't really true, that bein' that this were actually the first time he'd ever wanted ta fuck a television 'cos he remembert when he was a kid watchin' that show *I Dream of Jeannie* and the whole time he thought it oughta be called *I CREAM on Jeannie* on account'a that gal in the dumbass genie suit had a rack'a tits on her that'd make a fella wanna go on a milk diet fer life—shee-it, Hays wondered just how much cum landed on the floor from young fellas lookin' at that dumbass show'n jackin' their meat, and, well, not ta sidetrack, but Micah remembert another show back then that was always good fer a stiffer and a'corse that would be *Gilligan's Island* and Micah Hays often wished it was called *Micah Hays' Island* 'cos if it was then, by Gawd, Ginger'n Mary Ann would'a been walkin' around that island pregnant fer all four seasons, they would'a, and Micah even would'a fucked the poop out'a Mrs. Howell and then maybe wipe his dick off on that fussy hat'a hers. Why the fuck not? And...well, since we'se on the subject, *Get Smart* weren't too bad neither. Remember that gal named Agent 99? *Shee-it,* Micah thought, *I'll bet pork roasts ta gold bricks that between Max, the Chief, and Heimie, that prissy bitch had a quart'a cum pourin' out'a her cooze every day! Problee had the line producer'n the set director'n the gaffer'n the friggin' best boy dippin' their wicks in that pussy too. And after they was done, it was the property master'n the caterer'n the blammed negative cutter steppin' up ta have a go...*

Okay, so much fer television. What caught Hays' notice next was that new-fangled laptop computer, though Hays could think'a somethin' better fer Majora ta have in her lap. The active-matrix color screen glowed real purdy like, it did, and what was on it was this:

BEGIN MILNET MESSAGE

STAGE — NOTIFY
TO: "GEYSERITE"
DISCREETED PASSWORD AND ID-ALLOCATION COMMAND
TARGET-GRID POSITIVE — GPS-KH-3-UUHF CONFIRMED FOR AFFIRMATIVE-BI-MATRIX (LOW-GAMMA RECEPTION) —
MESSAGE: "GEYSERITE" REPORT TO THE FOLLOWING PROXIMITY —
— OLD HARLEY ROAD, LUNTVILLE, VA, 191 NE, 2004 E —
— NSA GRID-MAP/CLOSEST PLOTTED PROBABLE LOCATION —
—VFW POST 3063 —
DECRYPT AND DELETE
END MILNET MESSAGE

"The *hail* is this ballyhoo?" Hays asked himself as he stared at the screen. So engrossed he was that he didn't even take another glance at the TV where another chick in the same red swimsuit were now performin' CPR on yet another fella who'd been hauled out'a the water, and this here gal were a lot skinnier than that first blondie chick—she had short brown hair'n less eggs on her chest than Miss Brill the gals' gym teacher, but, hail, Hays would slick this tramp down with his spunk just as fast as the blondie, yes sir, face-fuck the bitch then pop a hard snot right'n her eye'n shoot the rest all over that flat-as-a-floor chest'a hers.

Yeah, that's problee what she needed, alls right, but then Hays looked in that opened briefcase on the bed, was about ta gander some'a the papers in there, but then...

"Sheeeeeeeeeeeeeee-*IT!*"

Someone were crawlin' inta the room through the winder!

## XI

Chief Kinion abstained from lightin' a Winston 'cos, see, when you was tryin' ta conceal yerself from someone else out in the middle'a the night, it weren't a very good idea problee ta be flashin' yer Bic lighter. So instead, after follerin' the felicitous Captain Majora to the Willis residence'n parkin' the patrol car a ways down the road, he crept up ta the house quiet as he could but noticed that the Captain herself wasn't goin' *inta* the house, she were goin' out past *behind* it. So the Chief follered on, he did, and even though he was wishin' a mite fierce fer a cigarette, it problee were good that he hadn't lit one on account'a the way this physercal exterion were causin' him ta huff'n puff, he'd more'n likely had a heart attack right then'n there, and if that'd happened then he'd never unravel this mystery now would he?

On'n on she walked, way down the hill behind the house inta the field, and what she done then was seemed ta take somethin' out'a her pocket'n look up at the sky, and then she just stood there doin' that fer what seemed a *dang* long time!

*What the hail's she got there? Binoculars? And what's she lookin' at?*

Well, by the Chief's judgment, whatever it was she were doin', she done planned ta do it fer a long time, so he figgert he oughta turn his attentions elsewhere fer a spell. Like, if she done come all this way out ta Doc Willis' house it were problee fer more than standin' out in the field behind the house'n starin' up in the sky, so's it seemed logical that the Chief might oughta thank about goin' *inta* that there house, and see if there was anythang out'a the ordinary.

Made sense ta him, at least.

The front door were unlocked so the Chief just walked right in, but all the lights was out and he didn't think it was too good a idea ta turn any of 'em on since Majora might take note'a that and figger somethin' was up. So the Chief stood there in the middle'a the dark house feelin' a bit foolish since he couldn't see nothin' but then thought to whip out his pen-light that he kept his keys on—shorely she couldn't see that!—and he moseyed around. A bit creepy, it were, snoopin' around a dark house when just earlier today they'd found a dead man in it, not ta mention a dead man who'd *disappeared*, and then, ta set the mood, it was unfortunate that he came ta remember way on back ta like maybe 1969 when he was maybe 22 years-old'n quite a bit slimmer he got off'a work at the compost refinery where he made a solid hunnert bucks a week, and he had hisself a *sportin'* Chevy Corvair (which would later be recalled by Detroit fer leakin' carbon mernoxide inta the front seat) and, see, there were this sorta heavyset gal who took'a fancy to him who at worked Hull's General Store right at the corner'a Layhill Road, and the Chief (who weren't the Chief back then a'corse) he summoned up the nerve ta ask this heavyset gal out (her name was Dory May, and she had bosom on her that looked like two heads stuck together under her blouse), and a'corse she said, "Why, shore, Richie, it'd just float my boat ta go out with a handsome fella like you!" and, see, "Richie" is what they called him back then, and what she said she wanted ta do was go ta the Palmer's Drive-In, and this suited the Chief just fine 'cos ever one knowed that when a gal wanted ta go to the drive-in what it really meant was that she wanted ta git down! So's the Chief picked her up in his Corvair, he did, and they droved out sharin' a large bucket'a fried chicken from the Bon Fire, and then crackin' inta a jug'a a Shine Sladder's moonshine which were pretty powerful stuff, it was, and the Chief figgert he must'a had one hit off the jug ta every four'a hers, but he didn't care 'cos just as soon as he parked his ride'n pulled that there speaker-thing-a-muh-jig into the winder, Dory May were all a'gigglin' and had her giant tits outa her top before the Chief could say licentious, not that he knowed what that word meant, but about just as fast she had her fat little hand 'tween his legs squeezin' his works, she was, and a right nice it felt, that's for shore, and 'fore he could even look up ta see what movie was showin', Dory May had his pants down'n his peter in her mouth lickety-split, she did. And since this was the first time his willy had *ever* found itself within the confines of a gal's mouth, the Chief was dag-straight celebratory, he was, thinkin': *I'se gettin' me a blow-job, I is! I'se gettin' my pole sucked!* But—

Well... the Chief didn't get his pole sucked fer long on account of what was plainly a problem'a faulty hydraulics. See, Shine Sladder's moonshine were powerful stuff, and it hadda way'a sneakin' up on ya, it did, and come ta think of it, the Chief had had more than a few pulls off'a that jug, and then—

"Aw, what'choo doin' ta me, Richie Kinion!" Dory May blurted out with that loud brassy redneck voice'a hers. "I been suckin' yer willy a good five minutes and nothin's happenin'! You done drank too much is what you done! It done give ya a case'a *whiskey-bisquet!* So's what am I gonna do with *that* li'l thang!" And, a'corse, she had ta point to the young Chief's crotch. "Shee-it, Richie, that looks more like a blammed baby's *pinkie* than it looks like a *dick!*"

Well, a might traumertizin' it was ta have his manhod referred to as a blammed baby's pinkie, but right afterwards she just huffed'n popped open the passenger door'a his Corvair'n slid her fat ass out, she did, and she said this: "Dang you, Richie Kinion! If you cain't give me a fuckin', I'll'se shore as hail find some fellas who will!" Then she slammed the door and stomped off, her big butt jigglin' as she huffed up to the first row and then wound up climbin' inta a shiny-gray 67 Chevelle full'a greasers and judgin' by the sounds that come out'a that car shortly after, she were gettin' 'zactly what she wanted. But young Richie Kinion were a bit desponderent by now, havin' his date run off in favor of a Chevy full'a fellas wearin' Macks'n t-shirts with packs'a Marlboros rolled up in their sleeves, 'specially after bein' thoughtful enough ta feed her fat ass all'a that fine fried chicken first. Anyways, his mascurlinity assaulted the likes'a which Alexander the Great assaulted fuckin' Persia, he did what most fellas would'a done: he drank some more. In fact, he drunk damn near the rest'a that jug'a Shine Sladder's shine and wound up passin' out, and it were hours later that he woke back up only ta find that he'd puked in his lap'n shit in his pants, yes sir, and when he looked out that Corvair winder, he could see these greasers pullin' a train on Dory May with her fat ass on the hood and not seemin' to object in the slightest, but at least the Chief woke up in time ta catch the last fifteen minutes'a the last of the triple-feature he'd bought two tickets for, and what it was was some flick about some lanky black fella fightin' off a bunch'a zombies in some piece'a shit house in Pittsburgh, and that's what the Chief thought of right now back in Doc Willis' dark house bein' that they'd seen the Doc's dead body and a few minutes later it was fuckin' gone almost like it might'a got up and walked off like, well, like a zombie.

*Aw, that was just a dumbass movie,* he thought.

But then the zombie tapped Chief Kinion on the shoulder . . .

## XII

"Jeanne Willis!" Hays exclaimed. Yes sir, that's who it was crawlin' in through that there motel winder and she was wearin' less than she was wearin' in them vacation pitchers Hays had seen this afternoon, and what that meant exactly was she was wearin' nothin' but fingernail polish.

"Why, hi there, Officer Hays," she said in a voice like warm honey once she were done comin' in through that winder and standin' buck nekit in front'a him and—hail!—Jeanne Willis had a body to make a brick shit-house jealous, why, she even made the gals on that there silly lifeguard show look like shit-smears on toilet paper—*that's* what a looker Jeanne Willis was, yes sir. Fuckin' tits like ripe, white fruit she had, and legs that was *made* ta be wrapped around a fella's back and a bush—

*Holy motherfuckin' sheeeee-it!*

See, this gal had a bush'n set'a lower parts on her that might make even the dang Pope lean back and do a Rebel Yell, yes sir. *Fine fur it was coverin' up that purdy girlcut; it looked like somethin' that should be in a fuckin' bon-bon box with a dang white ribbon tied around it.*

And right now the dutiful PFC Micah Hays couldn't thank of any other thang but untyin' that white ribbon.

"Be mine, Micah," Mrs. Willis breathed rather hotly whiles she were steppin' forward. "I've heard so much of your sexual prowess but that was back when I was married. Since then I've ascended to a grand, new hierarchy—"

"The *fuck?*" Micah Hays responded.

"Let me suck your dick . . ."

"Uh . . . shore," Micah Hays responded, and he was already so hard just from the look'a her and the seducterive sound'a her voice, it felt like he was carryin' around a marble bust'a Napoleon in his shorts.

Her smile beamed. Her hot mouth opened and her tongue came out and licked her lips, and at the same time her left hand ran up her sides ta her hooters which she then caressed quite provocatively and then that same hand slid right back down to her pie, it did, and she stuck a finger right up there and sighed. But that was her left hand.

In her right hand, she were holdin' . . .

*A fuckin' laundry sack?* Hays wondered.

Well, that's shore what it looked like, only it didn't look like it had much laundry in it. Hays tried to put the immediate situation into summation: *What've I got here? I got a dead doctor's nekit wife standin' in front'a me holdin' a laundry bag, and she's got a finger up her snatch, and she wants to suck my dick in the middle'a some phony Army gal's motel room with some silly lifeguard show on the TV.*

*What else have I got? I mean, besides a giant boner?*

Not much, at least not in the way of answers to the multitudinous questions posed by this predicament. Jeanne Willis took another slow step forward, her big bright eyes *wide* on Micah Hays, and— *Now if that don't beat all!* Micah thought—she was actually droolin' whiles lookin' at him, that's right a long line'a spit fallin' right out her yap. Micah knew full well he was hot property as far as gals was concerned—shee-it, they'd foller him down the street like he was one'a the fuckin' Beatles or somethin'! They'd stalk him, hide out in front'a his apartment, bust into his place, you name it!—but even he hadda admit he'd never seen a gal *drool* fer him. A'corse, this were fine with him 'cos noisy, sloppy, spitty blowjobs was the best.

"You're gonna let me suck your cock, aren't you, Micah?"

"Well, let me thank a minute. How's about . . . fuck yeah?"

"Let me see it . . ."

Never to deprive a woman'a her wishes, Micah whipped it out, er, well, not exactly *whipped,* on account he was already harder than a hammer handle—he hadda kinda *pry* it out, and after he done so, it was pointin' at her'n gittin' ta throb.

Her slow encroachment came to a momentary pause, and she gaped. "God*damn!*" she remarked. "That's the biggest penis I've ever seen . . ."

Hays shrugged, flexing the trophy. "Problee so, Mrs. Willis. Same as what most gals say once they git a gander."

She brought an astonished hand to her mouth. "Why, it must be almost ten inches . . ."

"No almost about it, ma'am," Micah Hays corrected, "and that's on an average day. I'se remember one time the Shiner twins was givin' me a double-header in the back'a their daddy's van, and they'se was all drunk'n giddy'n pitchin' a absolute *fit* over how big it was, so's one of 'em—Ellie June or Ruthie Sue, don't rightly know which one on account they'se both look 'zactly alike—she done snatched a ruler out her daddy's toolbox and—well, no pun intended—set ta measurin' my tool, and it measured ten and three-eighth inchers—no lie, ma'am."

Mrs. Willis gulped. "What, uh, what did you do then?"

What a silly-ass question! "Well, ma'am, I filled their yaps with cum, kept wood, ass-fucked the fudge out'a both of 'em, then went on to the bar and had me a few beers, er, not that's I'se prone ta usin' such language in front of a respecterble married woman such as yerself, ma'am."

"Ooo, and that's quite an impressive pair of testicles you have, Officer..."

Micah Hays cupped them in his hands, a proud display. "Yes, ma'am, big as eggs they is, and I don't mean hen's eggs neither, I mean duck eggs. I know that fer fact, Mrs. Willis, 'cos see one time I was cornholin' one'a the Kessler girls, and the Kesslers as you may know they have theirselfs a duck farm out 'tween here'n Crick City, and I'se fucked that gal in the butt so many times it were rumored she couldn't walk fer a week, but ta git back ta the point, see, ma'am, we'se was doin' this in one'a their duck-pens—see, the Kesslers *raise* ducks, then sell 'em ta Chinamen restaurants'n stuff in the city—and anyway I could plainly see all them duck eggs that'd been laid, and shore enough, they was the same size as my balls."

"You're quite a supernumerary, Officer," Jeanne Willis said.

"A *what?* Micah Hays said.

"An unparallelled reproductive specimen. You wouldn't happen to know your sperm-count, would you? Per cubic milliliter?"

"*Pardon* me?"

"Oh, no matter. I can index it later." Mrs. Willis opened that laundry bag then, and got ta pullin' out several things. One thing was somethin' that looked like a purple marble. Another was a hyperdermic needle. And the last thing, see, was somethin' of a very particular note to Hays: an empty 2-liter Coke bottle.

"Uh, ma'am?" he politely requested. "Before you git ta polishin' my knob, you mind answerin' a few questions?"

The way she was leanin' over just then afforded Hays a spectackaler view'a her tits hangin' down, and right between 'em he could gander her beaver-fur, he could. "Go right ahead, Officer," she agreed, and what she picked up from the contents'a the bag was that li'l purple marble thang.

"Like, did you murder yer husband Doc Willis?"

Jeanne Willis chuckled. "Oh, no, of course not."

"Well, someone shore as hail did 'cos shortly after he called the station ta report *you* as bein' kidnapped, we seen his body in the closet with his throat cut ta the neckbone, and five minutes after that someone not only took off with a bunch'a empty 2-liter Coke bottles 'zactly like the one ya just took out'a that laundry bag, but they also seemed ta take off with the Doc's body in his fancy Mercedes, and, see, I got me this danged funny feelin' that the person who done all that is you."

Her breath gushed through a wanton smile. "Never mind any of that for now. All you need to do, Officer, is look into the light . . ."

*The light?* Hays thought. *What light? The desk light, the ceilin' light? Bud Light?*

"This light—"

What she was holdin' 'tween her index finger'n thumb was that there purple marble thang, see, and then alls of a sudden all the lights in the room went out along with the television still showin' the silly show with all them Calerforna tramps in the red swim suits—almost like a power line had gone down somewhere, and what happened after that was—

*Dang!* Hays thought.

—that purple marble thang in her fingers started to *glow.*

A real dark light it was, dark purplish-blue and really weird, and to top that off, Micah hisself began ta *feel* really weird, like woozy the way ya'd feel after maybe throwin'g back three neat shots'a Maker's on a empty stomach, and that purple light just kinda . . . *bloomed* in his eyes such that it felt like the light were somehow gittin' inside his haid!

"You must do as I say," Mrs. Willis said but now it didn't sound a whole lot like her voice, kinda deep'n tony like maybe the way she'd sound if she were talkin' from the end of a sewer pipe. "Do you understand, Officer Hays?"

"Uh-uh-uh," Hays replied and noticed that his voice too sounded the same way and alls the while that nutty purple-blue light seemed ta be wrigglin' deep in his noggin' almost like the light were really fingers squirmin' 'round. "I'se reckon I understant just fine, Mrs. Willis."

But that ain't what he wanted ta say! What he *wanted* ta say was somethin' like: *You crazy nekit bitch! I'se arrestin' you fer suspicion of murder, I am! And ya kin ferget about the blowjob 'cos this is serious police business!*

"Good, good, Officer Hays," she returned. "Now, the first thing I need you to do is drop your pants . . ."

Hays dropped 'em fast, his big hard dong kinda wobblin' like the way a divin' board does after someone jumps off it. But what needed to be mentioned was that Hays done so under no volition'a his own. Once he heard her words, his body simply done it, so it seemed that whatever that funky purple light was, it were takin' command of his body but at least he could still think, and what he thunk was: *It's some kind'a hypnoseris! She's hypnertizin' me, makin' me do thangs against my will! Some kinda hippie mind-control or somethin'! I gots ta fight it! I gots to!*

But he weren't fightin' it too well now were he? Not after droppin' his police pants just as pretty as you please. And as the purple light seeped deeper into his brain, more'a her deep, wobbly, echoin' words came forth: "The Supremess will be pleased with your extraordinary contribution to her purpose, Officer Hays—"

*The WHO?*

"—and what's going to happen now is you're going to lie down on the floor and go to sleep, and I'm going to perform fellatio on you for an hour—"

*Over my dead*—Er, well, the thought of defiance didn't last long really 'cos, well, 'cos havin' a hot nekit gal suck his dick fer an hour sounded a mite dandy ta him...

"—and you're going to aspirate your semen into my mouth several dozen times—"

Hays weren't shore in spite'a his collerge education, but he figured that *aspiratin' semen* meant havin' a nut and this sounded a mite dandy to him too, but then a last trickle'a reason still remained in his mind: *I'se gonna blow my cockhock in her mouth several dozen times . . . in a blammed HOUR? Shee-it, even I cain't come THAT many times in a hour! It's plumb humanly imposserble!*

"—and this might strike you as humanly impossible, Officer, but I assure you, it is not. It's the Supremess' power that *makes* it possible, and just as I assure you that you will have several dozen orgasms—in my mouth—in the space of an hour, I can further assure you that they will be the very best orgasms you've ever had in your life—"

Hays' mind continued to reel. *The Supremess? Droppin' a couple dozen loads in a hour? The fuck's she talkin' 'bout?* But the more his thoughts continued to rebel, the more physically helpless he felt.

"—then you'll wake up later and everything will be normal, Officer Hays, so there's no harm done, is there?"

"Nuh-nuh-no, I guess not," Hays said.

"Then I take it you're ready to begin?"

"Yuh-yuh-yes," Hays said.

"Fine. But before we get down to businees, there's still one more minor thing I need you to do, okay?"

"Shuh-shuh-shore," Hays said.

Mrs. Willis placed the hyperdermic needle into his hand. "I need you to inject this syringe . . . into your penis..."

*Say WHAT?* That were 'bout the craziest thang he ever heard. *Ain't no way in a million years I'se gonna stick a needle in my fuckin' DICK?* he thought, but that's only what he *thought*. What he *did* was something else altogether.

*Holy everlivin' SHEE-IT! What the HAIL am I doin'?*

He took up that hyperdermic in one hand, pulled up his rock-hard pecker with the other, and began to point that sharp needle right at his dick-knob!

"Go on," Mrs. Willis ordered from behind the pulsing dark purple-blue light. "Be a good boy and empty that syringe into your penis..."

Beads of sweat crawled down Hays' face like fiesty ladybugs. His fingers properly gripped the syringe while the needle-tip lowered ever closer to his cock-helmet, and alls he could think was: *Fight it! Fight it!* For he figgered it out now, he did. *It's the light that's takin' over my will! It's that blammed evil purple light! Fight it!*

"Good, good, stick it all the way in," Mrs. Willis enthused.

Micah Hays cringed, his body unable to answer the commands of his brain, and what he felt next was the tip'a that sharp needle pushin' inta his cock...

"Don't worry, Officer Hays—" Jeanne Willis chuckled like a witch. "The needle's only a few inches long..."

## XIII

Chief Kinion was, by most folks' standards, and pree-verussly mentioned, a big man, so most folks might'a been more'n a tad surprised ta see a silly old zombie grab the Chief by his collar'n throw him clear acrost the foyer where he landed on an antique telephone table and completely demolished it as a result (and this formidable impact, ta be shore, demolished that there telephone ta boot!) Kinion rolled over like a dizzied walrus, blinkin' the grog out'a his eyes, and then lights snapped on.

Kinion looked up... and saw the zombie.

"Doc *Willis?* the Chief mumbled.

It were Doc Willis, all right: old'n skinny with his gray hair stickin' up, yes sir, and he was just as Chief Kinion had seed him last, wearing tan slacks and a casual navy-blue shirt—oh, and one more thing. The Doc had a knife cut runnin' from ear ta proverbial ear 'n deep enough to show the front'a the neckbone (or what would more clinically be referred to as the pharynxal medial pterygoid plates and petrous bone, fer those'a ya interested).

Yeah, the Doc were dead, all right, startin' ta rot as a matter'a fact, the skin on his old face turnin' sort of a neat shade'a green, not ta mention that his eyes had clouded all over. *A zombie,* Chief Kinion thought, and he weren't too far off, just like the zombies in that movie he'd took Dory May to in 1969 when the Chief couldn't get wood so's she'd run off ta pull a cunt-train with a Chevelle full'a snickerin' greasers.

But then the indisputably dead doc Willis did somethin' that none'a the zombies done in that movie.

The zombie dropped his trousers and took a shit on the floor.

"What the hail'd ya do that fer?" the Chief couldn't help hisself but ask.

The zombie didn't answer, 'least not with words on account the Chief didn't suppose zombies could talk. How this zombie'a Doc Willis *did* answer, however, was by haulin' up his pants, and then grabbin' the Chief again by the collar'n draggin' him kickin' and screamin' toward . . . Guess that?

That's right. He were draggin' the Chief right smack-dab toward that pile'a zombie shit.

And—oh, Gawd!—that pile'a shit were steamin', it was, and then it became quite apparent what the Doc-Willis-the-Zombie intended ta do—

The Chief's face was held less than an inch from that pile! And— ooo-eee!—did it stank! About the only thang that smelt worse than a pile'a shit was a pile'a *dead-man's* shit, shore enough!

—was ta push the Chief's face right straight down inta the shit-pile until he smothered!

*Aw, Gawd . . .*

The Chief's face were now just about ta kiss that big slab'a zombie fecal matter, it was, and he thought he just might die from the smell alone well before his face got stuck in it but . . .

*No dag zombie's gonna kill me, no sir! Not without a fight!*

But before the Chief could surge up against that zombie's intractable supernatural strength—which shorely he would've and then set ta open a can'a whup-ass on that servant'a Satan—he, well, what he done first was he burped hard'n heavy from all the viddles he et today, and when a man the size'a Chief Kinion burped, it can cause a fairly serious gastic hitch, it can, and when that hitch occurred, what happened next was the force'a that burp throwed the dead Doc Willis right off'a him, and . . .

*Thuh-thunk!*

The zombie was done throwed clear back into the front'a the stairwell, tripped, and landed with some force on the stairs themselfs, causin' the back'a the Doc's haid to impact quite forcefully with the edge'a the seventh step.

Then . . . nothin'.

The Chief drug hisself up, he did, and he were a purdy happy camper ta finally git his face away from that steamin' pile'a zombie shit, and then turnt ta see what up'n happened to his attacker . . .

"Well, I'll be . . ."

The zombie that were Doc Willis lay across the stairs with his head busted open like a coconut and alls'a his dead zombie brains muckin' up the carpet.

"Yeah-boy!" the Chief celebrated. "See what happens when zombies mess with Chief Richard Kinion!"

He clapped his hands and guffawed up at his victory, and when he were done guffawin', he looked down again and then he saw—

"What'n tarnations?"

He saw a hinged wood panel along the side'a the stairwell hangin' ajar.

*Hmm,* he thought. *I'se wonder what's behind there . . .*

Well, he found out right quick when he flipped that panel open'n saw a fuckin' set of wooden steps!

A set of wooden steps leadin' *down . . .*

Now, the Chief didn't really *want* to climb down them steps, no he did not, but he figgered it was his duty ta do so, 'specially given the oddities that were aboundin', and one oddity in particular bein' that he just watched a dead fella shit on the floor and then had ta kill him. Shore as chittlins was better fried than boiled, somethin' were amiss in this here house, and the Chief needed ta know what it was. So with more effort than was worth mentionin', he squeezed his girth into the opening behind that panel, and begun to descend them narrow steps.

Once he got down he found hisself standin' in the middle of what looked ta be a laboratory of some kind, fulla micrascopes'n lab tables'n test tubes'n what not. And linin' the walls was the big metal racks loaded up with boxes fulla blinkin' lights'n meters'n knobs. *A laboratory, it shorely is . . .* But weren't that the dangedest thing?

Yeah, and by the looks of it, Chief Kinion would know less about all this fancy equipment than he knowed about Naturalism in 19th Century Literature, but he'd shore like ta have a clue as ta what were goin' on down here, just as shorely as he'd like ta know what brung Doc Willis back ta life.

But, see, the Chief had et damn near over an hour ago, and when goin' so long without food, he found it hard to concerntrate, and shorely he'd need ta concerntrate if he expected ta figger out what was up with this here laboratory, and it just so happened that there was one apparatus in the lab that Chief Kinion recognized, right over there in the corner . . .

A refrigerator.

*Yeah, I wonder what kinda chow they got in there. I could shore use me a plate'a cold ribs or maybe a big pork-chop sammich, yes sir!* There were a consideration, however, in that most folks might not deem it too appropriate fer a officer'a the law to be helpin' themselfs to someone else's viddles without proper permission'a the rightful owner, but—*Hail!* the Chief thought, *It ain't like Doc Willis'll mind*

181

much, on account I just kilt his dead-zombie ass!

So the Chief hauled that there refrigerator right on open and looked in.

## XIV

. . . and suddenly all the winders shattered, from the outside in!

"That's it, that's it, Officer," Mrs. Willis' voice continued to flutter from behind that funky, hypnertizin' purple light. And, that's right, Micah, now almost totally lost of his free-will, had the point'a that syringe just about to sink inta his *dick-knob!*

*I cain't fight it!* Hays thought. *I'se helpless against her and her evil, hypnertizin', mind-controlin' purple light! I gots no choice! I'se gonna have to stick this needle inta my peter!*

But . . . could it be true? Could it be that PFC Micah Hays, God's gift to cracker women, was actually going to insert a hypodermic needle—several inches long!—all the way into his pride and joy?

"NO!" Hays yelled, and in a movement nearly too fast to be detected by the nekit eye, he dropped the syringe, whipped out his cool-lookin' mirrored sunglasses, and put 'em on, and suddenly his senses had returned!

"*I'se* in control now, bitch," he chuckled to Mrs. Willis.

'Cos, see, all that eerie hypnertizin' light were now reflecterin' off'a Micah's sunglasses straight back inta Mrs. Willis' eyes! She just stood there, blank-faced now, in a deep trance.

"Go ta sleep, bitch," Micah Hays ordered. "And don't wake up till I'se tell ya."

"Yes, Officer Hays," she droned back, and—*slap!*—she collapsed to the floor, her bare ass and back causin' the *slap,* and then that queer little purple marble fell from her fingers, the purple light abated, and the motel room lights snapped back on.

"Close call." Hays stuffed his penis back into his pants and zipped up, then looked out the front winder.

"I knew it!"

Shore enough, Doc Willis' fancy shiny-red kraut Mercedes were parked right out front. "*She's* the one who stolt it! *She's* the one who cut Doc Willis' throat, then hustled his body out the house ta confuse us! And *she's* the one who knocked all them boys out at the County Watch-House, and no doubt done the same thang ta all the fellas at the VFW hall!" Indeed, the deducterive Micah Hays had figgered it all out--er, well, not all of it just yet. Like what was with the dick-needle'n all that mumbo jumbo? And what was with the purple marble'n Coke bottle'n and alls that shit?

Then Hays looked back in Majora's briefcase, then gandered some'a the papers in there.

"Well ain't that just neat-o!" he said to himself.

## XV

Yes sir, the Chief opened that there refrigerator just *knowin'* there'd be somethin' good in there to drop right in his breadbasket, like maybe a big plate'a pork'n beans'n simmered onions, or funnelcakes'n molasses or maybe even some leftover cornbread—

"The *hail?*" he said when he pulled the door fully open.

Naw, see, there weren't nothin' of the sort in that blammed fridge, no sir. Absolutely ziltch ta eat. *Shee-it . . .* N'fact, alls that was in there was . . .

"Now wait just one minute," the Chief mumbled aloud.

Five 2-liter Coke bottles was what sat in the fridge.

A'corse, the Chief wouldn't mind a good, sweet slug'a Coke right now ta wet his whistle but it were quite clear that there weren't no Coke in *any* of them bottles; the Chief could see for hisself, in the bright interior fridge light, that all them bottles were filled with milk or somethin', somethin' white, so he took one out'n twisted off the cap'n took a sniff and—

"Lordy! What *is* that?"

"It's sperm, Chief," a voice came from behind. "Human spermatozoa and seminal fluid."

Well, the voice was such a surprise that the Chief spun 'round in somethin' close to shock, and what shocked him even further was to discover that the source'a the voice was none other than the stunning Captain Majora.

What *weren't* so stunning, though, was that she were pointin' that bigass Government Model Colt .45 right in his face.

"Captain Majora!" he exclaimed.

"Don't make any sudden movements," she said. "I'm sorry about this, Chief, but you're going to have to remain under arrest until you can be properly debriefed."

"Duh . . . *debriefed?*"

"That's right, Chief Kinion," she said in her tight, prim'n proper Army uniform, and, well, not ta sound sexist, but her tits were fillin' out the khaki top just dandy. "I'm afraid things aren't quite as they seem—"

"You shore got that right, ya lyin' tramp! Freeze!"

*click!*

"Hays!" the Chief rejoiced.

Yes sir, just in the nick'a time'n by the grace'a Gawd, it were none other than PFC Micah Hays who'd appeared as if from out'a nowheres, and even better, he were holdin' his service revolver right smack-dab up against Captain Majora's temple.

"You'se a ballsy bitch, ain't ya?" Hays said with a cocked grin, "thankin' ya kin hold my fine boss at gunpoint. Well you got just one second ta drop yer piece or else I'll'se drop *you* and yer li'l prissy, citified red bush ta boot, *Captain* Majora, or should I say *Geyserite!*"

Majora dropped her pistol, then went slump-shouldered. "How did you find out my classified codename?"

"Same way I found out you really ain't in the Army," Hays answered, "and the same way I found out what's *really* goin' on."

"Hays," Kinion stepped up, still holding the opened 2-liter Coke

## The Refrigerator Full of Sperm

bottle. "Dang good work, boy, just like the way I trained ya. But . . . what else is that ya got there?"

Hays picked up Majora's gun, then walked over to the lab table on which he placed Majora's briefcase and opened it. "All *kinds* of poop in here, boss. First off, as we already suspected, she ain't no Army officer. She's in the blammed F.B.I."

*Dang!* the Chief thought. Then he turned to Majora. "Is this true?"

"I'm afraid so, Chief Kinion," Majora answered. "It's all part of a federal disinformation strategy that's worked for fifty years. Impersonation of other agencies to decredulize the witness. The same with context—by fabricating the lie which claimed that Doctor Willis was involved in the selling ammunition technologies to terrorist governments, I was able to supplant myself in your midst, so to speak, by which I could investigate the *real* point of concern."

"Uh . . . huh," the Chief respondered. "Sounds more ta me like you're just plumb crazy." Then he turned to the PFC. "Hays, ya know what she just done tolt me? She said this here 2-liter Coke bottle is full'a . . . well . . . spunk."

"It is, Chief," Hays said.

Chief Kinion dropped the bottle immediatly, where it *thunked* on the floor, and since its cap was still off, it—*gullup-gullup-gullup*—emptied onto the lab floor. Chief Kinion gulped'n glanced down. It, well, it shore as hail looked like spunk comin' out that bottle.

And there was four more bottles full of it in the fridge!

"You're problee wonderin'," Hays postulated, "how so much petersnot come ta fill that whole bottle—"

"The average male ejaculation," Majora added, "comprises a liquid volume of 7cc's—about enough to fill an eyedropper."

Kinion's eyeballs went wide at the size'a the puddle on the floor. "Then how the *hail*—"

"Check it out, Chief. This briefcase is chock *full* of papers like this," Hays said, and handed the Chief a sheet.

Kinion's eyes remained bugged-out as he read:

185

*Edward Lee*

## TOP SECRET
### SPECIAL ACCESS REQUIRED/EYES ONLY
### TEKNA/BYMAN/UMBRA/SI

DEPARTMENT OF THE AIR FORCE
WASHINGTON DC 20330-100

OFFICE OF THE SECRETARY

25 May 1998

    SAF/AAIQ
    1610 Air Force Pentagon
    TO: DIRECTOR, FEDERAL BUREAU OF INVESTIGATION

    SUBJECT: CLASSIFIED REQUEST PER MEMORANDUM (GAO Code 701034); AFR 12-50 (CLASSIFIED) Volume II, Disposition of Air Force Records and Material

    (a) Identify pertinent directive concerning crashes of air vehicles not of terrestrial origin, investigations, wreckage/debris/dead bodies — retention, recovery, and evaluation.

    Dear Mr. Director:
    Per your request relative to the above memorandum, i.e., the incident concerning the Low Frequency Radar Array (LFRA) detection on 18 April 1998 and disposition thereof. This is the thirteenth documented contact of vehicles bearing this structural signature, and we can only anticipate similar subsequent "collection" activities. MADAM and HRMS pulses verify a contact-point in vicinity to a remote rural township, Luntville, VA. As in the past, I would like you to assign this case to Special Agent Dana Majora, whom we feel to be the best operative for the job.

    Attachment (TO): -MILNET
        -U.S. Air Force Joint Recovery Command
        -NSA (Interagency Liaison Office)
        Signed,

        William Jefferson Clinton
        PRESIDENT OF THE UNITED STATES
        1600 Pennsylvania Avenue
        Washington, DC 20012

## The Refrigerator Full of Sperm

"Tarnations!" Kinion bellowed. "This here letter's signed by the President!"

"Dang straight, boss," Hays confirmed.

"And . . . what the hail—"

Hays sliced a grin at Majora. "Captain—er, I should say *Special Agent* Majora. I thank it's only fittin' and proper that *you* explain the rest."

Majora's eyes cast down in dejection. "It's about I.G.E.'s, Chief Kinion—that's Intra-galactic Entities."

"The *hail?*" Kinion affirmed his confusion.

"Aliens," Majora went on. "A particular species we've identified as coming from the M34 Star Cluster; every 6 years and 25 days—in accordance with what is known as a an epicycular apogee, and by classified technological detection systems such as the MADAM—that is the Mass-Activated-Detection-Activation-Mechanism—and the H.R.M.S.—the High Resolution Microwave Survey—in other words, Chief, airborn-detection technologies which vastly exceed the capabilities of traditional high-and low-frequency radar systems, every 6 years and 25 days, this craft, in collusion with certain members of our own race, returns to earth in order to replenish a particular substance that their own race can no longer provide in order to propagate their civilization."

"Huh?" the Chief said.

"Sperm, Chief. The M34 alien race can no longer produce the necessary sperm to keep their civilization in a state of replication, at least not without help, I should say. Doctor Willis really had nothing to do with it—I implicated him in the specious primer-technology conspiracy for the reasons I've previously described—to divert the attentions of your own investigation from the actual truth. In actuality, it was *Mrs.* Willis who originally effected communicative contact with the M34 aliens, some 12 years ago, via her abuse of NSA radio-telescope receiving devices, after which she married Doctor Willis under a less-than-truthful guise so to embezzle money from his bank account in order to maintain contact with the aliens . . . and to assist them in their quest."

"Their quest fer . . . *sperm?*" Kinion queried.

"That's right, Chief," Hays piped up. "That's what these blammed aliens want from us. They want a good rasher of our petersnot ta keep themselfs goin' till the next time they kin come back. You know, Chief, our spunk, our peckerjuice, our dicksnot, our cock-hock, our—"

"Spermatozoa," Majora clarified.

Hays again: "And, see, them aliens was in cahoots with Mrs. Willis, and what she were doin' was givin' 'em the best locations fer gittin' the most dick-loogie in as short as time as posserble on account they can only be here fer a short time 'fore they gotta go back."

"It's called a straticular apogic-deflection window, Chief," Majora added. "Think of it as a window of opportunity. The aliens only have a space of about one day before they can arrive, achieve their collection priorities, and leave. If they leave late, they'll never get back to their own planet; earth's orbital angle would be off."

Hays were noddin'. "And, see, Chief, there's more. But first, I'se got me a question fer Miss Majora." He looked her right in the eye. "See, I bushwhacked Mrs. Willis back at your motel room when she tried ta do the job on me, but . . . she kept sayin' something about a . . . *Supremess*. The hail is that?"

"The alien flight technician. A female of their species. She is, in fact, the only occupant of the craft."

"And that craft is coming back soon?" Hays asked.

Majora looked at her watch. "In a matter of minutes, in fact. But she'll be in for a big surprise this time. No sperm."

Now Hays got it, but he felt the Chief deserved more of a explernation. "And likes I said, Chief, there's more. See, what they done is give Mrs. Willis this li'l purple marble which gives off this funky light that causes folks to become hypnertized'n go unconscious—"

"A low-yield millwave discharge unit which alters beta-

188

brainwave activity," Majora accentuated.

"Like all them boys at the County Watch-House?" Kinion pieced together.

"That's right, Chief, and she done the same thang at the VFW Post. Since the aliens gots so little time ta collect as much spunk as they can, they gotta go ta places with a high number'a fellas—ya know, more spunk fer the buck. And I'll'se bet their new-fangled radio-telescope frequencies done brainwashed Mrs. Willis inta doin' it."

"Precisely," Majora said. "You're very deductive, PFC."

Hays were all in a swivet talkin' 'bout all he'd figgered out on his own. "And, Chief, there's also somethin' else she does, see. Before she orders the fellas ta go unconscious, she makes 'em inject this stuff . . . inta their *wood!*"

"No!" Chief Kinion exclaimed.

"Your deputy is quite correct, Chief," Majora said. "It's a genetically-engineered oxytocin-nutrient which not only fuels the testes and the seminal vesicals, it enables the men and boys to achieve several dozen orgasms in the space of an hour. It's a libidinal stimulant, Chief."

But the Chief looked crosseyed at her, like he didn't know what'n tarnations she were blabberin' 'bout.

But Hays noticed this inflection, so he augemented, "What she means, boss, is that this stuff you inject in yer dick makes ya able ta have a bunch'a nuts real fast, and it were Mrs. Willis who done *sucked out* all that dicksnot and then spat it inta them big 2-liter bottles. It were the aliens who done gave her the stuff, and the purple marble, influencin' her by their fancy alien technolergy."

"It sounds ridiculous, Chief," Majora said, "but it's true, and PFC Hays is absolutely correct in all counts of his speculation— echnology, of course, being the operative phrase. It's an alien conspiracy to appropriate human sperm for their own devices."

Chief Kinion glanced again to that giant motherfuckin' puddle'a spunk on the floor. *Holy shee-it. That's a dang lot'a joyjuice, yes sir!*

*Problee enough spunk in each'a them bottles ta keep them aliens in spunk fer a LONG time! What a EVIL hoodwinks!*

"And as far as Doctor Willis being certifiably dead this morning," Majora went on, "yet being quite alive when you confronted him upstairs—it can all be explained by more of the technology that the aliens gave to Mrs. Willis in exchange for her assistance. A simple biogenic reanimation serum was infused into the corpse—by Mrs. Willis—and this produced a mute assistant for her objectives."

*The zombie,* the Chief calculated. But, yeah, the whole thang sounded purdy dickerluss, but the Chief thought he were beginnin' ta see it all. "But," he said, ta further his questions, "how do the aliens know ta come *here.*"

"Simple, Chief," Majora answered, "and this might sound ridiculous too, but it's true. Dr. Willis, even in his retirement, attended several medical conventions ever year. Upon such occasions that he was out of town, his wife took money out of his bank account to build a low-ohm, refractive radio-telescope receptor; it's buried in the field behind the house. See, simple. The aliens will be re-assuming a sub-orbital in just a few minutes, thinking they will receive the next cachet of sperm from Mrs. Willis. You may have noticed me earlier, out behind the house looking up into the sky."

Yeah! The Chief shore did! *And she were doin' so with a pair 'a somethin' that looked like binoculars!*

"I was using a specially made optical device that the Air Force Material Command was able to construct that will penetrate the alien stealth systems."

*Yeah,* the Chief thought. It sounded more *ridickerluss* than simple but how could he not believe it? All the proof was there . . .

"But there's still one more thing," Majora said, "and obviously, through his intelligence and perceptivity, PFC Hays has already figured it out . . ."

But when Majora and Kinion looked around . . . Micah Hays was gone . . .

## XVI

Yeah, Hays had read all 'a them fancy government classerfied papers in that red-hairt bitch's briefcase. He knew, and he was dang well pissed. *Bunch 'a evil aliens tryin' ta steal our dicksnot!*

He ran down behind the house, knowin' full well when the final embarkation would occur on account'a he seed with his own eyes the NASA trackin' infermation.

He knew, alls right . . .

And he dang shore knew what he was gonna do.

He stood back there, in the field behind the house. He looked up in the sky but weren't surprised that he couldn't see nothin' but stars. Alls he knowed was what he *needed* ta know.

*She'll be comin'. And she'll be thinkin' I'se the one with the spunk . . .*

Suddenly a great whirling wind rose; it seemed to turn circles around him, and nearly blew him off his feet. Blades'a grass and weeds'n dust rose like a friggin' tornado, and just as Hays thought he'd blow away like a piece'a straw—

*Fuckin'-A! Cool!*

A cone of light bright as the sun beamed down on him, and a second later—

*FFFZAPP!*

Hays were standin' someplace else. Nothin' at all like the breezy field behind Doc Willis' house but . . . *inside* somethin'. Someplace that were made of a bunch'a, like, honeycombed walls at all differnt angles, all drab gray, and it was cold in here, and he heard this steady hummin' in his ears, a low, black, warblin' noise . . .

OUTER LIMITS NOISE FROM DOOMSDAY

At once, though, Hays knew where he were.

*Jesus Chrast in a porn parlor! I'se right smack-dab in the middle'a the alien ship!*

—*You are*— a sultry voice fluttered in his brain.

From one of the honeycombs, a shadow stirred, then moved forward.

*Shee-it...*

The figure approached—it was short and thin'n all covered with slick gray skin, and had skinny beanpole arms'n legs. Problee no more than four-foot tall it was but with a big bald gray head like a upside-down pear. Another thang was the mouth: just like little slit'n two holes fer a nose. Purdy plain, though, that this were a *gal* alien, on account that she had pointy, gray tits on her rack-skinny chest'n darker gray nipples stickin' out long as golf tees, and 'tween her beanpole legs, Hays could see a li'l gash down there. *Not a bad cut fer a alien,* he considered. But then he noted—

The eyes.

*Dang!*

They'se was big as crystal-black tennis balls sunk in the skull. Oh, yeah, when Hays saw it, he knowed just what he were lookin' at...

"The Supremess," he whispered.

—*Yes*—

But it weren't like regler talkin' that this alien gal talked ta Hays. It were more like a scrapin' sound in his head that sounded like words. *Teleperthee,* he suspected.

—*Where are the collection receptacles?*—the Supremess asked.

"Oh, you mean them 2-liter Coke bottles filled with cum? Why, they'se down in the fridge, ya silly gray bitch," Hays was kind enough to answer.

—*You fool! Full-positive straticular apogee is about to occur!*—

"Yeah, I know, ya ditz, and that means you gots ta leave. Well this time you'se leavin' *without* them bottles'a peckersnot, so how do ya like *them* cookies?"

—*Go back and get them!*—the alien woman's telepathic voice

rocketed.—*Get them and bring them to me!*—

"Fuck you and the spaceship you rode in on," Hays replied, chucklin'. "I ain't doin' nothin' 'cept maybe bitch-slappin' the daylights out'a ya."

—*RETRIEVE THE COLLECTION RECEPTICALS! MY RACE CANNOT PROPAGATE WITHOUT THEM!*—

"Propergate *this,* spacecunt!" Hays grabbed his crotch and gave a squeeze. "I ain't doin' shit you say!"

—*Oh, yes you will . . .*—

Suddenly the Supremess' black-crystal eyes began to glow with the same danged purple light that come out'a Mrs. Willis' marble back the motel! Yes sir, that same evil, mind-controlin', hypnertizin' light!

—*You have no choice but to do as I bid*—the Supremess said. —*Step back into the egression beam, then retrieve the collection receceepticals, and bring them back to me at once*—

Hays stared, stock-still, and his voice droned: "Yes, my alien master. Your wish is my command . . ." Then Hays cut a big shuckin' grin, and he grabbed his crotch again. "In a pig's peehole, ya alien tramp!"

See, Hays anticerpated this, which was why he put his mirror-finished sunglasses back on when he went out into Doc Willis' back yard! The light weren't havin' no effect on him at all!

Then he dropped his drawers, sportin' a typical mighty erection. "Hey, hosebag! If it's cum you want, it's cum you'll get!"

Hays hauled the stupefied alien to the ship's floor. Then he hocked a good-sized spitter on his pole, pinned the alien bitch's six-toed feet back behind her ear-holes, and sunk every inch'a his pants-load right in her li'l gray alien pussy. A mite tight, it was, like *real* tight, yes sir, but he got ta puttin' some serious cockstrokes on her, and it soon became obvious that she didn't object. So little she was, though, it reminded him'a what it might be like ta fuck a kid, but . . .

*This ain't no kid!* he confirmed the truth. *This here's a alien overlord who's been stealin' human spunk!*

—*Ooo, ooo, what an earthling!*—she said hotly. —*Harder! Harder!*—

Hays pumped on as effectively as an oil derrick. "I'se plumb givin' it to ya damn near hard as I can, ya otherworldly whore!"

—*Harder! Harder!*—

Well, shee-it. PFC Micah Hays were never one ta deny a gal her desires, even if it were a *alien* gal! So's he got ta humpin' hard as he could yes sir, whiles the hot'n horny Supremess just kept shriekin' her orgameric bliss inta his head'n comin' like a Peterbilt with no brakes. And a right *good* her space-pussy felt, it did, real tight'n hot'n wet like a true tramp. And just when he's were fixin' to drop a shot'a snot like ta make a rhinoceros feel inadequate, he thought: *Now wait just one dang second! Cum is just what this evil alien bitch WANTS! So that's the one thang I CAIN'T give her!*

So . . . he'd give her the next best thing: the *box-humpin'* of her life!

*Yeah!*

And that's just what he done, he did. He humped the slimy alien bitch's bones like there were no tomorrow—

—*More! More! Harder! Harder!*—

Micah Hays complied, he shore did, slammin' her twat hard as a sledgehammer.

—*Harder! Harder!*—

And then he *really* turned it on . . .

She *screamed* in his head, so hard she were comin'! Perhaps she were the first alien ever ta have multerple orgasms! No, Micah Hays summoned all'a his discerpline, and he did not drop his wax, but by the time he were done givin' this bitch the kind'a hard'n fast fuckin' she needed, she were—

"Oops," Hays said when he looked at her.

The bitch were dead. That li'l cooze on her looked like a pile'a gray meat by now, with alls'a this thin gray blood leakin' out, and then big eyes in her skull were closed, and she just lay there like a bag'a twigs . . .

"Well, how do ya like that? I done busted her hole just like I done ta Miss Brill when I were a tot!" Shore, n'fact, Hays in his time had busted a fair share'a boxes with his giant dick, but this were the *first* time he'd busted a *alien's* hole . . .

*Shee-it. I done fucked the bitch to death!*

Suddenly the ship began to gyrate, probably some funky guidance computer on automatic. The apergee were here'n no doubt the ship would fly back to its homeworld.

This was one train Hays didn't wanna be on when it left the station . . .

He hitched back up his drawers—not easy on account'a the hard-on he still had—then stumbled back toward the middle'a the ship where he'd appeared. A white beam'a light glowed there, but it were startin' ta get real dim real fast.

Hays jumped in—

—and landed ass-first in the middle'a the field behind Doc Willis' house.

*Thank Gawd! I'se still alive! And—*

He grabbed his pantscrotch.

—*and still hard!*

## EPERLOG

So the evil alien bitch was deprived of her usual rasher'a human sperm, and so was her home world—Hays neglected ta reveal that he'd plumb up'n fucked her ta DEATH and busted her box ta boot— so who knew what'd happen? Would the alien race die? Would they hang on till the next apergee'n come back fer more joyjuice?

The answer: Who the hail cared?

And as it turnt out, Majora weren't quite the phony cooze Hays suspectered her'a bein'—well, shore, she was a lyin' redmuffed sleeze but at least she were still on *our* side. Only thang that happened afterward was that she hadda call some'a her cronies from the F.B.I. and they come around shortly to give Hays'n the Chief their proper "debriefing" and had 'em sign some paper called the National Security And Classified Secrets Agreement, which would be DOD Form 1501-95, agreein' that they wouldn't tell no one about what they'd seed, under penalty of law provided by the United States Code, violations'a which carried a maximum sentence of life imprisonment in a federal corrections facility and a one million dollar fine.

No big deal.

And as far as all'a them boys from the Watch-House and all'a them old VFW tuckers—them State Health Department buses weren't State Health Department buses at all but instead they were F.B.I. buses with phony markings!—and it was a federal medercal facility they'd all been took to, and soon enough they'se all woked up'n were just fine, and even better was they didn't remember a dang thing, not one of 'em! (A'corse, considerin' how much nut Mrs. Willis had sucked out'a all their peters, it'd problee be a while 'fore any of 'em shot a good load). Case closed, on to the next. So then Special Agent Majora thanked 'em both'n left, wishin' 'em well.

After which Hays elucidated, "Shee-it, Chief, no one'd believe us but we shore's hail know its true. Fuckin' aliens in league with a former scientist's wife in a evil plot to steal human spunk, and carryin' it away in 2-liter Coke bottles? A sassy chick FBI agent masqueradin' as a Army officer? Special alien drugs that make guys able to shoot dozens'a load in a hour? It's the most fucked up thing I ever heard, so fucked up it's downright perposterous! Sounds like one'a them weirdo science fiction stories only, like, a really *bad* one, like maybe the author didn't know what the fuck he was writin' about but he wrote it anyway. Anyhows, Chief, I'm outa here, I gots me another date with Jinny Jo, and lemme tell ya—" Hays grinned and grabbed his crotch—"my pole is hard as gnarled oak! I got me some meat to put in *her* pantry, fer shore! I'se gonna go on over there, treat her like dogshit, fuck her, wipe my dick off in her hair, then get the fuck out and go have a few beers with the boys. Later, Chief!"

Kinion looked up from his coffee. "Hays, wait a sec. Did you just say you hadda date with *Jinny Jo?*"

"That's a fact, boss."

The Chief rubbed his eyes. "Well, hail, ain't that the gal ya tolt me about this mornin' who hadda, well, you know—"

"Who hadda pussy fulla gonococcal pus? Yes sir, that's the same fuck-pig, Chief. Only I knows better now, so's I ain't gonna go down on her, no sir! I'd rather lick the bottom of a sewer grate. N'stead, I'll'se just hold my nose'n put a double rubber on my dick'n just bust her hole like it needs ta be busted, yes sir! And I guarentee it, Chief, she'll thank me fer it afterward."

Kinion waved an errant hand. He didn't even want ta think about it. "Fine, Hays. Goes have yerself a good time."

Hays turned to do just that but he stopped short'a the station house doors, and he slapped his thigh hard. "Dang, Chief, I'se awful sorry!"

Kinion's hooded eyes flicked up without much interest. "Yore sorry 'bout what?"

"I never *did* git ta tell ya why they called Martha the Tail."

The Chief let out a long, exasperated sigh. "Hays, I don't wanna know—"

"Aw, no, Chief, I couldn't do that to ya. A fella cain't be tellin' a story only ta leave off the end! That wouldn't be *proper.*"

"Hays," the Chief stated sternly, "I don't wanna hear."

"Aw, come on, Chief, I'se mean I tolt ya the part 'bout how I was fuckin' that old whore's pussy'n her pussy turnt out ta be fulla all these vagernul polyps're some shit, and whatever the hail they was, it felt like I had my boner stuck in a bag'a chicken gizzards, and then I tolt how after I creamed all over them polyps, she begged me ta fuck her ass, so's I did that too, boss, and put a *big* load up there too, but that weren't all, remember? Afters that she asked me ta pee up her tired ass and, hail, I still had 'bout ten beers in me just cryin' ta git out, so's shore, I'se fulfilled her third request'n pulled a giant beer-piss right up her poop-chute, I did, and then—"

"HAYS! GET THE HAIL OUT'A HERE'N THAT'S AN ORDER!" the Chief flipped'n just blew his lid.

Majora walked back in to say goodbye now that the case was concluded. Chief asked her out but she said, "No, I'm sorry"

"But . . . I kind'a thought you know . . . I mean, I could tell by the way you been lookin' at me that you were . . ."

"Attracted to you. It was all in the line of duty, Chief. I'm sure you understand."

"Huh?"

"For the same reason I faked Army credentials, I faked sexual interest in you, Chief, to make you more disposed to render information, and more likely to cooperate. This was a matter of National Security."

So the PFC shrugged'n did as he was tolt by his supervisin' officer. *Fine, he don't wanna hear the rest'a the story, then I'se won't tell him.* Seemed kind'a unfair ta Hays' though, 'cos not tellin' a fella the end of a story were almost as bad as readin', like, a novella with the end chopped off, and Hays *knowed* he wouldn't like that but— fuck it! He guessed he'd just have ta save the rest'a that story fer another time, he would.

Right?

So's Hays walked on out'a the station inta the middle'a the fine night. A'corse, the federal fellas had up'n took the shiny-red Mercedes along with the still-nekit'n unconscious Mrs. Willis, as well as the hyperdermic full'a alien libidinal stimurlent, and Hays imagined they done scooted Mrs. Willis' fine her bare ass off ta some government "debriefin'" facility, but, hey, that's the way it goes.

And what adjoined this here situation was that as Hays were leavin', he did take one last look back into the station through the front winder, and what he saw was a sad sight indeed.

*Aw, that ain't right...*

He saw the Chief still sittin' at his desk with his big kisser hangin' over that cup'a cold coffee'n just lookin' so dejected'n depressed, and it weren't no surprise considerin' how the Chief had such fierce hots fer Agent Majora but now he didn't have nothin' ta look forward to 'cept that beached whale of a wife snorin' like ta wake the dead back at the Chief's double-wide...

So that set Hays ta thinkin'.

The Chief were a good man at heart, and he shorely deserved better'n what life had dealt him so far, and when Hays glanced down to the other end'a the parkin' lot, what he saw was this:

Agent Majora fixin' ta git inta her government sedan.

And that's when Hays got his idea...

"Agent Majora!" he shouted out. "Hold up a sec if ya would!"

Hays trotted on over, wavin'.

"Yes, PFC Hays?" she queried, looking at him over the top of the car.

"Just one sec!" And then Hays finished trottin' over.

See, there were one thang he fergot ta hand over to them feds, and it weren't like he kept it from 'em on purpose, he just plumb fergot.

"What is it, PFC Hays? she asked, gettin' a bit testy.

Hays reached inta his pocket, then held up that neat purple marble 'tween his thumb'n forefinger, and when he pressed against it hard enough...

It began ta glow with that same dark-purple-weird-mind-controlin'-hypnertizin' light, and it were shinin' right inta Agent Majora's purdy green eyes.

"You ain't got no choice but ta do what I'se tell ya," Hays tolt her. "Do ya understand?"

Now Majora stood in a trance. "Yes," she droned back. "I understand."

"Good, ya red-hairt cum-dump," Hays said. "And you gots yerself a serious problem, see? See, Chief Kinion is the sexiest man in the world, right?"

"That," she agreed, "is correct."

"And you're so hot fer him, yer little red-hairt pussy's on fire, right?"

"That is correct."

Hays chuckled. "So git on back in there and *do* somethin' 'bout it, ya prissy bitch!"

Agent Majora nodded blankly, turned away from her car...and headed back toward the police station.

Well, shee-it. The case were closed, all right, all the commotion'a the day finished and everything set back ta rights, which were a good thang, indeed, but Chief Kinion still felt a mite glum, he did. Golly, he shore had hisself a giant crush on Agent Majora, but now she were gone and he'd more'n likely never see her again.

*Oh, well,* he commisserated. *Least I'se can always think back fondly'n remember her...*

He turnt on the radio, hopin' fer somethin' nice'n soothin', like maybe "Blue Moon," by the King, but what he heard instead nearly jotled him out'a his chair...

Evil, devilish, heavy-metal gee-tars crushed noise from the radio, along with'a voice like someone garglin' with rusty razor blades. "You shit at the moment of death!" the voice screamed, "and I feast on what is left!"

*Dag hippie satanic codswallop!* the Chief thought'n switched that radio off a mite quick. It was a dag sorry state'a world, when a southern fella could turn on the radio and hear *that* instead'a Elvis!

Then the station house door clicked open, and in walked—

"Agent Majora!" the Chief celebrated and damn near tipped over his desk gittin' up.

"Please," she said. "Call me Dana."

"Uh-uh-er, well, yeah, a'corse . . . Dana," Kinion babbled on. "So what brings ya back? Did'ja fergit somethin'?"

"Oh, yes, Chief, I most certainly did. You see, I forgot to make love with the sexiest man I've ever met."

Kinion cocked a smirk. "Hays already left—"

"Not Hays," she purred. "*You.*"

Well, the Chief about keeled over right then'n there when she up'n said that, but then he thought it must be some kind'a joke, 'least until she, well, started gittin' out'a her duds a mite fast.

And just as fast, the Chief was pitchin' a circus tent . . .

She sauntered over, just as nekit now as she was when he'd seen her in the motel room but somehow even more beautiful: her flawless white skin just a'glowin' in the office light, her red hair shinin' like new-spun silk, and her gorgeous, dumplin'-like tits pushin' out like they'se *wanted* ta be squeezed.

"Ooooooooh, Chief," she moaned, and then her soft hands set on his shoulders'n pushed him back down in his chair, and then she sat her cute l'il tush down on the desk, and she was lookin' right at him with a look in her wide green eyes that seemed to say, well . . . FUCK ME TILL I CAN'T SEE STRAIGHT!

Her voice issued from her lips like hot, thick honey. "Chief, all day long I've been trying to control myself but-but, the more I find myself in your proximity, the weaker I become. I feel so ashamed being so weak in front of you—"

*Be weak! Be weak!* the Chief's thoughts bellowed.

"—but I just can't help it! You are without a doubt the most sexually stimulating man I've ever laid eyes on, and pardon me if this sounds concupiscent, but-but-but . . . I need you to fuck me till I can't see straight . . ."

Well, the Chief didn't mind one speck 'bout her soundin' concupiscent, no sir. And he just sat there with his dick thumpin' in his trousers'n lookin' up at her, and then she moved one'a her purdy l'il feet up his leg'n let it set right smack-dab in his crotch, and

Chief Kinion thought he might just blow a gusher 'a peckersnot right then'n there. That cute l'il foot kinda fiddled down there fer a tad, as her breath gusted and her bosom heaved, and her nipples stuck out so hard he thought they might pop open'n start sprayin' blood in his face, he did!

"My sex yearns for your hot, pulsing manhood, Chief," her words oozed, and then *both* her purdy l'il feet rose up'n hooked around his ears, which gave the Chief more than a eyefull 'a her plush, perfectly formed, well . . . majora, them full soft-pink lips gettin' wet just as he looked, and that fine light-red hair tracin' over it.

It were a picture 'a desire incarnate!

Then her feet kinda hooked behind his head and . . . started ta pull forward.

"But first, Chief, please, please—I beg of you—*please!* Lave my hot, pink honeyhole with your big manly tongue!"

Chief Kinion sighed. Yeah, he could do that, yes sir, he could do it just as purdy as ya please, he could. Problee tasted like a l'il sugar cookie, so cute'n squeaky clean it was! Yeah, after all these years, finally—*finally*—the Chief were gettin' some 'a the reward he deserved fer a life 'a hard work . . . He were gettin' ta hobknob with the gal 'a his dreams—oh, yeah!—with the most perfect woman ta ever cross his path!

And goin' down on her snatch were just the appetizer! Purdy soon after, he'd git ta the main course: his John Thursday sunk deep inta her joyhole!

So the Chief stuck his big tongue right out'n—yes sir!—he buried it inta her poon like a weasel stickin' its head into a snakehole, he did, and he got ta lappin' away like a regler muff-diver, fer shore, and Agent Majora were startin' ta come right off, she were, and the Chief hisself, he were diggin' it too, pleasurin' so fine-lookin' a gal, and he just got ta lickin' up fierce on the adorable l'il clit, givin' her the velvet buzzsaw, yes sir, when—

*The hail!*

Alls of a sudden a stank rose like ta kick him in the snoot, it did, and then just as quick he felt somethin' hot'n snotty on his tongue, and when he pulled his face away, he took a hard hock'n watched a splat'a this stuff that looked like melted Jack Cheese hit the floor, and then he were gaggin' and backin' up on his knees, and he grabbed that wastecan by the desk 'cos, come ta think of it, he'd *swallered* some'a that cheese, and—

Chief Kinion threw up so hard'n heavy inta the wastecan that he thought his stomach might come up ta boot, and he damn near *filled* that wastecan, he did! And then he throwed up some more when he took a glance up at her box'n saw a whole lot more'a this cheesy stuff drippin' out. And then he realized 'zactly what that stuff were!

Gonococcal pus . . .

## ABOUT THE AUTHOR

Edward Lee has authored close to 50 books in the field of horror; he specializes in hardcore fare. His most recent novels are LUCIFER'S LOTTERY and the Lovecraftian THE HAUNTER OF THE THRESHOLD. His movie HEADER was released on DVD by Synapse Film in June, 2009. Lee lives in Largo, Florida.

## ALSO FROM
## deadite press

*You've seen Cannibal Holocaust. You've seen Salo. You've seen Nekromantik. You ain't seen shit!*

Brain Cheese Buffet collects nine of Lee's most sought after tales of violence and body fluids. Featuring the Stoker nominated "Mr. Torso," the legendary gross-out piece "The Dritiphilist," the notorious "The McCrath Model SS40-C, Series S," and six more stories to test your gag reflex.

**AVAILABLE FROM AMAZON.COM**

**"Squid Pulp Blues" Jordan Krall** - In these three bizarro-noir novellas, the reader is thrown into a world of murderers, drugs made from squid parts, deformed gun-toting veterans, and a mischievous apocalyptic donkey.

"... with SQUID PULP BLUES, [Krall] created a wholly unique terrascape of Ibsen-like naturalism and morbidity; an extravaganza of white-trash urban/noir horror."
- Edward Lee

**"Apeshit" Carlton Mellick III** - Friday the 13th meets Visitor Q. Six hipster teens go to a cabin in the woods inhabited by a deformed killer. An incredibly fucked-up parody of B-horror movies with a bizarro slant

"The new gold standard in unstoppable fetus-fucking kill-freakomania . . . Genuine all-meat hardcore horror meets unadulterated Bizarro brainwarp strangeness. The results are beyond jaw-dropping, and fill me with pure, unforgivable joy." - John Skipp

**"Super Fetus" Adam Pepper** - Try to abort this fetus and he'll kick your ass!

"The story of a self-aware fetus whose morally bankrupt mother is desperately trying to abort him. This darkly humorous novella will surely appall and upset a sizable percentage of people who read it... In-your-face, allegorical social commentary."
- BarnesandNoble.com

**"Fistful of Feet" Jordan Krall** -   A bizarro tribute to Spaghetti westerns, Featuring Cthulhu-worshipping Indians, a woman with four feet, a Giallo-esque serial killer, a crazed gunman who is obsessed with sucking on candy, Syphilis-ridden mutants, ass juice, burping pistols, sexually transmitted tattoos, and a house devoted to the freakiest fetishes.

"Krall has quite a flair for outrage as an art form."
- Edward Lee